Founders' Intent

Founders' Intent

By

Robert J. Ross

Published by JBeam Press
2019

First Printing: 2019

ISBN 978-1-7339559-1-1

Published by JBeam Press

JBeamPress@comcast.net

Ordering Information:

Special discounts are available on quantity purchases by corporations, associations, educators, and others. For details, contact the publisher at the
below listed address.

U.S. trade bookstores and wholesalers: Please contact JBeamPress@com-
cast.net

Dedication

This book is dedicated to the Founding Fathers' monumental effort during the 1787 Constitutional Convention to create a new form of federal government for a new country - one that's become the envy of the world and number one destination for immigrants from every continent.

Introduction

Founders' Intent unfolds through the eyes, words, and actions of an extensive cast of characters. Some are prominent, while others play only minor roles in the story. To assist readers, a list of all those characters is shown below, with primaries in bold.

Many of the places are real (certainly the locations in and around Charleston and Hampton Plantation, SC), some others are not.

Riggs Blanding, Army veteran and small business owner
    Galen Blanding, Riggs' father

Patina Gregors, graduate student and intern
    Alex Gregors, Patina's father

Richard, shift manager of the Wholesale Meat Market

Jason Tuttle, owner of Low Country Furniture Store

Rudy Hayes, Jason's attorney

Sonny Butler, U.S. Representative, 6th District, SC
    Dana, wife
    Luther Phillips, Chief of Staff
    Ripp Jennings, District Director
    Angel Johnson, Executive Assistant
    Gordon Asner, personal attorney
    Harry Loucks, Campaign Manager
    Everett and Davey Pelletier, pay-for-play supporters
    Jasper, property manager at Sonny's SC house
    Caprice Flowers and Starburst, golf caddies

Boggs Colman, President of the Food Services Union of America
    Dianne, wife
    Maddy, daughter and intern at the Library of Congress
    James Blaisdell, AKA **Ivan**, union enforcer

Donnie Edison, Chief, negotiating team
Manny O'Hara, Chief Counsel
Jack Andretti, Director of Public Relations
Paul Hayes, Director of Membership
Hondo, crowd-team manager

Neal Tanner, Pres & CEO, Nat'l Assn. of American Restauranteurs
Marjorie, wife, and Library of Congress Chief of the U.S./Anglo
Division, Acquisitions and Bibliographic Access Directorate
George Wickley, Chief Counsel

Charleston Historical Society, **Professor David Arkin**, President
Melba, receptionist

Charleston State University
Dennis Belton, Chairman, History Department
Dale Hartman, history professor
Franklin Ackers, economics professor
Zheng Wei, international economics professor
Professor Robin Cochran, new faculty member
William Edward Jackson IV, graduate business student

Janet Lewis, Forensic Document Examiner
Regina, assistant

Mark Chambers, SC State Senator and U.S. 6th District candidate
Sheila, wife

National Archive and Records Administration (NARA)
Juanita Menendez, employee

Library of Congress
Marjorie Tanner, wife of Neal Tanner and Library of Congress
Chief of the U.S./Anglo Division, Acquisitions and Biblio-
graphic Access Directorate
Piper Lawrence, a Team Chief under Marjorie

National Security Agency analysts: Ted Burnett and Jeanett

Chinese Embassy
Zhu Jianjun, Minister, Office of Economic and Commercial Affairs
Li Jun, Deputy, Office of Economic and Commercial Affairs

CEO of Sunrise Mechanical, Inc. **David Wang**, CEO

Jim Sparks, operative

WCHS Television
Betsy Harker, News Director
Jimmy Cooley, Station Assistant
Jennifer Rose, newsroom assistant
Jovita Schorre, news anchor

Dr. Rose, Tidewater Memorial Hospital

Shyrel Hayden, U.S. Attorney for South Carolina

FBI Charleston Regional Special Agent in Charge
Wilbert Haskell

Charlotte Williams, Solicitor, 9th Judicial District of SC

Charleston County, SC Sheriff's Office
Sheriff Barry Cobb   Jeanette, Deputy
SGT Winters, Evidence custodian
Dorothy, Public Relations Officer

Morris Brown, Charleston County Coroner

Committee of Detail, Constitutional Convention:
John Rutledge, Chairman, SC   Oliver Ellsworth, CT
Nathaniel Gorham, MA   Edmund Randolph, VA
James Wilson, PA

Contents

Acknowledgements

Writing *Founders' Intent* was a challenging, time-consuming, yet satisfying endeavor. Research, refining the story lines, drafting, and numerous re-writes all took time away from other pursuits, activities, and people I love.

Throughout that process, my wife **Joye** provided steadfast supported while I verbalized plots, and spent untold hours pecking on a keyboard (I cannot touch type). I thank her profusely once again for her unwavering encouragement and performing double duty while I was so engaged.

My brother **Jonathon**, an engineer by trade and a self-taught bagpiper, fiddler, linguist, and writer at heart, has been an inspiration and source of tips, techniques, and encouragement during this project. I thank him immensely for all his support.

Henry Rutledge, direct descendant of Founding Father John Rutledge, graciously hosted Joye and me at his family home of Little Hampton in McClellanville, SC, where he provided valuable personal insights into Archibald Rutledge Sr.'s life at Hampton Plantation and its furnishings.

Long-time friend and voracious reader **Dennis Benson** has regularly provided astute perspectives and asked searching questions that invariably lead to more realistic and interesting revisions.

Fayette County Sheriff **Barry Babb**, a standout lawman in the state of Georgia, walked me through multi-jurisdictional law enforcement issues to ensure I treated that dimension of the story with a proper degree of accuracy. Any errors in that regard are mine alone. I know he had many other tasks and missions on his plate when he found ime to counsel me.

I must acknowledge and thank attorney **Rudjard Hayes**, principal of Sanchez-Hayes & Associates, for his patient explanations of criminal proceedings, legal processes, and his words of encouragement.

Forensic Document Examiners **Jane Lewis** and **Joseph Parker** went above and beyond to provide insights into the scientific business of their science. They responded immediately and thoroughly to my blind requests for help. Thank you both so much for your generous contributions.

Jim O'Neill, concierge of the John Rutledge House Inn for sharing his considerable knowledge of Rutledge family and house history. He was kind enough to provide a personal tour of the upstairs room where John Rutledge drafted the U.S. Constitution.

David E. Murphree, Certified Sales Consultant for Tracker Boats in Leeds, AL took his valuable time to explain, in layman's terms, the workings of large outboard motors, bass boats, and their associated hazards and safety features.

Jayson Sellers, Hampton Plantation, for generously providing his extensive knowledge of the plantation and connecting me with the Rutledge family.

In addition to the contributors above, this project benefitted immensely from the thoughtful contributions of beta readings by **Charlotte Biskup-Godfrey, Paul Burton, Melissa Gilbert-Ross, Gil Harper, Elizabeth Huntsinger, Joyce Klaasen, Jane Lewis, Joseph Parker, Melanie Parker,** and **Sam** and **Tony Ross**. Thank you all for your enthusiastic assistance.

Prologue

A rchibald Hamilton Rutledge Sr. takes an admiring, sorrowful look at his cherished Hampton Plantation as an auctioneer opens bidding on many of its historic furnishings. Archibald and all the others are completely unaware that one piece holds an original document nearly two centuries old - a document with sweeping consequences for the nation and its major trading partners.

Thirty-four years ago Archibald returned from Mercersburg, PA to restore and reside in the Georgian-style house, following its occupancy by four generations of prominent ancestors. As South Carolina's first Poet Laureate, he composed more than a few of his 50 poems, stories, and books there on a mahogany desk that he remembers since childhood. Now in his 88th year, he'll use the auction proceeds to help buy Little Hampton in nearby McClellanville and bequeath the grand 300-acre plantation to the state.

His father, Colonel Henry Rutledge II, told him that ancestral Founding Father John Rutledge drafted a version of the U.S. Constitution on that very desk in the second-floor drawing room of his Charleston home on Broad Street. With that colonial legacy and a rumored compartment that Archibald never found, the desk held more treasured memories than any other item going under the auctioneer's gavel.

When part-time antiques dealer Galen Blanding submitted the winning bid for the desk, Archibald left the grounds to avoid watching strangers take away the revered heirloom and other cherished family treasures.

As Galen loads the antique into his truck, he watches late-arriving Charleston furniture dealer Kenny Tuttle bid on a harpsichord, a dozen cabriolet chairs, and two mahogany bedsteads. *I see he's in a bargaining mood today; wonder if I could parlay my new desk for the red leather recliner on his showroom floor?*

Founders' Intent

Chapter 1

2004

"**H**ey buddy, you running this place?" BC demands while aggressively closing the final six feet to his subject at the Wholesale Meat Mart.

Richard's already had an exhausting day struggling to keep a lid on prices without having to lay anyone off, and reluctantly turns to answer the late visitor, "It depends, who's asking?"

BC glares into his eyes, "Either you are or you aren't, asshole - it doesn't *matter* who's asking."

Richard's both surprised and baffled, *No way this is a late sales call, who is this reprobate?*

People variously whispered that BC meant Brutal Criminal, Barbarous Conspirator, or Berserk Crook. Truthfully, they all fit and regardless of which one is chosen, BC relishes any description that promotes his growing reputation.

Accompanying BC is a large muscular man from Tacoma who BC very aptly nicknamed when they first met. Since the accomplice bore a physical resemblance to a famous gorilla from the same city, BC nicknamed him after the celebrated simian: Ivan.

The packing house closed a half hour ago and Richard quickly concludes he's alone with an intimidating street thug and a human ape whose biceps are considerably more developed than his brain.

"Yeah that's me, I go by Dick. But listen, it's late and I've still got a pile of paperwork in the office. Come by tomorrow morning - I'll give you a cup of coffee and you can tell me what's on your mind."

"That goddamn paperwork, *that's* what's on my mind. You're screwing us over, all of us, with your price gouging and it's ending tonight. A new Benz out front with fancy vanity plates, a $500 sport coat and a Rolex, while we take it in the ass just trying to keep jobs at a few restaurants."

Their bodies are now a scant two feet apart, and every time the intruder opens his mouth, Richard smells his last putrid, half-digested meal. Ivan inches closer, just beside BC now and sneering with satisfaction at Richard's growing and very obvious anxiety.

Richard feels his neck hairs straighten, adrenaline kick in, a profusion of sweat, and his heart rate almost double. *Who are these goons?* "Look, we're both in business to make a buck. If you find a better deal, take it. I'm not going to fight you. Go for it - I don't care, even if you're under contract here."

While talking, Richard turns slightly clockwise to mask his furtive reach for a .357 caliber snub-nose revolver from inside his waistband. As soon as he grips the handle, he rapidly pulls the pistol from its holster, takes a step backwards, and points the pistol directly at BC.

"BC, the little fucker's got a *piece!*" Ivan blurts.

"I'm no sharpshooter, mister, but even *I* can put a couple of shots in your gut at bad breath distance," Richard tensely threatens. "Now both of you get the hell outta here."

BC and Ivan take instant notice of the revolver and the hollow point bullets visible in its cylinder. Neither man was expecting their quarry to be armed, much less with such a powerful short-range handgun. They momentarily fixate on the muzzle, knowing what a hollow point magnum bullet will do at this range. Both of them deeply respect the ability of its expanding petals to tear through their abdomens and utterly destroy vital organs. Independently, they both consider their next move very, very carefully.

BC slowly eases one step to the left, warily measuring Richard's response. That minor movement diverts Richard's nervous attention and aim ever so slightly.

Ivan instantly seizes the brief opportunity to lunge forward; Richard reactively squeezes the trigger, producing a deafening blast that reverberates throughout the building.

BC is incredulous - he grabs the fiery pain in his left shoulder and screams, "You shot me, you little cocksucker, YOU GODDAMN SHOT ME!"

The light little pistol's violent recoil throws Richard's arms upward and Ivan locks onto them with a vise-like grip that causes Richard to drop his weapon to the floor.

BC's eyes bulge, his jaws clench, and his forehead furrows in an instant rage. Ivan's seen him deranged once before, with gruesome consequences for the adversary.

"Hold the little prick, Ivan, so we can see what to do with his scrawny ass," BC commands over his pain.

Ivan hoists Richard off the floor in a bear hug and shakes him, deciding where to throw his terrified victim to inflict maximum retribution.

Richard struggles against his oversized assailant without any success until he delivers a powerful kick with his steel-tipped safety shoe squarely into Ivan's right knee. An audible 'crack' confirms that he's severely fractured Ivan's patella. Ivan's knee buckles and he shrieks, but painfully maintains his grip. Richard tries to gouge Ivan's eyes but his futile attempts only leave bloody fingernail ruts on his face.

"You little *shit!*" he curses while still gripping the struggling Richard, then head-butts him in retaliation

"Ivan! There, right there - stick his ass on that!" BC vigorously orders, pointing to a gleaming ½" diameter, stainless steel overhead butcher's hook.

Ivan turns and looks up at the hook, looks back at BC, and manages a thin smile over his intensely throbbing knee. More than happy to obey, Ivan agonizingly lifts his luckless victim up and impales his lower jaw on the suspended hook. Then he lets go and steps back to nurse his agonizing injury, wipe his face, and admire his gruesome handiwork.

Blood instantly spurts from Richard's jaw and mouth onto his jacket, pants, and the floor. His legs twitch uncontrollably and his body writhes in agony. He vainly struggles to lift himself free of the deadly metal piercing his tongue and palate, but his blood-covered hands cannot grip the smooth steel shank in front of his face.

Looking to exact a measure of personal retribution, BC catches his breath, stares at the man who just shot him, and charges forward

- landing a powerful gut punch into his trembling, struggling mark. Richard's quivering body jolts backwards in a violent arc, almost ripping it from its skewered lower jaw. He can't even scream, let alone free himself in the minutes before his lifeless body comes to rest on the cold, sharpened, hook.

"Damn, Boss, now that's some kind of *harsh*," Ivan proclaims in stunned disbelief.

"Nothing that asshole didn't deserve. Be careful, don't drip any blood around here and clean up our footprints. Don't see any security cameras, do you?"

Chapter 2

Fifteen Years Later

R iggs Blanding tenses with disbelief and growing disgust as his eyes focus on his father with laser-like precision. His teeth clench and his lips draw tightly as he leans forward with battle-worn eardrums to hear every syllable Galen Blanding reveals about the abject corruption that's about to destroy the family's property of three generations. "You *are* kidding, right Dad, you've got to be - the home, land, the whole place? I thought I left that kind of stuff back in Kandahar. Instead I come home to find it right here in Mt. Pleasant?"

"Doesn't matter where you are, Son, the common denominator is people - human nature. And politics draws out the worst of it – raw power grabs and the money and notoriety that come with it. For most of them, it never gets anywhere close to public service, it's just the means to achieve personal ends - getting what you want through the force of government instead of the market. I'm convinced it's a personality disorder."

A little confused, Riggs tries to reconcile Galen's latest update with the Charleston he knew before leaving for active duty. *What's happened? This is all so different – so much more antagonistic, aggressive, and relentless. No one could have taken dad's home then; what's happened here?* He knows dad's right, and slowly shakes his head, "Yeah you're spot on."

"Sonny Butler got the ball rolling a couple of years ago, just after you left for Afghanistan. He told everyone that Mount Pleasant just had to have a new highway to relieve growing congestion. The logical route was through Phillips Community, but they didn't want to deal with the racial politics and title searches for heirs' land," Galen says, referring to property passed down from slaves that would require long, complicated, and very expensive title searches. "So they rerouted it right through us, Park West, and Dunes West. It's affecting a lot more people than just your mother and me."

7

Galen had also served in the military, commanding a tank company in the 24th Mechanized Division's 4-64th Armor Battalion during Operation DESERT STORM. U.S. Representative Sonny Butler, on the other hand, never spent a day in uniform, feigning "the even greater need to serve America as an elected leader". Knowing he never walked-the-walk like so many of his military constituents, Butler learned just enough military history to at least talk-the-talk around the district's many veterans. They particularly liked hearing him recount major WWII tank battles. His riveting story-telling and presumption that audiences knew little, if anything, about those 75-year old conflicts were a blank check to fabricate what he didn't know or understand.

Riggs was becoming increasingly irate and disgusted as his father continued, "I did find out that a couple of Sonny Butler's old buddies wanted to drive up their land values though, and having frontage and curb cuts on a new major road would do that in spades."

"Sure, but you've been fighting it, right dad?"

"Oh, sure, along with some other people who were fed up with the kind of stuff they'd been pulling. We filled the city council meetings, but it didn't make any difference. Then Sonny won the 6th Congressional District seat. With that elevated perch for handing out even bigger political favors, the Council rammed it through and just grinned at us. We flooded the papers with articles, but people just don't want to get involved."

"Well, this really is a big, brown bag of it. I mean, I didn't serve to protect this kind of government. Do we have laws or don't we? They can't just do that." Riggs exhales and tries to settle down a little.

"Well they did do it, Son. Sonny Butler led the charge the whole way and he'll keep going until someone puts a boot on his neck. That's all they understand – power. Hell, he's probably fishing with his pals right now – one of 'em's got a really nice 70' Hatteras, a big sport fisherman yacht. Now I know how they afford those things."

Riggs reflects on what he's seen and experienced in the intervening years in the Army – peers fighting for key assignments, profiteering, and the sheer atrocity of war. *Maybe the place hasn't changed at all, it's been like this all along but I just never knew it.*

"Dad, I don't have any regrets about my time in the Army, but I'm out now. How can I help?"

Galen looked straight at his son, responding without a pause.

"Riggs, follow your own future. Your mother and I are going to try enjoying ourselves, and watching you succeed will be a big part of that. How *is* your new business doing?"

"Doing well, Dad. In fact, I'm thinking I need to take on some help, someone with some tech sense. The drone business is hopping – doing agricultural and construction surveys, mapping, inspecting power lines and cellphone towers. I'm even getting requests from realtors to shoot videos of high-end properties. Throw in a little event coverage and I'm a busy guy."

"That's great, Son," Galen smiles and vows to be as supportive as he can.

Riggs always strived to excel, and succeeded at just about everything he put his mind to – with the notable exception of playing the piano. After enrolling in ROTC at the University of South Carolina, he sensed a calling to the profession of arms and its cornerstones of duty, honor, and country. The day he graduated, he most willingly took his oath of office... *to support and defend the Constitution of the United States against all enemies, foreign and domestic.*

Within months, he completed the Infantry Officer Basic Course in preparation for a two-year stint as a ground-pounder. The Army promoted him to 1st lieutenant before he served in his primary branch – Military Intelligence. He pinned on captain's bars after four years of service and finished the MI Officer Advanced Course. Subsequent assignments found him serving as an armor battalion S2 (staff intelligence officer), and assistant S2 at brigade level.

Riggs thoroughly enjoyed, trusted, and respected the uniformed leaders he worked for, soldiers he worked with, and those he led. He was on a team that lived and breathed similar values - men and women who worked under trying conditions and could be trusted. He also thrived in the intricate, fast-paced life that's inherent in warfighting units.

The Army recognized his outstanding potential and selected him to attend a fully-funded master's degree program in Operations

Research and Systems Analysis at Stanford University. His early selection for promotion to Major identified him as a fast-mover.

During his second tour in Afghanistan, a Taliban fighter deto-
nated a roadside bomb under his HMMWV. The machine gunner
died and doctors evacuated his driver to the Landstuhl Regional Med-
ical Center in Germany with a mangled stump of a right leg. Riggs
suffered a concussion, burns, and a fractured ulna in his left arm. He
recovered in Afghanistan and assumed duties in the HQ intelligence
collection section of Regional Command-East. He frequently thought
about his crew and their families and privately interrogated himself,
*Did I do everything I could've to avoid it? Should I have insisted on
taking another route, looked at more intel reports? Looked even
harder for signs of a buried IED?* As their leader, those questions
would always hide in a reserved, corner of his mind. Sometimes an
unexpected action, sight, or sound would raise them again: hitting a
pothole or a bump in the road. You never forget.

"Your mother and I are glad you're out of harm's way and home
safely, but I was really a little surprised when you hung it up. You
seemed to like it, and it sure provided the kind of challenges you
thrive on. I just thought it was a fit that would've lasted longer."

"To be honest, Dad, I did too, especially at first. I certainly found
it a noble calling. Too many of the last years in service had me doubt-
ing too many of the people pulling the strings, though. Not so much
on the uniformed side, but politicians and the suits. Guys with an attitude just like Sonny Butler's. No consideration for the mission and
no moral compass - or if they have one, it points straight down. I just
didn't feel like I was fully committed anymore."

"Yep, politics draws that kind of people."

"I began to feel complicit – enabling national decisions to save
their political careers. Decisions that caused too much death and injury to ordinary Americans doing extraordinary things."

Galen had similar thoughts when he served, but threats to America's interests seemed more clear-cut during the first Gulf war.

"The politicos weren't going to change the equation, but I could,
and I finally did. I don't regret my time in, but now I'm trying something different. Completely different."

Galen nods in agreement.

"Who knows, I may even take on Sonny Butler."

Galen turns towards Riggs, proud but a bit surprised and curious about that last remark.

Founders' Intent

Chapter 3

Contributors

"Congressman, your 2:30 is here," Chief of Staff Luther Phillips announces on the intercom to South Carolina 6th District Representative Sonny Butler. Butler stands up and walks to the front of his desk where he'll greet them, "Yes, Luther, by all means, show them right in." Always one to distance himself from failure and take credit for success, a particular quote accurately captures Sonny's egocentric nature, 'He's a self-made man who worships his creator'.

Luther enviously admires the visitors' $6,200 Brioni suits as he escorts them from the anteroom into Sonny's office.

"Everett, Davey, always such a pleasure to see you both, especially all the way up here in Washington." Years in public office taught Sonny that the most important attribute for any politician is sincerity. Once he learned how to fake that, the rest was easy.

"Sonny... oh, excuse me, Congressman... "

"No, no, Everett, we've been friends for way too long to let titles get between us – please, you know it's still 'Sonny' to both of you." *He just assumes he can call me 'Sonny'? That's an awfully presumptuous way to greet a U.S. Congressman – I haven't seen <u>him</u> win an election, or even run for office. Jesus, what I have to put up with for donations...*

"And I've got to say, you're looking more fit every time we meet – you've got to tell me your secret."

"You're looking pretty damn good yourself, Sonny, and I like your step up in the world – an office here in the big leagues."

"Well, the office and location get better the longer you're here, and that's where long-time supporters like both of you are so important. But you've come all the up from Charleston, what can *I* do for *you?*"

"It's the Charleston Air Force Base expansion and renovation. There's a ton of federal money in that one and we're going to need a little help getting an edge with our contract bid."

Everett's brother Davey chimes in, "We know of two other companies who're in the hunt on this one too. It's over a $175 million, so winning it would give us plenty of juice to continue working with key supporters like you, Sonny."

Sure, they've got fat wallets, but they're still just a couple of uncultured hicks - no class, no discretion. He might as well have just come out and said 'bribe'. And who's got a recorder in their pocket – to play when they're looking for payback?

"You two know, of course, that I'll do everything I can to help you on this one, just because I *am* your representative, that's what I'm elected to do."

All three of them manage a wry smile, knowing full well it's a straight pay-for-play proposition.

"Happy to look into it, fellas. I believe I know just the man in the House Armed Services Committee who has a thumb on the Readiness Subcommittee. He sits on the other side of the aisle, but he's also a South Carolina boy - let's see if he knows a helpful contracting officer in the Army Corps of Engineers."

"We'll leave all the twists and turns in your most capable hands, Sonny, and thanks so much - knew we could count on you."

"I'm happy to help, and be assured that we won't end up with a fiasco like that big Army project in Korea that SK Engineering and Construction got caught up in. I've got to tell you, though, people are always on the lookout for questions about privileged contract info, but that just means we've got to get creative, or find a vulnerability - and everyone's got one."

"We're on kind of a timeline too, Sonny - the government's Request for Proposal is due on the street in about a month, and contractor bids will probably be due back about six months later."

"I understand completely, men. I may be able to wriggle a way in through my seat on the Education and Workforce Committee, too. I'll look for a link to wages that you could include in your proposal." *Got to remind Luther to hang on to any useful contract info I could use to leverage donations from the other two companies if either of them are smart enough to come see me with a donation.*

"That'd be wonderful, Sonny, really wonderful. Listen, we're not flying the jet back until later tonight, let us take you to one of those dinner places with lots of Michelin stars."

"I'd really love to, but Luther's already got me double-booked for a couple of events tonight that I just can't get out of. You know I'd much rather be with both of you, but I'm having to spend way too much of time fighting off that upstart state senator who's trying to connive his way into my seat. Hell, I've got to spend most mornings telling voters the truth about his campaign lies. I'll hold you to a rain-check when I get back to the district though – count on it."

"OK, Sonny. Still, we'd like to leave a small contribution with Luther on the way out."

"That'd be too kind, my friends, too kind." *But if it's really just a small one, don't expect any big favors.*

Luther leads them out and returns to the office, "Sir, one more item... the Tidewater Preservation Corps invited you to be keynote speaker to their annual meeting in January. I'll go ahead and tell them you're unavailable."

"Yes, by all means, send my regrets - with the usual blather about how much good work they all do and how honored I am just to be invited." He pauses and grimaces at the problems they've caused to a few of his most generous supporters. "They're a joke - constantly getting in the way of some of my biggest donors' projects with crap about turtles, birds, or sawgrass – I don't even know why they'd send me an invitation, much less want me as their keynote speaker. I must be putting on a better environmental show than I thought!"

"Yes Sir, I'll send your regrets."

"The problem with those people, Luther, is they just don't have any money and never lift a damn finger to help my campaigns. Then they turn right around and ask me to do something for them. With nothing but time on their hands, they delude themselves with a self-generated sense of importance; just a shallow clique of human im-pediments who bask in a false, self-contrived superiority. They don't have any *real* purpose in life, so they compensate with phony crusades against those of us who actually *do* work. They anoint themselves with lofty-sounding titles like 'wildlife warriors'. It's all just to appease their fragile consciences with a bogus moral justification for their actions to 'save the world'. Actually, they're nothing more than a meddling pack of limp-wristed daisies."

It's quite a condemnation by someone who treasures his secluded home among the undisturbed flora and fauna on an inland island west of Charleston's constant bustle.

Luther turns towards the door to leave when Sonny grins and suddenly stops him. "Luther, hold on just a minute, I've got a better idea. Let's go ahead and accept the invitation – tell them I'd be thrilled and honored to participate in their event as keynote speaker."

Luther looks surprised and completely confused, "Really, sir, you want me to *accept* the invitation?"

Sonny smiles and stares at Luther, "Yes, just for now, though. In the meantime, look for a junket, preferably some warm overseas place that'll take priority over me actually going down there to speak. Then, about two or three days before the event, call them to 'express the congressman's deepest and most sincere apologies' for having to abruptly cancel for extremely urgent national business. After spending all their money on ads and invitations announcing me, the whiners will be up against the wall getting a last-minute no-name replacement from under some lily pad."

"Nice touch, Sir, kind of a stealthy kick in the balls they'll never see coming."

Sonny smiles his confirmation, winks, and aims a finger at Luther. "Oh it's not that bad, Luther, and you've got to have a little fun along the way, even with your enemies." Then he gazes out the window with a satisfying smirk. *Damn I love this job, being at the front of the formation and picking winners and losers.*

It's only 3:10 and he feels like he's already accomplished a full day's work. *Nothing on the calendar tonight, I think I'll surprise Dana with an impromptu date night this evening.*

Chapter 4

Who Are You?

"Oh crap, Dad - I'm going to be late for a client meeting!" Riggs apologizes and jumps into his four-year old Toyota Camry to speed off to his appointment. Charleston traffic's always been a nightmare, and didn't get any better when Boeing built its commercial aircraft assembly plant there six years ago. Caught in today's snarl, he's still fuming when he looks down at his phone for an alternate route.

Suddenly and unexpectedly, the safety belt digs deeply into his lap and chest as the car slams to an abrupt halt. The forced stop hurls his head forward and he hears the grill crash into a SUV stopped in front of him.

Riggs has a fleeting flashback of Afghanistan: an explosion and his HMMWV landing on its side in a ditch. His pulse races and he momentarily freezes to instinctively listen for enemy fire. *It wasn't an IED. No small arms or machinegun fire and no mortars.* Then he checks his vision, hearing, and limbs. *Check, check, and check. No blood, I think I'm OK, how's everyone else? Wait, I'm back in the states - no crew to get injured.* He sits still and takes a couple of deep breaths to clear his head.

Then the practical side of the collision sets in, "Oh crap! I *really* don't need this," he complains while looking at the Honda Pilot SUV ahead of him. Its heavily tinted windows obscure whoever's inside, *Are they all right? Any kids hurt?* Riggs gets out and briefly looks at the damage; the Honda doesn't appear to have any - even a Charleston State University "Computer Whisperer" sticker on the rear bumper is intact.

The door opens and the driver looks back to see who just plowed into her. *Who's this bonehead going to be - an 80-year old? A drunk? A texting teenager or some self-styled macho man?*

She strides towards his car in a black soccer uniform and he quickly tries to gauge her attitude, "Are you OK? Anyone else in the car? I think I'm good. Doesn't look like any airbags went off - that's always a good sign."

Her eyes narrow as she stops a mere three feet away, plants her feet, and stares directly at him.

"You just ran into me. *I* stopped, like the red eight-sided sign says to - just like *you're* supposed to do. Wouldn't it be a whole lot easier to use the brakes like everyone else does?"

She is pissed*. What part of her life did I just turn upside down?*

She isn't ranting, sobbing, screaming, or incoherent. She's direct, confident, and in total control of herself and the situation. She scans him from head to foot, then her large brown eyes pierce his in a practiced effort to rapidly assess any potential threat – a reaction that's become second nature since a traumatic event during college.

Riggs feels like he's being sternly raked over the coals by a seasoned prosecutor. *Is she going to sue me or something? Who* is *this person and what am I in for?* he asks himself as he looks at her and back at the two vehicles. Hers has a little paint scraped off the tow hitch where his radiator ran into it, that's it. He's not so lucky, as an expanding pool of fluid underneath his Camry testifies.

Riggs assures her, "It looks like your vehicle's fine, certainly better than mine. I'll go ahead and call the police."

"I'm all right," she says, "nothing broken or bruised - mostly just surprised. It really wasn't even that much of a bump."

Well that's *good to hear, maybe she isn't going to sue me after all.*

Only then does Riggs really look at her, and he likes what he sees very much. She's amply demonstrated that she's no shrinking violet. She can think clearly and communicate effectively. She speaks without starting sentences with 'So' and doesn't throw a 'like' in between every couple of words. Physically, she's about his age, tall, shapely, very fit, with large brown eyes and a brunette ponytail. No visible tattoos or body piercings. Her lips and perfect teeth would make a fabulous smile, but he certainly isn't going to see one of those today.

Most notably, she isn't wearing a wedding band.

Riggs extends his right hand and introduces himself, "I'm Riggs, Riggs Blanding and I really apologize for this. I'm just glad you aren't hurt. I guess we need to exchange insurance info?"

She lightly shakes his hand, "You're right, we should exchange information - you *are* insured, aren't you?"

Riggs thinks, *Do I look that irresponsible? You'd think her car was totaled.*

"Yes, of course I am, and I'm sure they'll make your scratched tow hitch look brand new," he tells her with a tinge of humorous sarcasm.

She turns her gaze from the cars back to him without acknowledging his attempted humor, but then softens just a little, "I'm glad you're not hurt, I'm sure all this can be fixed." *Well he certainly isn't 80, drunk, or a kid.*

They pull out their cell phones to photograph each other's insurance card and the damage to the vehicles as a cruiser pulls up.

Riggs asks, "Listen, I really feel bad about this, can I make it up to you, maybe over lunch this week?"

"I don't think your car's in much shape to go *anywhere* this week," she says with a not-so-subtle smirk.

Well, she didn't say 'no', I guess that's a good sign. He turns and looks at the pool of fluid under his car, "Oh, yeah, I guess you're right. But I can use my company van while the car's in the shop. How about tomorrow?"

She ponders for a few seconds and Riggs wonders, *Is she being coy, trying to remember if there's anything else on her calendar, or just trying to decide if I'm worth her time?*

"I usually don't go out with anyone who's guilty of vehicular assault..."

"It must be my lucky day, then," Riggs interrupts. "The case isn't even on the docket yet, and innocent until proven guilty, right?"

Well, he's certainly quick on the uptake, isn't he? She tilts her head and looks at him, "I'll make an exception, today only. Meet me at Ahab's on James Island, by Folly Road, about 11:30 so we don't have to wait for a good table."

"Ahab's? Haven't been there, but I'll find it on the GPS."

"Just make sure you check the GPS *before* you take off. I don't want you running late because you hit someone else while you're looking at your phone."

Ouch! I guess I deserve that "OK, great, see you there at 11:30."

She returns to her SUV, waits for the traffic cop to take down her information, and wonders, *What did I just agree to, and with whom? I don't know anything whatsoever about a guy I'm meeting for lunch tomorrow; better have an exit strategy, a get-out-of-date free card.*

Riggs smiles and looks at the picture of her insurance card: Patina Gregors.

Immediately after the accident, Riggs takes an UBER back to his business, goes directly to his computer, and logs onto facebook.

Patina Gregors... can't be too many of those here he thinks while typing her name into the search space. He's relieved to see that she's got a current page and he zeroes in on her cover photo - a younger Patina on a beach, hugging a guy a bit older than her. *Who's that – a boyfriend? Former husband? Someone she's in a long-distance relationship with? Maybe even a Sugar Daddy? Wait a sec, what am I getting into with this Patina person? She seems so put together, so why isn't she with anyone? What am I missing?*

Riggs begins scrolling down her timeline, which doesn't include too many posts, but at least he can view them. She graduated from Duke University in 2006 with a BS degree in Computer Science. Friends' comments on other posts show that she'd traveled to the Caribbean and apparently lived there awhile.

He clicks the Friends tab, but doesn't recognize anyone. Then he clicks the Photos link, *Hmmm, some nice pics of historical places around Charleston, I wonder if she took them or just re-posted someone else's?*

One picture, labeled 'John Rutledge House, 116 Broad Street', reminds him of a building he visited with his father when he was very young. Riggs doesn't find anything under her name on any other social media sites.

Well, Miss Patina Gregors, just who <u>are</u> you?

Chapter 5

Ahab's

"Hi, Patina," Riggs greets as she walks through the door at Ahab's the next day. He immediately recognizes her in mid-thigh shorts, a simple pastel-colored pattern top, sandals, and sunglasses. "I'm so sorry again for yesterday, and I gotta say, it's a lot better seeing you today for lunch than it was over my bashed-in car. I've already got us a spot on the water." He habitually selected a seat with a wall at his back, one that offered clear lines of sight ahead and to the sides; this one also happened to be perfect for lunch.

That's nice, he's already picked out a prime table - very thoughtful. He's pretty cute, too, and buff. I hope he isn't living in his parents' basement. I wonder who else is in his life?

Riggs walks her to the table and pulls back her chair. *I love it – she's on-time, no excuses about deciding what to wear or problem-hair. And, yep – she's a real looker with a perfect set of stems – long, toned, and tanned. I hope she isn't high-maintenance or some pushy feminazi. I wonder who else is in her life?*

"Why thank you, kind sir. And what is this?" Patina points to a colorful gift bag on the table as Riggs seats her.

"A little restitution," Riggs replies with a smile.

Patina's touched, and looks down at the bag, "Oh, how very thoughtful, but it isn't necessary. Or is this in lieu of an actual lunch?"

Riggs nudges the bag towards her. She unties the ribbon, pulls out a sheet of colored tissue paper, and reaches inside to feel something round, cold, and metallic. *What in the world...?*

"Oh, and you're such a romantic too," she says just a bit sarcastically while pulling out a can of black Rust-Oleum spray paint that matches her tow hitch.

Riggs nods sheepishly, "I can't take all the credit, the insurance company promised to reimburse me."

Patina looks down, momentarily blushing just a little herself. *I'm not getting any bad vibes, that's always a good sign, isn't it?*

Riggs cautions himself, *There's that smile; just don't do anything too stupid!* Then he hears an Andrew Lloyd Webber ringtone from Patina's purse, which she ignores.

I'll take that as a sign she's either very polite or I'm interesting enough that she'll catch it later. I'll take either or both!

"Looks like a nice place, do you eat here often?" he asks.

"I come as often as I can for the seafood, a breeze, and the view. This is the first time I've done it for a can of spray paint, though."

"Well, I'm glad you did, it makes my punctured radiator worth it. I hope I didn't make you late for anything yesterday."

"No, not really. I was going home to change after a league soccer game. I started playing in college, mostly as a diversion during a rough spot when I thought I was going to lose my sanity. Riggs noticed that Patina suddenly became decidedly pensive, as though the recollection was of a grave past experience.

Then she laughingly said, "Later, I guess I secretly just wanted to be like Mia Hamm - she's still my soccer idol."

'A rough spot'... breaking up with the guy who was with her on the beach? "No problems with your SUV?"

"No, well, nothing I can't fix with this can of paint."

"Good, I'm glad you made it home in one piece. Was the rest of the afternoon a little less eventful?"

"Oh sure. After I changed, I ran an errand. I'm earning my master's degree in computer science and electronic networks. A classmate moonlights as an audio-visual tech at the Charleston Club and he asked me to sub for him during a big political event there in about six weeks. He walked me through the lighting, projection, and audio equipment."

Riggs knew of the place, located on a prime block of South Charleston near Waterfront Park. An opulent entry to the carefully-restored building led into a foyer with a hallway and magnificent wooden staircase. Authentic period furnishings and original colonial artwork adorned rooms where the political, business, and social elite routinely gathered. It was expensive and very useful for making high-level contacts. He also thought that too many of its members, like

Sonny Butler, were much too pretentious, disreputable, or both for his liking.

"Did you get there in time to meet your friend?"

"Yes, it worked out fine. They have a pretty standard projection and sound system. I even hooked up my laptop to see if it'd work as a backup."

Patina found Riggs genuinely interested, so she continued, "I also get some computer networking practice as an intern at the Historical Society of Charleston. They needed someone to update their IT and I like history – it's been a perfect match."

"Always nice doing what you like, but history and computers seem like an odd combination," Riggs says.

"I guess so, but I enjoy them both. Computer systems work pays pretty well, so I can indulge my historical interests. I also run their monthly children's workshop where I show the kids how to make old-looking documents."

"You mean you're training the next generation of forgers?" he playfully teases.

She looks at him and says "No, they're all too sweet for anything like that; the projects do turn out pretty well, though. We start with heavy paper and color it with tea. They write with fountain pens and a special ink, then crumple it a little and warm it up in an oven to make it look and feel old. I know it sounds a kind of artsy-craftsy, but we all have a lot of fun and I've got to say, I've made some pretty authentic-looking documents."

"Do you get to research old places and things, or have to stay in a cubicle dusting cobwebs off antiques?"

"Funny you should ask, A friend thought that my working there qualifies me as an antiques expert and he invited me to look at some old things at his business."

"Does he run an antiques business?" Riggs asks, hoping to find out how serious a friend he was.

"No, it's actually just a family furniture store. Jason and I met years ago when we were sophomores in biology lab." She pauses and considers what she's about to suggest. *He's kind of charming and seems alright on the surface, but he did just run into me yesterday. I don't really know him, his friends, where he lives, or what he does.* She defers her suggestion until learning more about her appealing lunch date.

"I do some woodworking and refinishing myself, but it's been on hold forever," Riggs says.

"How did you get into that?"

"My father had a small construction company, and sometimes he restored old buildings around the city. I still remember riding in his truck to a big three-story house on Broad Street when I was just five years old. When I was in high school, he brought me along as free labor. I figured the quicker I learned some skills, the sooner I could use them instead of carrying lumber and cement around the sites."

"Just so I get this straight, you learned carpentry just to avoid doing manual labor?"

"Guilty as charged, Ma'am."

"Actually, it sounds kind of fascinating to reconstruct old buildings; were there any historical ones? Did you ever find anything neat in them, other than an occasional ghost?"

"Sometimes. Dad collected fixtures that owners were throwing out or they gave him to help pay their bill - stuff like leaded glass doors and transoms, old furnishings, wrought iron-work, and used bricks."

"A man after my own heart! What'd he do with it?"

"Sometimes he and mom sold the items at flea markets, and sometimes he traded them. He really wanted a red leather recliner at a furniture store and traded some old desk he picked up at an estate sale out east of town; he still has the recliner."

"If you liked woodworking, what took you away from it? I'm thinking it was probably girlfriends," she says with a coy, inquisitive smile.

She's probing, that's a good sign, right? Or maybe she just likes talking about relationships, regardless of who's in them.

"What really took me away from woodworking was twelve years in the Army, first as an infantry platoon leader, then as an intel officer – planning and managing intelligence collection with drones."

Patina reflects, *An Army officer – don't meet a lot of them around here.*

"I found it all technically challenging - fascinating, really, and I'm using that training and experience to run my own drone business here in Charleston now – aerial surveys, inspections, and a little photography."

"Well, a girl doesn't hear *that* every day. Drone photography, huh? I do some photography too – mostly historical sites and architecture. Maybe you could show me some photo techniques with a drone."

"If it has to do with drones, I'm your guy."

She smiles and makes a mental note to follow up on his offer – there are some magnificent old buildings that she's only been able to shoot at ground level or from the roof of her Honda.

"When did you get out of the Army?"

"Just a couple of years ago, and I still think about it from time to time. I took a few months off playing hooky from life. As a leader, I had a real problem ordering soldiers to carry out what I thought were flawed policy decisions. Politicians have no idea what service members endure, and the families of the married soldiers are a whole other dimension." Riggs' lighthearted tone and manner turn serious as he looks towards the river and sincerely appreciates its tranquility. The question arose again, *What could I have done to avoid losing a soldier and having another suffer a mangled leg?*

"Did *you* have someone at home?"

"My parents and a couple of college buddies. Back then I dated someone pretty seriously, but she married someone else while I was away and they moved out of state."

Patina takes it all in and enthusiastically deems him fit for her suggestion.

"I have an idea. Tomorrow, why don't you come with me to look at the old furniture pieces and tell us what kind of shape they're in. If they need a little work, maybe you could get back into woodworking."

Riggs smiles and sees her do the same. Hers was even more engaging than he'd imagined. *Once in a great while you feel an immediate, deep, almost electric connection with someone – one* *that's <u>real and</u> undefinable. She's absolutely mesmerizing.* "I guess I could do that, but there's one condition."

"What would that be, that I buy the next lunch together?"

Riggs laughs and shakes his head 'no'. "I was hoping you'd help me *make* our next meal together," he hints.

Patina blushes and thinks, *For someone who just ran into the back of my Honda, he seems pretty sure of himself. Maybe it's that Army training and experience.*

"Here's the condition: give me the address so I can meet you there instead of having to follow you too closely."

"OK," she laughs, "That's a deal, give me some digits and I'll text it to you."

As they eat seafood salads, Riggs notices her polished manners – she doesn't shovel in her lunch and is refined without being pretentious. She's also very well groomed – hair, nails, and just a light touch of mascara, all very natural looking. The colorful top shows off her modest appealing curves, and her shorts and sandals complete the perfect picture.

After lunch and further conversation, Patina reluctantly pushes back from the table, "Riggs, this has been the most enjoyable lunch I've had here, thank you so much – I can honestly say that I'm glad you bumped into me."

"Do you have to go already?"

"Afraid so, I've got an afternoon class I have to catch." She stands up, walks to his side of the table, and beams the smile that Riggs is already falling for. He melts as she leans over and gently kisses his cheek, "Thanks again for the wonderful time, soldier, it's been awesome. I'm looking forward to seeing you at Jason's tomorrow."

Riggs stands up and hugs her, "Can't wait, Patina. See you then."

Riggs watches her glide out of the patio with her gift bag. *After spending an hour together, I've got more questions now than when she walked in – and I was an intel guy! She's beguiling, gorgeous, technically savvy, and isn't seeing anyone. But I think <u>that</u>'s about to change.*

Chapter 6

Low Country

After battling traffic the next day, Patina and Riggs pull into the parking lot of Low Country Furniture, go inside, and link up with Patina's friend Jason.

"Hey strangers, I hope you brought a dumpster," he greets them. "I need to clear out a room so we can refurb this place.... economy's growing and people are buying a lot more furniture."

"No chance with a dumpster, Jason," Patina replies with a broad smile, anxiously anticipating a valuable discovery. "This is my friend Riggs Blanding – we just ran into each other this week," she says with a knowing smile at Riggs.

"Hi, Riggs, I'm Jason Tuttle. Thanks for helping out. This stuff's been around way too long and we're expanding the showroom; it's all gotta go."

"Hi, Jason, nice to meet you too. How long have you known Patina?" He glances at Jason's left hand, relieved to see a wedding band.

"We met back in college, and still do a little work together through the Historical Society. Sometimes they want old pieces for staging houses that are on a tour."

"Sounds good. I'm no antiques expert, but Dad used to buy, sell, and swap things from work sites and I moved a lot of it in my time."

"I can identify with that. My dad used to get loads of older furnishings, clean 'em up a little, and sell them. Maybe they did some business together. For a couple of years now we've been slowly getting rid of things that never moved; what you see here is the last of it."

Jason leads them through the showroom and down a hallway. They pass two busy offices to arrive at a partially filled storage area. Jason turns the rusted doorknob and pushes the door open with his shoulder. There are no operable lights inside, but a ceiling light in the hall provides enough illumination to keep the trio from tripping over anything.

"Here they are, Patina – treasures from the past!" Jason announces as he steps aside.

Riggs looks into the room, sneezes from the dust, and reflects on the many other dark rooms he had to go into for meetings with Afghan tribal leaders. *But you're not there, you're back home. It's OK to go in.* "Jason, your original assessment was spot on; this looks like it's long outlived its usefulness." They turn on their mobile phone flashlights to better survey the room.

Patina is much more positive and walks the few steps over to two chairs. She certainly isn't an antiques expert, but even her brief experience at the Society convinces her they're worth a professional's look. Jason is determined to fan Patina's excitement about the furnishings and start clearing the room.

Riggs moves by the chairs, a wooden filing cabinet, and stops at a mahogany desk, "Looks like this one's been here awhile."

Jason glances at it, then looks at Riggs, "Yep, for as long as I can remember. Dad said it came from a plantation auction; he thought it may be valuable and took it in on a trade. I guess it wasn't too valuable because it never sold – probably because of the shape it's in."

After another minute in the room, Patina designates the chairs, cabinet, and desk for recovery. Jason, less physically fit than Riggs and Patina, enlists one of the stock boys to help load the items into Riggs' business van.

Patina's thrilled, Jason's relieved, and Riggs is resigned.

"Thanks again, Jason; these look like great projects – even if we find out they aren't antiques. I'm sure Riggs can get them back into shape," Patina says.

"Just remember, all of this is on a one-way trip. The chairs, cabinet, desk, and anything that's in them - it's yours now and I don't want anything else to do with any of it."

"Yeah, yeah, we got it, Jason," Riggs assures him with a smile.

"Are you sure you don't want to take any of cobwebs and these boxes of loose papers?" Jason chides.

Riggs rolls his eyes, *another project* he thinks to himself before leading Patina back to his house. Once there, she's giddy with expectations and can't wait to share her find with the Society's staff.

Riggs surveys the pieces more closely. *This stuff looks like the kind of junk Dad used to trade. If it is, dad clearly got the better deal!*

"The chairs are wobbly and we'll have to at least re-glue the joints, lightly sand the pieces all over, and apply a coat of wood preservative. You can still just put them on Craigslist and be done with it. The desk is another matter – these two legs that are almost falling off have broken tenons and it's got some major cracks on the side panels and back."

He raps his knuckles along the desktop and doesn't give a second thought to a distinctly hollow sound at the right rear, "I don't think it's worth repairing unless it belonged to someone really famous, like George Washington."

Patina turns her face towards him with a disappointing look.

"Patina, I've got to clean up. Let's tackle all this stuff later. I'm hungry, how about you?"

"What're you thinking?"

"I've got all the makings for a chef's salad, but I'll need another chef in the kitchen. Do you know where I can find one who won't eat too many of the fixings before they're served, and who isn't covered with cobwebs and 200-year old dust?"

"I think I could clean myself up enough to help out," she says while running her fingers down his ribs. "Oh, you're ticklish, aren't you?"

They work well together, preparing dinner and serving it on Riggs' patio.

"Are you re-invigorated enough to jump back into wood-working now?"

"There's a little interest, but my plate's really spilling over building the business. It seems like someone's coming up with a new drone feature or capability every week. Nowadays, if I get tired of flying it manually, I can plot a course on the computer right here at home and upload it for the drone to fly. Or I can launch it and designate someone or something for it to follow automatically – just amazing. Maybe you need to tutor me on some computer skills, though."

"I don't know, you look like a pretty tough case to me. I mean, just look at the way you handled yourself with a cell phone GPS," she teases.

"That only happens when I'm around smart, beautiful, intriguing women..."

She grins with a poorly concealed acknowledgment, "Now I *know* you're laying it on,"

"Who said I was talking about you," he replies with a smile.

Patina laughs while balling up her napkin to throw at him.

After dinner they walk around the neighborhood, greeting a few of Riggs' neighbors and stopping to pet a pair of golden doodles.

"They're adorable, Riggs, and so affectionate. Ever think about getting a dog?"

"I love them, but I don't think they'd like my schedule – most days I'm away from the house all day."

"Put a fence around the back yard and use your carpentry skills to install a doggy door. It's just so wonderfully uplifting when they greet you at the end of a long day."

Right you are, Patina Gregors, but I'd much rather have you greet me at the end of the day!

Chapter 7

Loose Paper

The following Saturday afternoon, Patina drives to Riggs' house and finds him in the garage.

"Hey, Riggs, you working on the furniture already? I bought us a couple of smoothies and blueberry scones."

"Hi Patina, thanks – that's perfect, but this stuff isn't." He lays his sander on the workbench and walks over to give her a warm hug, "You ready to check everything out?"

She's a bit disappointed with his initial report and puts the refreshments on a workbench and hugs him back, "Yep, I'm ready. Working IT at the Society has its rewards, but I'd like to add to their real mission. Maybe I can do that with one of these. Oh, and you look like pretty good company, too."

Her heartfelt embrace and smile are more than enough to keep Riggs' motivated. "For as old as they look, the chairs aren't too bad; the wood's sound and I've already re-glued a few joints."

"That's a good start, I guess."

"The filing cabinet's not too bad either, but the slides need a little work if anyone's actually going to use it."

"And the desk?"

"It was probably quite a piece in its day – made from nice wide mahogany boards with straight, fine, even grain. It's really rot-resistant and probably came from Cuba. That's the good news."

"And... I'm sensing there's some bad news?"

It's a casualty of some rough handling and termites. Mahogany has some natural resistance to termites, so it's better than if it was pine or spruce, but it's still pretty well shot. I'm surprised it didn't fall apart during the move over here."

Patina walks over to the desk and leans on a pullout leaf that almost disintegrates in her hands. "I see what you mean. Have you checked to see if there's anything in the drawers?"

"No, but go ahead, then we can load it into the van with some other stuff I'm hauling to the recycling center today."

Patina looks through each drawer in turn, finding some nondescript papers among the roaches, cobwebs, and wood dust.

"Nothing here. I was hoping to at least find some papers signed by John Adams or Thomas Jefferson," she jokes.

After looking at the chairs and cabinet, they load the dilapidated desk into the van.

"Too bad we didn't save ourselves a trip by tossing it into Jason's dumpster last week," Riggs says.

"Yeah, yeah, there could've been a real find in there. Let's eat and I'll help you haul it away."

An hour later, they arrive at the recycle center and back the van up to the area designated for yard waste and wood. An operator waits nearby before using his tractor loader to consolidate the small stacks of branches, shrubs, and Patina's desk into a large pile they'll shred into mulch at the end of the day.

As fit as they are, they have no trouble pulling the old desk out of the van and onto the ground. They high-five each other and get back into the van. As Riggs is pulling away, the equipment operator moves in to scoop up the desk and add it to the large pile.

"Good, got that done," Riggs declares as he starts driving towards the exit. Then he hears an attendant hailing them from behind.

"Oh great, now what? Was I supposed to pay a fee, or don't they let us mix wooden furniture in with yard waste? I *really* don't want to take that thing back to the house."

Riggs stops and rolls down the window. "Something wrong?" he asks the approaching attendant.

"Hey Mister, you just dropped off that desk, didn't you?"

"Yes Sir, is there a problem?" *Here it comes...*

"You tell me. You probably didn't see it, but when I dropped it onto the pile, it smashed and this fell out." He hands Riggs a large waxy envelope with some old writing on it. "Thought you might want it."

That's a relief. "OK, thanks so much, we'll look at it," he says as he hands the envelope to Patina.

"I guess it was stashed somewhere in the desk we never saw. I wonder what it is – probably more old records."

"Who knows, maybe it's Jason's first pay stub," he jokes.

Patina looks at the envelope, "Riggs, the envelope says 'Committee Notes No. 3, August 6, 1787, JR.' That's over 230 years ago, what do you suppose it is?"

"A committee that decided to buy the Low Country Furniture building or something?" he replies sarcastically. "Open it; maybe whatever committee it was drew a treasure map, or kept some money inside."

Patina carefully slips her finger underneath the envelope flap and lifts it. She looks inside to find a sturdy sheet of linen paper with hand-written cursive text and five names at the bottom – only one of which is familiar to her: John Rutledge.

"Whatever it is, it's got to be *some*thing if it's this old."

"It may be. If it is, put it back in the envelope and you can take pictures of it for the people at the Historical Society. That way you don't have to handle it as much."

"That makes sense."

At the house, Riggs carries the envelope to his workbench, takes the page out, and carefully sets it down under better lighting.

"What do you think, history master? Any idea what it is? I don't see John Hancock's name, or anyone else's I've heard of."

"It could be some old business correspondence, I guess," she opines, hoping it's actually much more significant.

Patina, an excellent photographer, went to her SUV for her camera gear. She always kept it close for opportunity shots, especially the historical subjects that viewers frequently complimented her on. Her left brain handled the technical effects of aperture, shutter speed, and ISO settings, while her right brain intuitively used lighting and composition to capture her visions.

She returns with an old tried-and-true Nikon D3 professional digital camera body mounting a 24-70mm lens and an SB-800 flash. Riggs clears the workbench and spreads out a towel for better background contrast.

Patina turns on the flash and rotates the flash head to bounce its light off the ceiling for a more diffused effect. She sets the mode to "A" and ensures a tack-sharp focus with an *f*8 aperture setting. A quick check confirms that 200 ISO is dialed in to minimize noise. She composes and shoots a picture of the page.

Even though he's been watching Patina prepare for the shot, the bright flash stirs a memory of the IED explosion. *That image is seared into me; I'll never forget it, can only try to accommodate it.*

Patina glances at the back screen to confirm the correct settings, then points the camera towards the chairs and file cabinet.

Patina transfers the picture files from the camera's digital storage card to her laptop and opens them in her photo-editing program.

"What do you think, Riggs? Looks like we can print these and I'll bring them in Monday," she says with more than a hint of pride.

"Yep, they look perfect, just like their photographer. The experts at the Society should be able to see everything they need to know from them," Riggs compliments as he rests a hand on her shoulder.

Patina prints the pages with Riggs' printer, looks at them briefly, and hands them to Riggs for inspection and a bit of hoped-for admiration.

"They look great, Patina, but why the two smudges in the center of every page?"

She grabs the prints and examines them; Riggs was absolutely right. "Damn it! That's from some trash on the camera sensor. I haven't cleaned it in months because I hardly ever change lenses. Let me take care of it," she says, a little embarrassed.

She exports the file to Photoshop, taps the "J" key on the keyboard, and uses the editing tool to blend the spots to the exact same color as their surroundings. "There, that'll do it. Now I'll just print the edited versions and we're all set."

The printer groans and stops.

"Damn it! It's always something – the computer won't talk to the printer, the paper's jammed, it's low on ink, or needs a program update," she grouses. "Now it's out of paper! Well screw it; these do a great job of showing the furniture and this one clearly shows the document date, all the text, and the names. Professor Arkin should be able to use it to tell whether it's significant or not."

Patina closes her photo programs and makes a mental note to clean the camera sensor.

Riggs puts consoling hands on her shoulders and leans forward with his cheek next to her hair. Patina puts her hands on his and squeezes them.

"Mission accomplished, Patina. Let's have a glass of wine on the back-porch swing."

"That sounds perfect, I'd love to."

On the way to the kitchen she spots a Baldwin upright piano and stops in front of it, "Riggs, you didn't tell me you played the piano."

"Oh that, it's something Dad picked up years ago on a job. He and mom thought they'd turn me into some kind of keyboard prodigy, but never had much success. How about you?"

"I play a little," she says coyly.

"Really? Let me pull out the bench for a quick serenade."

She browses the sheet music as she sits down, "OK, anything in particular you'd like to hear?" she asks while focusing on a few song-books in the music rack.

"Surprise me, I'm game for anything from country to classical."

Patina sits erect, addresses the keyboard, and warms up with a short étude.

That's already better than I ever played, he thinks.

She begins with a two-measures prelude, then continues with melody and chords as she softly sings, "Night time sharpens, heightens each sensation…"

Riggs recognizes the words from Andrew Lloyd Webber's 'Music of the Night', "You do opera too?"

"Oh no, not really," she laughs. "I saw *Phantom of the Opera* years ago and loved the songs – I played them so many times I can still do a couple of them from memory."

Well, I'm certainly impressed. Is there anything she doesn't do?

Patina stands up and accompanies Riggs into the kitchen to get a couple of glasses while he uncorks a bottle of Chianti.

"You know, Patina, I've really enjoyed working this project together. I didn't think that getting back to the shop would be so enjoyable, but it is and you're the reason why." He leans towards her and kisses her forehead, "Thank you."

She looks up, warmed by his sentiment, and even more pleased that he told her.

"Well, Mr. Riggs Blanding, I find myself looking forward to seeing you, too. Let's go outside and enjoy ourselves on the swing." She steps forward, hugs him around the neck, and returns a kiss.

"Well that's certainly worth hauling furniture for."

They walk to the swing holding hands and their wine, with absolutely no idea how significant their discovery is and the perils it'll bring.

Chapter 8

Trash or Treasure?

J ust after Patina sits down in her cubicle at the Charleston Historical Society on Monday, Professor David Arkin arrives.

"Good morning, Melba," he greets the receptionist, "All ready for another grand week?"

As the Historical Society's Executive Director, Dr. Arkin sets an admirable example of punctuality and politeness. His manner is also reassuring, helping Patina avoid feelings of the shock she underwent in college. Among his many professional attributes, he has a well-respected eye for early American furniture. There are few better authorities on South Carolina history than Arkin, and Patina is excited to support him with what may be a discovery for the Society, even if it's a minor one.

"Knock, knock," she announces as she leans her head into his office. "Can I get a quick minute before things get crazy?"

"Good morning, Miss Gregors, how may I serve you? Is everything all right with the computers this morning?"

"Oh, yes sir, they're all fine, at least for the moment." Patina then quickly summarizes the events that lead to her seeing the furniture and her admittedly unstudied assessment. Arkin listens attentively, but without any anticipation of finding something meaningful. She looks for raised eyebrows or a focused look to indicate some interest, but doesn't see either. She also surmises that he's not interested in spending much time on the matter.

"Patina, I appreciate your commitment to the Society's purpose, but right now I'm struggling to develop a theme for our annual donors' event. We desperately need the funding, and that'll require something new – some signature exhibit with real impact. I'm afraid it'll have to be something much more significant than a couple of old pieces of furniture."

Patina lowers her gaze and her shoulders sink. *Am I making a fool of myself?* She walks a few steps to his desk and lays four pictures on it.

"Not to rain on anyone's parade, but excited friends and strangers often tell a similar story – 'It could've been George Washington's!' they say with hopeful enthusiasm."

"I took these pictures of three old furnishings and one of an old paper that was in a desk we had to throw away."

Dr. Arkin puts his coffee cup on a bookshelf, hangs up his jacket, turns around, and walks to the desk. He bends over and looks at the pictures of the chairs and filing cabinet.

"Well it looks like they're in fair shape for their age, and if I had to say, possibly from as early as the late 1700s or early 1800s. Before you get excited about their possible value, though, I have to say that I don't believe on first inspection that there's anything distinctive about them, nor are they particularly rare. In fact, they have the characteristics of fairly common pieces – inexpensive, functional items that business owners would've picked up for office staff. Unremarkable, really."

Patina shrugs.

He continues, "I'm sorry I can't report that they belonged to anyone of note. Someone decorating a period house may want them, but I can't imagine an established museum vying for these."

Patina sighs and picks up the three furniture photos.

"I understand, and thank you so much for your time and expertise, Dr. Arkin."

"I took this last pictures of a document we found in the desk. I know it's old – look at the date, and it has five signatures on the bottom. I checked on them - they're five of the Founding Fathers and the first one is John Rutledge from South Carolina."

Arkin's demeanor and interest instantly transform as he sits down and looks at the last photo. His concentration narrows when he reads the text and carefully examines each name.

"My dear, tell me again where you got this."

"I took the picture myself, it's a shot of an old-looking page my friend and I found in an antique desk."

"This is interesting, Ms. Gregors, *very* interesting indeed."

Patina feels partially vindicated and manages a smile.

"John Rutledge was the colonial President, then Governor, of South Carolina and one of our state's delegates to the 1787 Constitutional Convention in Philadelphia. Since these other four men were also delegates to the Convention, the signatures alone would make it a treasure if they're original."

Patina's excitement grows with the revelation.

Suddenly, Dr. Arkin's face absolutely illuminates, becoming much more animated than she's ever seen him, "I've been searching for something unique, something dramatic that the Society could use as the centerpiece for the donors' event. You've no doubt seen the mannequin we're assembling – it's John Rutledge's great grandson, Colonel Henry Rutledge II, right down to the original Civil War belt buckle and officer's sword. Henry was a colonel in the Confederate army at age 22, so it'll be quite an attraction. But this document, this would round out the exhibition perfectly! We could feature it in the Rutledge Room, on a floor display that includes a note explaining its relevance." Arkin is fascinated now, and feels like a weight has just been lifted from his shoulders.

"My friend Riggs does woodworking, I'll ask him if he'd make a display stand."

"Oh, that'd be splendid, Ms. Gregors. Then we could place the U.S. flag to the display's right and the state flag on the opposite side. Between them, we'll have South Carolina's Revolutionary War flag," he excitedly points to a blue banner with a white crescent and palm tree attached to a stout pole with a traditional spearhead on top.

"That looks awfully intimidating."

"The flag bearer certainly hoped the enemy thought so too. Since he couldn't handle the flag and a sword or pistol at the same time, it was his only real weapon during an assault."

"The whole exhibit would look striking under the ceiling light, just in front of the Colonel Rutledge mannequin."

Arkin enthusiastically nods in agreement, just barely containing himself. "I suggest we consult Dr. Dale Hartman on this matter, he's an academic acquaintance who's a history professor at Charleston State University. I believe he wrote his doctoral thesis on the

Constitutional Convention, or at least some of the events surrounding it. I'll send him an introductory email and you can arrange an appointment through his assistant."

"Thank you so much, Sir, I'll call first thing tomorrow."

Patina was more than anxious to finish her day and report the breaking news to Riggs. *This could be a real find!* For now, she looked up Dr. Hartman. He joined the university's faculty four years ago and sat on several doctoral committees. A number of routine accolades followed his name on the faculty page, but none were very recent. She couldn't find any outside interests or activities he was associated with.

It was difficult for Patina to concentrate on work, but when her day finally ended, she sped over to Riggs' house. Pulling into his driveway, she finds him in the front yard picking up tools after completing some overdue yard work. He wasn't a gardener, but could mentally escape in the manual chores of keeping the place looking nice.

"Hey Patina, what's up?" Riggs asks, "You look pretty excited."

"You won't believe it!" she says as she runs up and hugs him.

"The furniture belonged to George Washington?" he jokes.

"No, not the furniture – it's old, but pretty ordinary. The document though, it may have actually been handwritten by the Founding Fathers!"

"Well that certainly sounds like a contribution to the Society mission – good on ya! Let me put these tools away, then tell me all about it. Will you give me a hand and get my hoe?"

Patina pauses, grins at him, and playfully teases, "I thought *I* was your ho."

Riggs turns towards her, smiles broadly, and shakes his head. *Well, isn't she just full of surprises!*

She smiles back at him, "Riggs, Dr. Arkin wasn't interested in the furniture, but he was *very* interested in the document. He said it could be original notes from the Constitutional Convention."

"Really? And that's a big deal? I guess that gets me off the hook for furniture repairs."

"No, listen, this could be huge. He wants it to be the centerpiece at the annual donors' event, mounted on a wooden display stand that you could make."

"Oh, a stand that *I* could make?" he asks as she comes over to hug and kiss him.

"He also said we ought to show it to one of the professors at the university, an expert on that period. Will you go with me?"

"I don't know much about early American history, so I don't know what I can contribute to the discussion. But I'm happy to go with you if I don't have a client then. When are you going to see him?"

"Oh, I don't even have an appointment yet. Why don't you check your business bookings and I'll call his office tomorrow morning."

The ordinary start of their investigation belies what lies ahead from unexpected directions.

Founders' Intent

Chapter 9

At Any Price

The mood is significantly more intense in Silver Spring, MD, where Donnie Edison, the chief contract negotiator for the Food Services Union of America, is nervously briefing his union's president.

"Boss, we're already getting a ton of push-back from the other side of the table about increasing health benefits. We can probably move 'em if we don't press for wages too, but there's no way we're getting anything worthwhile in *both* directions. I think we've got to keep looking for a good bump in the healthcare package first."

President Colman's face reddens and his brows wrinkle. He stands up and sticks out his chest like a silverback gorilla intimidating a predator. He scans the roomful of officers and glares at Donnie for an uncomfortable 10 seconds. Everyone in the room tenses under his caustic stare.

"*Looking for?* Donnie, we're not just *looking* for a health care bump. This is the *big* one, the do-or-die. If we get whipped on this, I'm through as union president because the rank and file will vote in two months for one of those assholes who says 'Colman couldn't get it done, elect me'. And make no mistake, shit rolls downhill, so all of you are through too. Hell, the whole damn union could go wobbly." *Christ, I'm way too far down the road to find another gig like this one - hell, all of us are.*

Suitably intimidated and embarrassed, a red-faced Donnie looks down at the floor.

"We *really* gotta come away from the table with something I can bring back to the membership. Sure, I'd love to get health care *and* a wage bump, but that's out of the question now. Besides, most of our wage contracts are guaranteed by the federal minimum, and that's solid. So drill into the health piece with everything you've got - *that's* going to be our push. Next time, we'll squeeze 'em really hard to increase the wage multiple. And they can afford it, they just don't want to."

"We'll have to throw 'em a bone somewhere, boss."

"Fall off a little, but *just* a little on the number of regular hours before getting overtime. And believe me, those assholes can pay for that too."

"Don't forget to keep jamming it up the suits' butts about how Amazon's going to pay at least $15 an hour, even to part-timers. Seattle raised their minimum to $16, and California pushed its to $11. That'll soften 'em up for health."

"Got it."

"Donnie, don't let 'em push you around on health care."

Donnie gives an obligatory nod, "I'm on it boss."

Colman's temples begin sweating. He rolls up his sleeves to cool down, paces the floor, then fixes his stare on public relations chief Jack Andretti.

"How we doing on press releases, Jack?"

"On top of 'em, boss. We keep talking about our health demands. Haven't had any real pushback in the press, social media, or the internet."

"Damn well better not. God knows I shovel enough advertising money their way. OK, keep it up. Paul, talk to me about membership"

"Sure, boss, they like what you're doing to shift health costs off their backs and onto management's." Out of this month's three and a half million total food service workers, just over 265,000 are on our rolls, and that's been climbing.

"You need to ramp it up – we gotta be the biggest dog on the block when it comes to raw numbers. They making any noises about pay?"

"Well, there're always some, mostly those starting out at the federal minimum rate."

Everyone in the room knows that many of the members and union officials aren't actually paid the federal minimum, but a wage that's *indexed* to it. Even though the fed hourly rate is $7.25, workers indexed at 1.5x earn almost $11 an hour.

"Yeah, I remember some of those wage wars, they were knock-down drag-outs. But, hey, what can I say - wages are still the holy grail. If the union stands for anything, it's got to be wages."

"Sure, Boss. Nobody really understands the whole multiple thing anyway. They just look at the bottom number on their pay stub and don't care how the pencil-necked green eyeshades come up with it. That's part of the beauty of it. When our people hear about the fed's $7.25, they know they're earning more than that, so they're happy with us. When the public hears it, they think it's low and they sympathize with us. They don't have a clue that's just the starting point for what we actually take in."

"Good, good, don't give me any downturns."

"Even though the Fed's minimum is lower for tipped workers, some of them are coming aboard too. I think they're seeing we can really do something for everyone in this next contract."

Boggs Colman seems relatively calm for the moment and turns back to his Public Relations chief, "Jack, you're sending my letter out to all of 'em, including new members?"

"Yes sir, it tells 'em how you've always fought for them, and will go to the mat with every one of the asshole owners who're trying to get rich off their work."

"I just wish it really did call 'em out – asshole owners."

"It doesn't say that exactly, but it's pretty close, like you wanted."

"OK, thanks - all of you."

On the way down the hall after the meeting and out of anyone's earshot, Donnie and Jack compare notes.

"If he was half as involved in-between contract years as he is during them, he wouldn't be so damned uptight about the election in two months," Donnie confides.

"Amen to that, brother. He used to be a real fighter for working stiffs. Now that he's finally in the big corner office, he's all about his new Cadillac and the condo at the shore we're not supposed to know about."

Boggs Colman worked hard, smart, and sometimes forcefully, starting as a teenager in Charleston. He'd been happy to land a fast food job and put in long hours, but quickly learned about nepotism when a manager skipped over him to promote a well-connected shirker. That happened a couple of other times, which motivated Boggs to join the union. It also motivated him to put the manager in the hospital for two days.

"Didn't he really mess up some guy in South Carolina, a supplier?" Donnie asks.

"That's the story going around with people down there. When he was a district director or something like that, restaurants were cutting back on hiring and hours because they said meat prices were going through the roof. Some prick who sold the meat kept jacking the rates, which was killing the little guys. The union higher-ups asked Boggs to pay him a visit."

"A 'business' call?"

"Yep, *hard* business. The guy was some foreign shit who made the mistake of pulling on Boggs and popping off a shot – would've killed him if he'd aimed any better. It messed up the boss's shoulder and golf game, though – he still fades his drives. They say Boggs and some union muscle from the northwest left the little prick hanging from a meat hook."

"Did that really happen? I thought it was a rumor."

"I think it really did - it's the kind of thing BC would've done back then."

"Hanging someone from a meat hook – damn, that's hard core, even for Boggs."

"Yeah, sure is. He was already on his way up the ladder, and the union kept rewarding his persuasive skills, devious thinking, and willingness to put 'em all to work whenever they asked him to. I don't even want to think how far he'd go if anybody got in the way of locking in this contract."

Chapter 10

Across the Table

"Colman's really starting to dig in and ramp up the public propaganda on this one," Neal Tanner tells his contract negotiating staff.

Tanner, President and CEO of the National Association of Restauranteurs, was just as anxious to stonewall contract negotiations as his opposite number Boggs Colman was to accelerate them. Dragging them beyond the union's November election would almost certainly ensure Colman's defeat and provide Tanner with a much less-combative adversary.

A management friendly outcome would also bring Neal Tanner to the attention of the search committee for Burger Joints' new CEO. Leading a Fortune 500 business like Burger Joints national fast food chain was Neal's lifelong ambition, and he wasn't about to let Boggs Colman impede it. Neal was also keenly aware that an unsuccessful negotiation would end his tenure as the Association's President and CEO – the stakes were far too great for directors to retain him after any such a debacle.

"Neal, we're throwing all the right points up and we both know what any sort of walkout would do to their strike fund – it's just about empty," Jim Olson, his negotiations team chief, tells him. "They're coming at us hard on the health care, Neal, and that stuff is expensive, *very* expensive. When the companies pay for it, their profitability drops and can easily take a fatal hit. Then investors pull their money out and move it where they'll get a higher return. Too much of that and the companies implode – stock prices fall, the Chinese buy them, and everyone loses... management *and* workers."

Another adds, "And don't forget all these states, cities, and companies that've jumped on this 'livable wage' bandwagon. Everyone loves free stuff, and it's generated some real momentum and a ton of popular enthusiasm among the union rank and file and leadership."

Neal angrily waves his finger and abruptly stops them, "I *know* all that - now tell me something I *don't* know – something different we can jump out of the starting gate with. Who's thinking outside the box for a really innovative strategy we've never used before? Something from left field, something they're not prepared for and won't know how to respond to? Find something that'll keep 'em tied up just long enough to frustrate the membership and dump Colman?"

"I hear you, Neal, at least in principle. But I'm not sure what kind of move that'd be or what it'd look like," another director tells him.

An increasingly desperate and frustrated Neal Tanner berates, "Gentlemen, do I have to do *all* the thinking here? You haven't told me *anything* new. We need a way to slow down the negotiating momentum on health costs, overtime rules, and 'give em whatever-they-protest-for wages. Those are all the rage until you run the financials on them. It'd be a hell of a lot easier to negotiate with a new union president instead of that Neanderthal Boggs, so go back to your offices, put some batteries in your thinking caps, and let's get things back on track."

When someone lays out all the pieces, they can put them together - even when it's complicated. But coming up with something new and bold... I'm not holding my breath for that crowd's Eureka moment. But that's exactly what we need.

Neal returns to his corner office, worrying about the negotiating strategy, its outcome, and his personal future.

Chapter 11

Cabal

In Washington, D.C., Congressman Sonny Butler shares every bit of Boggs Colman's re-election angst - he's all too aware of his uncomfortably slim first-term victory. His stomach literally twists at the thought of losing his innumerable congressional perks and power to dispense favors and punish political and personal enemies.

Butler formed and abandoned countless alliances as a Charleston County Councilman and state senator, and hasn't hesitated to do the same in his current office. Promoting an expensive, questionably useful road in Charleston County was small potatoes compared to other deals he was orchestrating from Washington. He wasn't about to relinquish that hard-won power and prestige to an ambitious young challenger.

"Get Boggs Colman on the phone," Sonny tells his loyalty-over-morality Chief of Staff Luther Phillips.

Hometown friend and union president Boggs Colman only had to fight off challengers every four years, but as soon as Butler was elected, he had to immediately start campaigning for his next election. And that took money - lots of *other* people's money.

"Boggs, I know you're hip deep in contract negotiations and reelection business, so I just wanted to see if there was anything I could do for you and the membership."

"Hey there, Sonny, I certainly do appreciate the offer, especially in light of everything you've got going on with your bill in the Education and Workforce Committee. I guess the real question is what can *I* do for *you*?"

In reality, both men knew all too well that Sonny would do as little as possible for as many votes and dollars as he could get, and Boggs would donate the least amount of money necessary to keep Sonny's influence. Like everyone else, they were always trying to fly first class for a coach fare.

"That's mighty kind of you, Boggs. I hope you know I always have time on my calendar to stop by and say a few words at any event you've got – I heard some pissant from Baltimore's trying to wiggle his way into your seat this time."

"Yeah, sure is, but I'm doing everything I need to so that never happens. Thanks for reaching out though, Sonny, and you know you can count on me and the membership in South Carolina to turn out for you. I've already submitted this year's contribution plan to the board to rubber stamp. After our max direct contribution to your campaign, we'll funnel the rest to a super PAC - these days, it takes a village!"

"I knew I could count on you for all that, and I hope you know how much it means to me to turn out the rank and file in November."

"Don't give it a second thought, Sonny."

"Listen, Boggs, have you considered leaning on the restaurant owners and their families a little harder, kind of up-close and personal? I'm seeing some of that in the news, and it looks like it sends a real clear message."

"Not really, but I'm open to anything; tell me more."

"Here's the way it looks to me, Boggs. The suits don't give a second thought to making a mess of your members' lives and paying such cheap wages that your guys can't even *take* their families out to eat. Why not give the suits a taste of the same crap they're dishing out?"

"OK, I'm listening."

"I know a guy named Hondo who can whip up demonstrations for anything you want. Why not get some pros to go to the suits' houses in their fancy neighborhoods, knock on their doors and tell 'em they're pieces of crap – right to their faces. Or to their wives' faces. Show up at the end of the driveway in the morning when mommy takes their precious little clones to school. It really gets to the wives and kids, and they'll lean on hubby at the dinner table the way you *never* could at the bargaining table. It works *really* well on the timid ones!"

"I like the sound of that, I'll get one of my guys on it. What do they charge?" *There's no way I'm paying more than $7.00 an hour to some herd of street-level agitators.*

"Get some of his other guys to follow the suits and families to restaurants or shopping malls and give 'em a face-full there, too – that'll make 'em think twice about stepping on your guys while they're living the high life."

"I'm sold, how do I get a hold of the guy?"

"Get a pen and I'll give you a number. Just don't pay him any of the money you're steering my way!" Sonny jokes.

Sonny hangs up and goes back to work on a labor bill he wants to submit to the Education and Workforce Committee. It's a bit of a long shot he's coordinating with some cronies at the Department of Labor to mandate additional health benefits for workers in the restaurant business. Any federal pressure he can exert on the owners will be leverage Boggs can use in contract negotiations... and become further indebted to Sonny.

Within two days, Boggs' accomplice of many years and union Chief of Membership Paul Hayes contacts Hondo.

Chapter 12

Anniversary Dinner

"**H**ondo is it?" Paul Hayes asks into his cell phone.
"Yeah, this is Hondo, who am I talking to?"
"My name's Paul, and I'd like to talk about doing some business. I need some small groups to show up at a few homes and restaurants within a week."

"That's what I do. I can get some of them out on the streets this week and the rest early next week. School's in session, so it cuts into my labor pool. I do business at the Starbucks on Wisconsin NW, Center Metro Level. About 10:00 tomorrow morning?"

"That'd be great, thanks, Hondo."

Paul meets Hondo the following morning and ever the bargainer, negotiates hours, wages, travel expenses, confidentiality, and liability. Neither side even considers raising the issues of benefits, especially health care or paying the minimum wage.

Paul slides a single piece of paper across the table, "Hondo, I need a group at each of these home addresses when their neighbors are driving to work or coming home – lots of visibility. I also need some people on a short string in the evening to show up at restaurants or shopping malls when I call you. Can you do that?"

"Too easy, but you've also got to pay the on-call people for the time they're on stand-by."

"Sure, I understand - I can do that."

As advertised, Hondo has a couple of small crews at the home addresses Paul provided.

When Neal Tanner looks out his kitchen window two mornings later, he sees a group of five college age males and females walking back and forth with signs on the sidewalk in front of his house:

WE WANT HEALTHY KIDS TOO

> HEALTH CARE – YOU HAVE IT, WE DESERVE IT
> GREED KILLS
> HEALTH CARE IS A RIGHT
> PEOPLE BEFORE PROFITS

Neal's shocked, *What the hell? They aren't even <u>old</u> enough to have families. How'd they know where we live? There's no way they're restaurant workers.*

"Marge, come over here to the window, look at this - I don't believe it."

Their kids come downstairs, the youngest one crying, "Mommy, what's going on outside? Who are those people, and why are they carrying signs in front of our house? What're profits? I'm scared!"

"They frighten me, Neal, are they dangerous? I've got to take the children to school today," Marjorie confides while trying to hide her primal fear from the kids.

"I don't know what they're capable of and I'm not waiting to find out; I'm calling the police right now. This is extreme, it's absurd, and I can bet who's behind it."

"Behind it? They aren't just some angry workers?"

"I'd bet the farm that Boggs Colman and his damn union set this up, I'm sure of it."

That evening Jim Olson, Neal's negotiating chief, backs a silver Lexus out of his garage to take his wife out for her 48th birthday dinner. A pair of union eyes watches their departure and the observer alerts Paul Hayes, "Mr. Hayes, he's just pulling out now with a woman in the car – must be his old lady."

"Good, follow them and call me when they arrive wherever they're going. Don't let 'em see you."

"Yes sir, I'll do it."

As soon as the Olsons drive down their residential street, the observer sits upright in his car, starts the engine and follows them from a couple of car-lengths away. Area traffic is unusually light for metro Washington this evening, and the Olsons pull up to their favorite Italian restaurant 18 minutes later.

The union observer dutifully picks up his phone and dials, "Mr. Hayes, they're going into the Borgo Italia by the intersection of 644 and I-95. What should I do now - wait until they come out?"

"Just tell me what they look like and what they're wearing, then you're done for the night. Thanks for the good work." Paul relays the restaurant location and the Olson's physical description to Hondo, who forwards it to an on call four-member team.

The team arrives at the restaurant in 16 minutes with a plastic bottle of colored vinegar and a flask of urine. A female member of the team enters first to survey the layout and find the Olsons... sitting against the left wall under posters of northwest Italy's Cinque Terre National Park. She goes back outside and briefs her teammates. They're all convinced they're social and economic justice warriors battling immoral forces of evil.

Each member is dressed in non-descript clothes and wears a cap and tinted glasses; the two males are sporting low-grade costume moustaches. The four of them push through the front door, abruptly brush past the hostess, and begin screaming at the Olsons, "Hate mongers! Racists! Fascists! Robbers! If we can't eat here, you can't either! Get out! You owe us the same health care you have!"

The frantic manager can't dial 911 fast enough, not knowing if his restaurant will erupt in violence at any minute. In addition to any violence, this is devastating for business.

Jim Olsen and his terrified wife also have no idea what's happening or where the melee is headed; they're completely shocked. He reaches across the table to tightly hold her trembling hands and they both crouch lower in defensive postures. Jim instinctively reaches for his butter knife without any conscious thought of what he'll do with it.

"Jim, what's happening? Who *are* these dreadful people? Why are they doing this to *us*? What are they going to do? I'm petrified!" she sobs.

One paid demonstrator quickly moves behind Olson's wife and empties the foul-smelling urine on her hair and new dress, "See how you like that, you greedy capitalist bitch!" he gleefully cackles.

His partner splashes colored vinegar over Jim and his expensive suit before signaling his co-conspirators to quickly escape. The astonished staff and older diners don't think about taking a cellphone video, which might've been of questionable value anyway, considering the subdued lighting and fast action.

Hondo's teams continue to assault officers of the National Association of American Restauranteurs over the next several days. Boggs Colman beams wider with each day's report. *Nothing's too extreme when it comes to looking out for the rank and file* he reflects as he looks up and out the window to admire his new $81,520 Cadillac Escalade in its reserved parking space.

Chapter 13

The Expert

"Edwards? *Edwards?* Which fools made *that* moronic oxygen thief a department chairman?"

Professor Dale Hartman seethes in his plain third-story office at Charleston State University. He literally grinds his teeth while reading about former classmates who've been appointed as department chairs, or in one case, a dean. Every two months he pores over the accomplishments of yet another fellow alum without ever seeing his own name in Stanford Magazine. *I'll be damned if I'm sending in updates like these limelight-grabbing noobs; my work speaks for itself and the editorial staff themselves ought to write me up.*

Resignedly, he knows everyone else draws the same conclusion he does – Dale Hartman never made the ivies; he's nothing more than a mediocre, no-name faculty member at a small undistinguished state university. The repetitive absence of his name glaringly reiterates his stagnation.

Hartman tightens his jaw as well as his grip on the magazine, then spitefully slams it on the desk in disgust. He's written several notable articles in the past, but nothing of peer interest recently.

Characteristically, he consoles himself by disparaging others, *My piece three years ago was the most original insight ever published about the influence of the Founders' personalities on the Constitution, and none of these so-called brilliant minds appreciated it– if they even understood it!*

Dale Hartman's sole form of physical activity is walking up three flights of stairs so he can avoid other faculty members and students who take the elevator to the third floor. He attempts to cover his slightly balding scalp with a comb-over, cautiously experimenting in front of his bathroom mirror to avoid any snickering comparisons to Donald Trump. His stout physique, ordinary stature, and pedestrian manners contribute to his self-deprecation.

Hartman lives alone in a two-bedroom condo that only occasionally sees a male friend or two join him for a card game. Most other nights he listens to a collection of classical music CDs or reads great novels in hopes of acquiring taste to burnish his image.

No other faculty member comes close to my knowledge of the Constitution's origins, ratification, and role in early American development - not a soul among them! But, no, Chairman Bentson continues to run the History Department and dictate academic policy to me. When'll they see the light? He often repeats the mantra to himself and a few confidants who find him slightly delusional.

After research, Hartman's greatest pleasure is exercising authority over teaching assistants and students who must suffer his abusive critiques with virtually no recourse. This semester, he's taking particular delight in tormenting a student whose visible attributes conspicuously eclipse his own. That student is younger, of course, much more physically fit and better looking, gregarious, and ever so popular with the ladies. Any of those traits alone would irritate Hartman to no end; taken altogether, they absolutely infuriate him.

Passing back midterm exams during an early class provides a perfect opportunity to gloat over that student, "Mr. Jackson is it? You seem to have utterly failed to grasp even the most fundamental concept of the Founders' view of federalism. The readings in your syllabus provide excellent explanations; have you read or done *any-thing* outside of class - anything at all?"

Hartman relishes watching Jackson submit to his authority and fidget with each sentence, "In fact, it appears that you're failing to achieve even the minimum standards for passing the entire course..." In the midst of the harangue, Hartman quickly glances at Jackson's attractive coed friend, whom he's hoping to impress with his dominance over the popular student. *Now who's the big man on campus?*

After the morning class, Dale Hartman smugly struts down the hall and sees the department's newest faculty member walking towards him, young Professor Robin Cochran. *Old Chairman Bentson finally did one thing right – hired a little eye candy to light up the halls!* Hartman knows, but chooses not to recognize nor appreciate, that her work is rigorously documented and two of her peer applauded articles were recently published. He alters his direction to intercept her.

"Dr. Cochran, right? Good morning, I'm Professor Hartman, Professor Dale Hartman. I was at the faculty mixer last week, but didn't get a chance to welcome you to the University." Hartman would never admit the truth, that he wasn't about to embarrass himself in front of several eminent colleagues who were fawning over her.

Continuing her stride, Dr. Cochran turns towards him. "Oh hello, Doctor, that's very kind – thank you ever so much. Listen, I'd really love to chat, but I'm already late for a meeting, perhaps some other time?" she says over her shoulder while continuing down the hall. *What'd he say his name was? He's a professor here? I thought he was some geriatric administrator.*

Hartman's inability to attract and hold a woman's attention adds one more dimension to his self-denigration.

To be sure, Dr. Hartman is very well versed in the overall aspects, as well as details, of the Constitution's impact on the young, developing nation. He steadfastly clings to the idea of a breakthrough moment that will thrust that knowledge onto a broader, more prestigious academic stage - propelling him to the higher office and admiration he's convinced he so justifiably deserves.

I just need one chance – I'll take it from there. One stand-out opportunity that I could turn into a tour-de-force would guarantee me being on the short list for chairman here. That'd do it, that's all it'd take.

Professor Dale Hartman has no idea, of course, that an intern from the Charleston Historical Society and her friend are about to present him with just such an opportunity.

Founders' Intent

Chapter 14

First Look

P atina is her usual punctual self, arriving ten minutes early for the 9:30 AM appointment and looks around the parking lot for Riggs. *He knows how much this means, where is he? Better not have run into someone.* She keeps scanning the lot while walking into the faculty building.

Riggs greets her in the lobby with a hug, "Hey, good lookin', been waiting on you – I'm hoping you brought smoothies and scones this morning."

"I thought it was your turn, trooper, " she says while lovingly poking him in the torso.

They look at each other, smile, and sneak a quick kiss.

On the third floor, the administrative assistant who serves two newly-minted PhDs and Professor Hartman welcomes and invites them to sit on a small sofa outside Hartman's office.

Within minutes, Hartman approaches from down the hall, "Are you waiting for me? I don't recognize you as any of my graduate students or doctoral candidates." His tone is brusque and snobbish.

"No Sir, we're not students. I'm Patina Gregors and this is my friend Riggs Blanding. I intern for Doctor Arkin at the Charleston Historical Society. He referred us to you in regard to a document we found."

"Oh, yes, I remember, David sent me an email about that. I'm Professor Hartman, follow me," he coolly commands while unlocking the door to his cluttered office.

Riggs notes that Hartman neglected to extend his hand, emphasized his title of 'Professor', and didn't say his first name. *Probably to ensure that we underlings don't get any ideas about being on a first name basis with his highness, the arrogant ass; reminds me of a couple of colonels I used to work for.*

"Well, come in and show me what David was so interested in," he grouses.

Like Riggs, Hartman also notices and admires Patina's athletic figure and strikingly good looks. He also immediately and correctly concludes that she wouldn't be the least bit interested in him even if they were much closer in age. *Damn, she's fine, why do they always go for brawn instead of brains? I bet she'd be all over Jackson - that dimwitted self-styled Adonis in my Constitutional Studies class. Hasn't she noticed what's hanging on my walls? And this boyfriend of hers, does he even have a GED?*

Riggs looks around at Hartman's four 'I love me' walls, completely covered with personal certificates, diplomas, and photographs. *I'm surprised he doesn't have his 1st grade report card hanging up.*

Patina presents Dr. Hartman with a folder containing the page-sized photograph of the document. Hartman scans it, then his eyes go straight to the signatures on the bottom. He bends forward and squints at the five names, then sits back up and reactively raises his eyebrows. He makes a deliberate effort to mask his enthusiasm - playing his cards close to the chest to gain control of wherever the discovery may go.

"Where did you get this?" Hartman asks without so much as glancing at Patina.

"I took it myself."

"Yes, yes, of course, but the document in the picture, where is *it*? Who has it and where did it come from?" Hartman blurts out as though he has a right to know and she's somehow obliged to tell him.

Patina immediately realizes from his tone and reaction that she and Riggs are on to something very significant.

"Riggs and I discovered the original page a couple of weeks ago. We didn't want to handle it any more than was absolutely necessary, so I took this picture. It captures the colors of the original paper and ink very accurately."

Hartman looks at it even more closely, becoming more excited. He doesn't offer an opinion regarding its authenticity, but makes a mental note to compare the signatures with known originals.

"The date coincides with the Constitutional Convention. It's possible these men were delegates to the Convention; by all means, I'll check on that. *Of course they're delegates, Dale – hell, our own*

*South Carolina delegate Rutledge chaired the Committee of Detail.
What have these two rubes stumbled onto? Most importantly, how do
I get it from them?*

"Oh, naturally, authentication goes without saying," Riggs says
in a thinly-disguised mocking tone. "Patina already looked them up
– they clearly were delegates."

Patina shoots him a quick look that says 'Can it, buster'.

Hartman condescendingly scowls at Riggs and continues, "Some
of the delegates to the Convention simply wanted to improve upon
the existing Articles of Confederation, under which the colonies re-
linquished a limited degree of their authority to a federal government
to prosecute the Revolutionary War. Virginia delegate James Madison and others came with a very different idea. They saw a unique
opportunity to create an entirely new authority – with a Constitution
for a completely new and different type of federal government."

"Yes, sir, I'm familiar with that," Patina says.

Hartman glances at her with a slight sneer. *Is this little tart trying
to impress me with some superficial bit of internet knowledge she just
picked up last week? How dare she interrupt a professor!* "As with
any large assembly dealing with extremely consequential matters, the
55 delegates organized over a dozen committees to examine certain
very contentious subjects, such as slavery and the proportion of each
state's representation in the new federal government. I'll check to see
if these five delegates were serving on one of those committees."

*What a blowhard. You need a PhD to find out who was on a
committee writing the U.S. Constitution?* Riggs pulls out his
smartphone and seconds later reports, "Here it is right here in Wikipedia: 'Rutledge chaired the Committee of Detail that produced the
first complete draft of the Constitution'."

"Then this could be actual handwritten notes from that committee!" Patina says.

"Not so fast young lady, we can't get ahead of ourselves and
jump to conclusions. Proper research deserves precise academic ri-
gor, not a simple two-minute Google search that you students rush
into nowadays. Fortunately, I have all the requisite training and experience to conduct the meticulous work this requires. You'll have to

provide me with the original document, though." *Can this be? Can these possibly be actual notes from the Committee of Detail? That would be absolutely ground breaking!*

Patina ignores the document request and Riggs is getting fed up with Hartman's arrogance. He steps in front of Hartman's computer keyboard and types 'Constitutional Convention' into the search bar. "Mr. Hartman, I'm pretty good on Google, I'll find out what they did on the committee in no time."

A more discreet Patina thinks, *Probably not a smart move, Riggs.*

Hartman immediately pivots towards Riggs, aghast that anyone else would dare use his workstation. The completely flustered professor recoils in shock, "You've probably never been associated with higher education, young man, but it's proper to address me as either 'Professor' or 'Doctor'. And that university computer is for my exclusive use. You have to get off of it this instant."

Just like that idiot colonel in Kandahar. Riggs rolls his eyes, steps away from the keyboard, and changes the topic, "The notes talk about commerce and what the federal government would be allowed and prohibited from doing with wages. How would that relate to the Constitution nowadays?"

Hartman pauses, *Commerce? Anything dealing with commerce would have a colossal impact on our 20 trillion-dollar economy! Gotta get these two on their way so I can go through this in detail.* "I haven't read the text, so I really can't address that properly. Commerce is hardly mentioned in the Constitution, there's just a single clause about it in one of the Articles. Although brief, that single clause has been interpreted to assume colossal importance to our economy."

"OK, the Constitution, clauses and all, has been around for over 200 years, hasn't it all been figured out by now?"

"Constitutional scholars, liberal and conservative lawmakers, special interests and their attorneys, lower federal courts, and the Supreme Court itself have argued certain aspects of the Constitution since the document was ratified, my young friend. Administration lawyers even argued before the Supreme Court that it served as an authority for the Affordable Care Act," Hartman pontificates while admiring Patina.

"So, I'm guessing anything dealing with a part of the Constitution about commerce is still up for debate?"

"Precisely, young man. Here, let me confirm the exact wording on my computer." Hartman conducts a quick search, "Yes, here it is, Article I, Section 8, Clause 3, and I quote,

"The Congress shall have the power... To regulate commerce ... among the several States..."

"That's it? Congress has the power to regulate commerce among the states? No more explanation than that?"

"Yes, that's it. Other than precluding the feds from passing commerce regulations that favor any seaport or state, the word never appears again - that's all the Constitution has to say about it. Depending upon their objective, people have fought fiercely over the years for legal decisions that favor their purposes. For example, what does 'regulate' entail?"

Riggs presses, "Why was commerce even addressed in a document as fundamental as the Constitution – didn't they have more important matters to include?"

Patina speaks up, "The Revolutionary War debt was a driving force behind it. Some Founders thought that a limited degree of federal authority would promote commerce and provide tax revenue to retire that debt."

This time, Dr. Hartman throws a condescending look at her, expecting both her and Riggs to unequivocally understand that he is the cardinal constitutional authority in the room and they should conduct themselves accordingly.

"That's true, young lady, and in large part it did so by providing federal authority to negotiate foreign trade deals that balanced European access to our markets with our access to theirs."

Patina listens and looks away. She isn't impressed by his title, his certificates, what he says, or his thoroughly pompous speech and mannerisms. Hartman, of course, is *very* impressed with all of them.

Hartman proceeds to his desk and pecks at his keyboard, "Now that I'm in my notes, let me just check on the committees."

Riggs looks closer at a number of the certificates and awards on the walls, finding them all rather dated.

"Yes, here it is. The five delegates on the document comprised the Committee of Detail, which met from July 24 through August 6, 1787 with the task of preparing the first draft of the Constitution. John Rutledge chaired the committee, so, yes, this *could* be his personal notes from a session." *Got to get these two out of here.*

I bet he just read that in Wikipedia, and it sure didn't take ten minutes and a degree, Riggs thinks. "Why didn't the committee just write the note's more comprehensive language directly into the Constitution so there wouldn't be so much confusion later on?"

"Remember, young man, the Constitution enumerates those very few authorities the federal government *has*, not the infinite others it *doesn't* have and are reserved for the states. The Founders would have believed it obvious and completely unnecessary for the Constitution to state that the federal government has no authority to intervene between an employer and employee to dictate such a detailed matter as wages. That would clearly be left for states to consider."

"How significant would these notes be, and why didn't anyone know what's in them before?" Riggs asks.

"Like the convention at large, the committee's business was conducted in absolute secrecy. Given the monumental scope of their task, though, Rutledge could have easily found it prudent or even necessary to maintain notes of some kind. It would be highly unusual for any of them to survive a committee session, though. Other than James Madison's record of the general proceedings, I'm unaware of any other examples."

Riggs nods.

"Such notes, then, could be exceedingly significant. They could provide a fresh new, authoritative insight into the Founders' actual intent, one that is quite divergent from Supreme Court decisions about the vague, very brief clause that *was* ultimately included in the Constitution. That would have enormous, far-reaching consequences."

Patina says, "I had no idea there was still so much controversy."
Of course you didn't, you amateur, wanna-be historian, Hartman thinks. "Then there's the matter of authenticity too. It'd have it be verified by the NARA staff or a contracted examiner. The Library of Congress may also render an opinion," Hartman quickly interjects to reassert his authority.

Patina responds, "Oh, yes sir, of course. Authentication goes without saying." *The NARA, the National Archives and Records Administration? This may be quite the find after all.* She makes a mental note to figure out how to get an opinion from the NARA.

"Young lady," Hartman inquires, "I'd like to keep this photo until you provide the actual page if you don't mind."

"Of course, professor, but I'd really appreciate your keeping keep us in the loop through the Historical Society."

"Certainly, and now the document itself. It's absolutely *vital* that you turn it over to me as soon as possible so I can take three steps. First, secure it from damage, degradation, or theft. I have access to secure, fire-proof, humidity-controlled storage facilities here at the University. Second, that I determine its authenticity, which I can coordinate through my colleagues at the NARA. And third, to obtain a legal opinion on the document's relevance to the Constitution and appropriate Supreme Court decisions."

"That all makes sense, Dr. Hartman. Then the document may be important or even have historical significance?" she asks without making a commitment.

"Well, it's interesting and I'll be happy to look at it more closely when you deliver it to me. Right now, though, I'm due at my weekly faculty meeting," he says dismissively without emotion or apparent interest in her and Riggs. *Get out of here so I can read this and look at the signatures – this is a very rare and imminently significant discovery indeed!*

"Thank you, sir. Riggs and I'll see ourselves out."

In the hall, Riggs leans over the assistant's desk and asks, "Ma'am, how long will Dr. Hartman be in the faculty meeting this morning?"

"This morning? No, not this morning. He attends his weekly faculty meeting tomorrow after lunch. He doesn't have another appointment today until 2:30."

On their way out of the building, Riggs turns to Patina, "Yep, this guy may be smart on the Constitution, but he's a shady, lying weasel. I don't trust him."

"And did you catch how he just assumed he'd get the document and be in charge of everything, like we had no say in the matter at all, much less Dr. Arkin and the Society?" Patina says.

"Like I said, he's a pathetic little weasel."

Chapter 15

This Can Be Big, Very Big

D r. Dale Hartman spends the next hour enthusiastically transcribing the handwritten text into a Word document with the fervent hope that the page is genuine. *Is this it? Can this actually be IT? Has fate finally provided me with the means to fulfill my destiny? I'm the first, the very first authority to see a substantial new constitutional document!*

Hartman savors every syllable, word, and sentence on the photograph. He struts and pokes out his diminutive chest like a conquering superhero. He can't ever remember being so self-assured. *I may just ask Professor Robin Cochran out to dinner! No, I'm definitely going to ask her out!*

Hartman was intimately familiar with the budding republic's need for addressing interstate commerce, and it made perfect sense that a Constitutional Convention committee would consider the vital matter.

He leans closer to the photograph, fixating over the stylistic cursive writing. It's legible, but only with some effort. He begins to slowly read the version he's transcribed, softly out loud:

"The Union has both a legal and moral responsibility to settle the consolidated debts of the states from the war just ended, according to the terms of those obligations. The Union can best accomplish this task through federal negotiation of trade with other countries, resulting in the collection of tariffs on foreign goods sold in these United States.

"Robust commerce within and between the states shall increase the demand for European goods and substantially support this necessary effort. Barriers to commerce between the states, mainly coastal states' imposition of tolls and duties for goods traveling from their ports to inland states, would substantially diminish this vital federal effort. Inland states would reciprocate, leading to further reduction in necessary commerce, anger by the respective states' populations, and possible violence. The federal government, therefore, has a just and vital interest in preventing such actions through their regulation.

"The states are encouraged to compete to provide products and services through their choices of what they shall produce, their design, materials, techniques of manufacture, labor arrangements, promotion, distribution, and the legal frameworks the states create to either promote or curtail the formation and conduct of such activities. Along with true free trade across state borders, this will best decide what businessmen choose to produce in their states or choose to produce in another state.

"The federal government shall be authorized to prohibit measures that states impose uniquely on the goods and services imported from other states; they shall especially be prohibited from imposing such measures as import tariffs, duties, and taxes on products originating in another of the states. Authority is reserved exclusively to the several states to regulate within their boundaries the manners of design, production, labor arrangements, and sales.

"It shall be the sole purview of the several states to establish and enforce all manner of labor wages within their boundaries as they may decide.

"These provisions and prohibitions are to be considered as they have been written, and not to be interpreted to the benefit or detriment of any specific state or party to manufacture, agriculture, or commerce.

"We committee members do hereby unanimously agree that these provisions recorded above are the true sense of the convention delegates at large."

Yr. Most hble. Servt., J. Rutledge, Chairman, SC
Appt'd Mbr. Oliver Ellsworth, CT
Appt'd Mbr. Nathaniel Gorham, MA

Appt'd Mbr. Edmund Randolph, VA
Appt'd Mbr. James Wilson, PA

Professor Hartman leans back, takes a very deep breath, and considers the overwhelming significance of what he's just transcribed onto his computer. *My god – this could be absolutely devastating to organized labor, it's monumental! Yes, this IS it! THIS is my opportunity! This must be exactly how Howard Carter felt when he stumbled onto Tutankhamun's secret tomb a hundred years ago!*
He beams to himself and imagines the momentous impact his masterful treatise will have on fellow academics, institutions, the courts, and history. No one will be able to ignore or dispute his scholarly preeminence... or question his right to the title 'Chairman Hartman' on the door to his large new office on the ground floor. *No more trekking up three flights of stairs!* He basks in self adoration for several very pleasurable, gratifying minutes.
Hartman goes on to spend the entire afternoon gleefully refreshing his knowledge of the committee's work, the commerce clause, and how the combined information can benefit him. Suddenly, he snaps out of his fantasy and focuses on the imperative to possess the actual document. *That little vamp never told me where it was, and <u>that's</u> what's essential – not just a picture of it.*

The next day, Hartman dials Dr. Arkin at the Historical Society to pick his brain. He can barely conceal his excitement after getting right through.
"Good morning, David, Dale here at the University. I just wanted to thank you for steering your intern my way; she dropped off a picture of a purported document that I assume you've seen?"
"Oh, yes, good morning, Dale. You're right, Ms. Gregors *did* show me her photo – she brought it in about a week ago. I haven't seen the actual document, but it certainly deserves some follow up. I plan on using it as the focal point of our annual fundraiser. What were your thoughts?"
Hartman sidesteps the question to hear Arkin's assessment first. "I just had a moment to look at the photo before having to attend

another meeting, but I did notice the names at the bottom. Some of the text bears a closer look too," he stalls.

"You're right, Dale. The date, signatures, and the fact that it said 'Committee Notes' support the premise that it was prepared during the Constitutional Convention."

"I agree, I think you're exactly right," Hartman says to keep Arkin going.

"As I recall, it mentioned commerce; could it relate to federal authority over commerce? If that's the case, the document could be as useful as the Federalist in conveying the Founders' intent regarding the fed's commerce role, couldn't it? I imagine that's always a matter of debate, with significant and far-reaching consequences. I'm not sure how extensive the impact would be on overall wages and employment, you'd probably need to talk to an economist at the university.

Good idea about an economist – I should've already thought of that, damn it! And yep, Arkin picked up on the same point that struck me right between the eyes – that the Founders intended to explicitly reserve wage matters exclusively to the various states.

Partly to show off his knowledge, Hartman follows up, "This wasn't an issue for the first 150 years. It's only since FDR's[1] Supreme Court Justices' interpretations that it's made any difference."

"I didn't know those details, Dale."

Scholars have minutely dissected what 'commerce' meant to the founders. They thoroughly examined its definition in period dictionaries, its context throughout the Constitutional convention, usage in the text of the Constitution itself, the states' ratification conventions, and the Federalist Papers. All supported 'commerce' to mean trade or exchange, rather than the broader 'all gainful activity'.

Hartman drones on with his lecture, "Two professors tried to ascribe to Pennsylvania Constitutional Convention delegate James Wilson a broader definition of commerce - one that included labor-and-wage transactions. Wilson's remarks at his state's ratification convention much more closely refer to commerce as trade or exchange, instead of a broader definition that would include wages. In

---

[1] Franklin Delano Roosevelt, Democratic U.S. President from 1933 to 1946

fact, all of the eight uses of the word 'commerce' in Pennsylvania's ratification report support the narrower meaning."

Dr. Arkin listens intently, hoping to pick up any interesting facts or stories he can include in his display. "What about the first part of the Commerce Clause, the one that authorizes the feds to 'regulate' commerce?"

"That's fairly well established too, David. One of the earliest scholars of the Constitution, St. George Tucker, a Professor of Law at William and Mary College, concluded around the turn of the 18th century that the clause gave no constitutional right to control inter-course between any two or more parts of the same state. I think it's obvious that an employer and employee are two parts within a same state." Hartman glows with confidence that he's on top of the discussion with his colleague.

"Well, you certainly know your stuff, Dale. I clearly referred Ms. Gregors to the right person - my hat's off to you."

"David, how many decisions have the Justices handed down that couldn't have considered what we're looking at now?"

"Dale, I couldn't tell you, just not my area of expertise.

Hartman attempts to reassert himself, "I think we have several matters before us, David: security of the original document, preservation, and authenticity. Anything else?"

"No, you've hit the key points, Dale, but we also need to compare it with Madison's convention notes and the Federalist Papers to see how it supports or conflicts with them."

Hartman winces, *Crap, I should have brought that up!* "Exactly. As I recall, Madison's #42 discussed commerce. Madison also wrote in Federalist #45 that 'The powers reserved to the several States will extend to all the objects which, in the ordinary course of affairs, concern the lives, liberties, and properties of the people, and the internal order, improvement, and prosperity of the State.' That's certainly consistent with the 'no federal wage' part of the document.*"

"Dale, you must have #45 sitting right in front of you to be able to quote it so quickly."

"Well, I have been doing some preliminary research. If the kids found a valid supporting document of this magnitude, it'll provide invaluable new insight. I'll take the lead, of course, since I have the University's full resources at my disposal." Dale Hartman has staked his claim and hopes Arkin won't push back or harbor any notions of co-authoring the explosive study that will catapult him to fame.

Dr. Arkin chafes at Hartman's automatic assumption of taking the lead. Arkin and the Society were always having to look for different angles to maintain a flow of donations, and a newly-discovered original Rutledge document would certainly stimulate more than a few checks.

"Well, Dale, I'd certainly like to remain closely involved. John Rutledge helped write the state constitution, served as a delegate to the Continental Congress and Constitutional Convention, as well as serve as a U.S. Supreme Court justice. We have an entire room devoted to that favorite son and his descendants."

"One more thing, David," Hartman continues without acknowledging Arkin's comment, "Will you tell your intern to bring the original document to me as soon as she can – it's *absolutely imperative* that I properly secure and preserve it here."

"So nice talking with you Dale, as always," Arkin says indifferently.

Chapter 16

More Questions Than Answers

R iggs and Patina leave Professor Hartman's office and duck into a coffee shop at King and Calhoun Streets in downtown Charleston. Patina's almost giddy over the prospect of contributing to the Society's fundamental purpose. To her, it's becoming a mission – one that fulfills her need for meaning and substance. Riggs is more reserved, but as dedicated to helping Patina as he was to supporting his men in Afghanistan.

"Patina, I listened to my gut when we left Hartman's office and asked his admin assistant about the 10:30 meeting Hartman told us he had. The assistant said the faculty meetings were on Wednesdays and his calendar was clear today until 2:30. I don't trust the guy and he sure was interested in getting the original paper from us."

"Maybe he's just really concerned about keeping it safe and pre-serving it," she replies.

"He wants it alright, but for completely personal reasons. Did you see all the crap on his walls?" Either way, Riggs begins to feel on guard, knowing that in all likelihood they now have a rare, conse-quential, and invaluable historical document. He was much less aware of the attendant risks it brought.

"Patina, if this is anything close to what Hartman thinks it is, it's a *really* big deal, a critical part of American governance – virtually a decisive footnote to the U.S. Constitution itself. Protecting the page and getting it into the right hands is as much a responsibility as what I swore to in my commissioning oath – to support and defend the Constitution."

She pauses to reflect, "I hadn't thought it like that, but yeah, you're right."

"At the far end of possibilities, it's genuine and could substan-tially impact everyone the way he said it could. If that's the case, who stands to gain and lose from it? Labor and management, of course, but also how about everyone who uses their products and services?

How would you even put a value on it? How do you keep a growing number of people from taking advantage of us? Or worse, taking it by force?" They begin to ponder the many possible foul outcomes.

Patina listens intently and then adds, "That makes sense; then it'd have tremendous monetary value to certain people and organizations. We ought to tell Jason - he didn't have any idea something like this was in the desk, much less what it could be worth."

"I agree; anything that affects the wages of millions of workers and the financial stability of entire companies would certainly draw people out of the woodwork, and some of them wouldn't take 'no' for an answer You know Jason better than I do, can you call him?"

"Sure. Do you think we should bring the actual document in to Dr. Hartman for safekeeping?"

"Maybe some time, but not now. Besides the fact I don't trust him, we need to learn more about what we're dealing with. And there's the whole thing about what precautions we should take to preserve it. The less handling the better, of course, and we need to use gloves when we do touch it and the envelope. We should probably avoid sunlight completely and minimize exposure to artificial light. What about humidity? Is there an optimal level? Before taking it to anyone, we just have to get smarter about everything."

"Professor Hartman also talked about security and preservation. It's in your gun safe now, what else do you think we should do?"

"The safe is solid, it's got a full-time dehumidifier, and it sure beats the storage room at Low Country Furniture. Still, it isn't the Smithsonian. And it's in my house – not where I want thieves to be poking around."

"Why don't we put it in a bank safety deposit box, I have one I've used for about six years. I'll just tell the professors we're working through some concerns, but they're free to keep the pictures for preliminary research. I know Hartman will press me on it; maybe he wants to look at the paper, ink, and the envelope, too."

"There's no way that bow-tied narcissist has the training, facilities, and tools to do any kind of legitimate examination. He just wants to be in control."

When they finish their coffees, they drive to Riggs' house and carefully place the envelope into a sturdy plastic bag that Patina holds on the way to her bank. After securing the package, Riggs suggests, "Let's pick up some groceries, go home and get an early dinner going."

"You do the grilling and I'll make a salad. You like wine or a beer?" she asks.

His dad Galen tried to convince him he needed a Big Green Egg, but Riggs preferred the practicality of his propane grille. At the house, he applies some Mr. P's rub on the chicken and pops it on the grille. Patina's Greek salad and white rice complete the evening menu.

"This is turning into something of an adventure, Patina; does it measure up to all the others you've had... minus me colliding with you, of course?"

"Well, I've got to say it *is* getting interesting, and even a bit intriguing, but so far it hasn't taken us on any far-flung trips to Bangkok, London, or Budapest."

"Should it? Is that where you want to go, or places you've been and want to return to?

"No, I haven't been to any of them. We did move some when I was younger. Mom decided to travel when she graduated from college and ended up on St. Thomas in the U.S. Virgin Islands. She was an artist – started with water colors and then moved on to metal sculpting. That's where she came up with my name. She married a Danish businessman there named Alex Gregors and they had my older brother Richard two years later."

"Oh, you've got a brother. Does he live here in Charleston too?" *Is that who she was hugging on her facebook page?*

"He did for a while," she looks down and her expression and tone immediately turn melancholy, "but he was murdered after hours at work when I was a sophomore in college. Both mom and I were completely devastated."

Riggs recoils, "What? Murdered? Patina, that's terrible! I'm so sorry." He steps forward and holds her, gently stroking her hair for a minute while he tries to fathom the impact of such a catastrophe.

"What happened? Who did it? Did they catch the guy?"

"No, it's been a cold case for years and I'm not sure they'll ever close it. I still go by the sheriff's office every few months to see if they've made any progress and volunteer to do legwork for them. I'm even on a first-name basis with the evidence custodian, SGT Winters. I do some online research, but I always feel like it's not enough. Maybe that's why I play so hard at soccer – to burn off those feelings."

Riggs nods in shared sorrow, still holding her. "You shouldn't feel like you've let him down, because you haven't - and I'm sure he wouldn't want you to. "

She turns her gaze away from Riggs. "Don't be too sure of that."

"Why, what do you mean?"

"I cancelled plans to come home from college then. If I hadn't, he'd have come earlier and wouldn't have been around when the guys came to the plant."

"Patina, you, you can't take on their guilt."

She looks back towards him, unconvinced.

"Where was your dad?"

Patina looks down again, then quietly says, "That's the other family tragedy - Dad died helping neighbors during hurricane Gilbert. I wasn't even in school then. That was 1988 and it was the most intense Atlantic hurricane on record at that point. He saw a neighbor's roof blow off and went over to help them come to our place. A flying piece of debris hit him."

"I'm so sorry, Patina. He sounds like quite a Samaritan, and gutsy too. From what you've told me and what I've seen, there's no doubt you inherited the best characteristics from both of them."

She looks up at him, then rests her head against his chest as tears run down her cheeks. Riggs presses her against himself and gently strokes her arm.

After dinner, Riggs and Patina clean up the kitchen, sit on the couch in the den with glasses of wine, turn on Netflix and watch an episode of *Justified*. Before falling asleep next to Riggs, Patina wonders, *Marshal Raylan Givens caught the bad guys in that series; would anyone ever avenge her brother's real-life killer?*

Chapter 17

Economics

An increasingly anxious Professor Hartman wastes no time scanning his University Faculty Guide for an economist with actual business experience, and finds him on the first page of the Business College's web site: Franklin Ackers, Professor of Economics. He calls immediately.

"Hello, Doctor Ackers, Professor Dale Hartman from the History Department here. I've very recently discovered a historical document that will have monumental economic implications and I'd like to discuss them with you - at your convenience, of course."

"Hardiman, is it? I'm not much of a historian…"

"I'm sorry, it's 'Hartman', Dale *Hart*-man."

"My mistake. As I was saying, I'm not much of a historian, but I'm happy to meet with you. Tomorrow around 3:00 PM – does that work for you?"

"Yes, it does, thank you and I'll see you then."

Hartman again senses he's on to something that will propel him to his rightful place among academia's luminaries of history.

"Doctor Ackers, what a pleasure to meet you, and thanks so much for agreeing to get together on such short notice."

"Certainly. Now tell me how an old economist may be of assistance with your historical document."

Hartman lays Patina's photo on the table and hands Ackers a printed transcript of the text. Ackers pores over the document with only modest interest until he reads the 4th and 5th paragraphs.

"I don't understand this, Dale, it says the federal government is *prohibited* from establishing a minimum wage, when clearly it's done so and the Supreme Court's affirmed that authority. There must be some mistake."

"Those Supreme Court decisions were based on severely stretched interpretations of the Commerce Clause of the Constitution, which has been challenged repeatedly. This document significantly elaborates the Founding Fathers' intent *behind* the Commerce Clause, but I only recently discovered it. Obviously, the Supreme Court Justices didn't have the benefit of reading it when they decided in support of federal minimum wage legislation."

"Do you mean the fed's minimum is actually unconstitutional, and therefore illegal?"

"Yes, exactly - that's my informed professional conclusion, but it's something the courts will ultimately have to confirm. My interest right now is understanding the range and magnitude of economic impacts when those decisions are reversed. What do you think?"

Ackers slowly leans back in his chair, stroking his chin and contemplating the enormous number of factors necessary to quantify such a fundamental correction, along with the many inevitable and unpredictable consequences.

"Very interesting question, Dale, fascinating actually. You're talking about an extraordinarily significant change in the foundation of labor rates across an extensive number of entire industries, with many spread across the country - coast to coast and every state in between. My friend, the impact would be extraordinary... no, I'd have to say it would be *seismic*."

Hartman beams at the prospect of introducing such a consequential document to the country - and significantly elevating his notoriety.

"Dale, the matter would have such an impact that wage earners en masse would crucify any representative, senator, or president who supports the reversal. The justices would be absolutely pilloried. On the other hand, business leaders would no doubt laud the action."

Professor Ackers turns in his chair to face his computer, "Let's start with a few fundamentals. The federal minimum wage was last adjusted in July 2009 to $7.25; the Bureau of Labor estimates that only about 2 - 3% of America's hourly workers, or two million, actually earn the federal minimum or below."

"That's quite a few people, but not nearly as many as I'd have thought," Hartman says, wrinkling his frustrated brows.

"That's true Dale, but there're about ten times that many who're referred to as 'near-minimum' workers. They earn less than $10.10 an hour."

"That's more than the fed rate, why is that relevant?"

"Because that's the number of electors who would benefit from any increase in the federal minimum to or above that amount. That's a very powerful incentive that vote-hungry politicians and the living wage crowd hope to leverage into another raise in the federal rate."

"OK, I know that federal adjustments apply across the whole country in one fell swoop. So absent a single federal standard, proponents would have to mount separate legislative efforts in individual states or cities?"

"Yes, and they know that some of those states would never establish minimum wages – preferring to let the open market sort it out, just like it does for T-shirts and avocados. The impact doesn't end there, either. There's another whole population of workers whose wages are contractually indexed to the federal rate. They'd also like to see one federal action applied across the board instead of fighting separate wage wars in cities and states."

"It gets more complex the farther down you dig, doesn't it?"

"It absolutely does, Dale. And don't forget that both labor and management know that it's often easier to manipulate minimum wage legislation within state governments than it is through a majority of both houses of the U.S. Congress and the President. Some groups may *want* to kill the federal wage and fight it out at the state level, while others may opt to *avoid* state-level fights and work it at the federal level."

"Yes, I see. No matter which camp you're in, there're pros, cons, and lots of room in-between for fighting. It'd be a labor-management nightmare that an entire range of players would variously encourage or oppose."

Dale Hartman is only now beginning to fully grasp the pervasive effects that would cascade throughout the United States, but he gives only a fleeting thought to how broadly and deeply it would affect individual workers and their families. *But, hey, that's not my problem – I'll still be on a state salary, and that'll go up handsomely when I publish my paper and get named department chairman. Then there'll be speaking engagements, book-signings, a documentary, and who knows... even a movie?*

"Don't forget the lawyers. It'll be a decade-long battle," Ackers adds only half-jokingly. Both professors agree there'd certainly be an untold number of lawsuits, counter-suits, and appeals.

Ackers stands up and rubs his chin in contemplation, "Dale, you've probably already surmised this, but those notes could have implications beyond any domestic company or industry. With today's global economy, impacts would reverberate internationally."

"Yes, I suppose that makes sense, Dr. Ackers - how extensive would it be?" *This just gets better all the time – international notoriety!*

"Rather than responding to that myself, let's see if my colleague, Professor Zheng Wei, is in his office down the hall – he's our lead authority on international economics. I'd like to hear his thoughts on the matter myself."

Dr. Ackers calls Zheng and invites him to the office to briefly discuss the matter.

Minutes later, Dr. Zheng knocks on Ackers' open door, "Dr. Ackers, you sounded so much more animated on the phone than usual, how might I assist you?"

"Dr. Zheng, may I introduce Professor Dale Hartman of the University's History Department."

Hartman, oblivious to Chinese protocol, puts his left hand on Zheng's shoulder while extending his right to shake hands. Zheng stiffens slightly, but is used to such American faux pas, especially in the casual south. Zheng leans forward slightly at the shoulders and extends a business card with both hands, face up and towards Hartman. Hartman, again oblivious to Chinese business customs, grabs the card without so much as looking at it and shoves it into his trousers pocket. He doesn't return a card of his own, and Zheng cringes inwardly. *This particular American is especially crude - worse than most. How did he become a professor? What could someone this coarse possibly know or say to excite Professor Ackers?*

Ackers outlines Hartman's discovery and its very real potential to abolish existing federal minimum wage laws. Zheng, knowing

Ackers' distinguished business experience and meticulous analysis of complex business issues, becomes much more interested.

"Professor Zheng, we wanted to include you in this discussion due to potential international implications. What do you think – how would you gauge the impact of the U.S. federal minimum wage being repealed?"

"That *is* an interesting and complex proposition, Dr. Ackers. I imagine it would ultimately result in moving wages in one direction only – lower. By how much, I have no idea, nor can I speculate right now how many workers would be affected, especially in those many jobs that are indexed to that wage. It would also be necessary to specify which industries they worked in. Suffice it to say, though, that lower wages would reduce production costs, resulting in less expensive American products. I cannot think it would be immediate, but would unfold over a number of years."

Hartman can hardly contain himself with the idea that he and his forthcoming essay will have international visibility and impact.

Ackers chimes in, "Less expensive U.S. products would then be more competitive in the global market place, re-routing some overseas demand to America. Since there'd be no American tariffs on those same U.S. products, it would further amplify the benefits to domestic consumers."

"You're exactly right, Professor Ackers; trade patterns would impact America's largest trading partners – the European Union, China, Canada, and Mexico."

Professor Dale Hartman becomes almost light-headed and strains to mask his excitement.

A week later, Zheng Wei accepts a courtesy invitation to a meeting hosted by the South Carolina Governor, the state Department of Commerce, and state Chamber of Commerce to present a comprehensive package of incentives to the CEO and staff of Chinese manufacturer Sunrise Mechanical. Sunrise's planned U.S. heavy equipment assembly plant would bring hundreds of well-paying jobs and millions in tax revenue to the state.

Following the formal presentation and an hour-long Q&A, the attendees retire to an elaborate reception, where Professor Zheng spots old friend Li Jun.

"Jun, so very, very good to see you again, is your family here? Are you a businessman with Sunrise Mechanical now? Will you be working here in South Carolina?"

"No, Wei, I still work at our embassy in Washington. I knew you were on faculty at the University here, so included you on the embassy's official guest list. My family is in Washington, but sends you this little gift." He hands Zheng a small box modestly wrapped in red paper.

"You work in the Chinese Embassy?"

"Yes, in the Office of Economic and Commercial Affairs for Minister Zhu Jianjun – he's the Chief of the Office. That is why I'm here today. The American president's tariff talks are quite unsettling on markets and will surely make U.S. products more competitive here in America – affecting many of our workers."

"Yes, of course, Jun. I was just explaining as much to two professors at the university last week. One of them has just discovered an old U.S. document that is certain to challenge the U.S. federal minimum wage."

Li Jun is shocked as he looks directly at his old friend, then pauses and reflects for a moment, "It would not be to our advantage for U.S. labor rates to fall; it could only make our trade and employment challenges so much worse."

"Yes, as I said also."

Zheng Wei elaborates on the document's relationship to the Constitution and SCOTUS[2] decisions, as well as the extended process that would unfold to reverse those decisions.

Li Jun carefully takes detailed mental notes that he'll pass on to his superiors at the Chinese embassy tomorrow.

---

[2] Supreme Court Of The United States

Chapter 18

Running Out of Time

Delta Kappa Delta fraternity is known throughout Charleston State University as the party house, and social chairman William Edward Jackson IV invariably leads the activities. This Friday night's bash at the house won't be any different.

Billy, as the brothers knew him, didn't have the grades to follow in the steps of his father and grandfather at Duke and Vanderbilt - partying consumed too much of his attention. Even with an expensive prep school education and offers of generous donations to both universities, their deans of admission refused Billy's admittance in exchange for what would have basically been a bribe.

His lackadaisical academic attitude also extended his undergraduate time and beginning of his MBA studies.

Billy wakes up in the fraternity's sleeping porch just before noon. After a 15-minute shower, he throws on some cutoffs and a sweatshirt to go downstairs. In the hall on his way to the dining area, he checks his mailbox and pulls out an official-looking envelope, *Palmer & Palmer, Attorneys at Law... Mom's and Dad's personal lawyers, what the hell is this?*

Billy opens and reads the brief notification,

Mr. William E. Jackson IV,

As the trustees of your father's irrevocable trust, it is our responsibility to inform you that the terms of that instrument allow you to withdraw up to one fourth of the principle amount upon earning your Masters' Degree in business administration by your 24th birthday and reaching the age of 25.

Failure to earn your Masters' Degree from a SACS-accredited university as stated above shall adjust the date you may withdraw any amount of the principle until age 30.

Please arrange with The Charleston State University to provide this office with a certified copy of your Masters' Degree diploma upon graduation.

Original Signed

"I've gotta *have* my MBA by age 24? I thought I just had to be actively *pursuing* it. Holy crap, I'm not going to make it! This is bullshit!" Billy hangs his head in sheer despair.

Another brother looks at him and laughs, "Hey bro, you look like shit, what's up?

Billy looks up at the brother with a 'screw you' look.

The brother goads him a little farther, "One of your hoes send you a Dear John text?"

Billy looks back at the letter, *If I don't pass every class this term and next, I'm toast. I don't have time to make up a busted class, and I'm tubing that damn Constitutional Studies electives; hell, I only signed up for the damn course because of that coed. I won't have the degree in time! That trust's got about $3 million in it and I'll need to get a chunk of as soon as I can so I don't have to slave like Mom and Dad do.*

After considering his very limited options, Billy books an appointment with the course instructor - his nemesis, Professor Dale Hartman. Two days later, he's waiting outside Hartman's office.

"Professor Hartman, I'm in a serious bind. I'm just a couple of points short, and I *have* to pass your class. What can I do? Anything!"

Dr. Hartman lights up with the inner satisfaction of knowing he can again lord over and control someone, and the fact it's William "Playboy" Jackson, this term's special target, makes it ever so much more gratifying. He relishes the moment of absolute authority, then begins his often-told mantra, "As I explained on the first day of the course, *I* don't determine your grade, *you* do. I simply record for the

Registrar what you've chosen to achieve, or in your case, chosen not to achieve."

"Yes Sir, I understand completely, Professor, but I'm in a really serious box here. There's got to be *some* kind of extra credit I can do."

Hartman, ever mindful of his own real-life failings, is completely unsympathetic to anyone else's – especially someone who's as popular with the ladies as Billy. "As you must also know, I don't assign extra credit projects, Mr... what's your name?"

"It's Jackson, Sir, my name is William Jackson. People usually just call me Billy."

Hartman continues to savor his dominance by watching Billy sweat, squirm, and beg, "There's been ample opportunity during the semester to master the course material to passing standards; you *do* know that, don't you?"

"Yes Sir, but, Sir, I'll do *anything* – research, reports, a special project, *anything* you need me to do."

"It's out of the question, Mr. Jackson, and besides, it wouldn't be fair to the other students. Now I'm sure you understand, but I have work to complete so *I* don't fall behind in *my* responsibilities."

Billy leaves, more despondent than ever. *That asshole, he could do something, he just doesn't want to.*

Chapter 19

Comrades in Need

I.M. Pei, the late Chinese-American architect who designed the Louvre's glass pyramid in Paris, chose warm beige-colored French limestone walls for The Embassy of the People's Republic of China in the United States of America. Within those walls at 3505 International Place, N.W. in Washington, D.C., national representatives and very senior non-governmental leaders regularly discuss and spar over topics of national security, forced technology transfer, and currency manipulation. In every session, as in human nature at large, participants aspire to maximize their benefits and minimize concessions. Nowhere is this more obvious than with matters of economics and trade.

In the embassy, Li Jun updates Minister Zhu Jianjun on yesterday's news from his academic friend in Charleston.

"Minister, I have some new and quite unusual information to share with you." Li Jun explains the discovery of the old notes and their potentially explosive impact on SCOTUS decisions, American wages, and China's world trade.

Within two days, Minister-Counselors' representatives from the embassy's Office of Economic and Commercial Affairs, Congressional, and Economic Affairs Sections meet in the embassy. They're particularly interested in discussing which industries would be impacted by a repeal of the fed's minimum wage and how significant it would be to their homeland's economy and employment.

They are intimately familiar with the enormous volume of annual trade - $520 billions of exports to, and $130 billions of imports from, the U.S. It's easy for them to conclude that reducing even a small percentage of that colossal volume would result in significant losses of Chinese income and jobs. They are quite distressed with the prognostications and associated disastrous consequences.

"How many workers will be idled for every billion yuan of products Americans buy from themselves instead of our workers? The Europeans would also buy American, too. We are facing 300 million old people by 2030 who will require a sweeping reallocation of priorities and resources, with fewer workers to provide them. That's only a decade away, when U.S. courts would decide the wage matter. Which provinces would be hit hardest? How will the provincial committees Secretaries of the Communist Party react?"

"Yes, and how many more dissidents and how much more social discontent will arise from those lost sales and jobs? The Party doesn't need any more unrest in these troubling times. Only three years ago The Hague's International Court of Justice wrongly rejected our historic and legitimate rights in the South China Sea. A million people openly protested against our Chief Executive in Hong Kong. There's a potential mass migration from the Democratic People's Republic of Korea, and America's growing defense budget - the list has a hundred lines. We must do all that we can to interrupt this professor's document quest and to assist his foes."

"Yes, comrades, and also be mindful to take advantage of the time available to stop the threat - it is still vague and the U.S. courts will ensure that the actual damage is deferred to the future. For now, we should contact our friend at Sunrise Mechanical for his counsel on this matter."

"Yes, yes" they all agree.

Sunrise Mechanical CEO David Wang, like many Chinese in America, has taken an Anglo first name and places it before his family name to simplify dealings with members of Congress, financiers, and clients. As a highly successful and experienced Wharton MBA graduate, the embassy often confers with him on weighty commercial matters dealing with Americans. Wang is a master of the major relationships, actions, and nuances necessary to advance broad agendas through the complex and often arcane labyrinths to achieve desired results. The week after the embassy discussion, he is again prepared to advise a countryman and greets Minister Zhu Jianjun with a genuine smile.

"Jianjun, your family is doing well and your health is good?"

"Yes, thank you, and yours too I presume?"

Wang nods an affirmative response. "How may I help you serve the Central State today, Jianjun?"

Zhu Jianjun explains the collective ministers' discussion and their recommendation to seek additional ideas going forward. Wang listens and jots down a few key points. When Jianjun is finished, Wang quickly reviews his notes and ponders for a moment before talking.

"Jianjun, you present a troubling issue for us and the Central State. We shall find out which American workers' unions know about the paper and will oppose its use to overturn the federal wage. Perhaps we can support them with money, behind the curtain of course, and let *them* be a public face to get named in the fights to come."

"Yes, thank you. Please let me know what resources you may need from the embassy."

"Certainly, Jianjun. I can also talk with our lobbyists who know those in the U.S. Congress we should donate to. Both lobbyists and politicians are quite clever at derailing, delaying, and amending legislation, even when it makes no sense or it's against their country's interests. They have very little national allegiance or long-term purpose, but do only what is needed to retain their authority and prestige. All are obsessed with power, entertainment, and the personal status they attach to money."

"Truly a weakness. It is a blessing that we are not."

"Yes, I agree, and a weakness we often leverage. Should I arrange for social media campaigns?"

"No, we will task our offices in the homeland to discredit those who favor repealing the federal wage. The academics should be an easy target, along with leaders in any trade association who want to repeal the current law."

"Does your friend in Charleston have more information on this matter and the names of the professors? Have they done any preliminary analyses?"

"I'm sure he can provide us with more, which I will send to you by courier. Wang, the Central State appreciates the help of a son."

"Of course, it is my duty and honor."

Li Jun reaches back to Professor Zheng Wei at The Charleston State University to collect information about Professors Ackers and Hartman, a transcript of the document, and initial economic impacts that Ackers and Zheng had hurriedly calculated. David Wang's lobbyists furnish additional information about on-going contract negotiations between the National Association of American Restauranteurs and the Food Services Union of America, as well as that union's close relationship with U.S. Representative Sonny Butler.

Minister Zhu Jianjun prepares and transmits his comprehensive classified report to Beijing and anxiously anticipates an especially laudatory response.

Chapter 20

This Makes No Sense

H ighly-sensitive antennas at the National Security Agency Hawaii (NSAH) in Kunia, Oahu collect thousands of electronic signals around the clock. Tonight, they pick up Beijing's response to Zhu Jianjun's report. The Hawaii Cryptologic Center's computers in nearby Wahiawa filter, analyze, and assess the signals intelligence data using sophisticated algorithms to identify key words, patterns, and anomalies that suggest a foreign threat.

A classified Chinese embassy transmission with the names of a U.S. Congressman, three American professors, presidents of a powerful national union and trade association, and the CEO of a major foreign corporation immediately raises flags that scream for human review. The computer prioritizes its machine-generated alert to telecommunications information systems officer Ted Burnett.

Included in Beijing's response to their ambassador in Washington is a new directive: TAKE IMMEDIATE ACTIONS TO OBTAIN OR DESTROY NEWLY-DISCOVERED HISTORIC DOCUMENT REFERENCED IN YOUR REPORT (COPY INCLUDED).

Ted scans the transcript and asks a colleague's opinion, "Jeanette, what do you make of this – heard of any of these guys before?"

She reads the translated Chinese government message and scratches her head, "Nope, doesn't make any sense to me either - looks like a real odd combination of players though. We know the congressman's a U.S. citizen, so we'll need a warrant from the FISC[3] to do anything more than continued monitoring. Are you going to push it up the chain of command?"

"Given their positions, you bet. Hell, a U.S. Representative? Why's the Chinese embassy interested in him, some professors, and

---

[3] Foreign Intelligence Surveillance Court

a Chinese businessman? Must have something to do with money, and probably lots of it. I wonder if they have access to classified info?"

Ted's all too aware that contract employee Edward Snowden, now living in Moscow, worked in this very office six years ago before leaking thousands of classified NSA documents. America's enemies exist in every form imaginable and he has to be constantly vigilant.

The NSA informs the FBI's Counterterrorism Division, which reviews the initial signals intelligence and deems it worthy of further investigation. The Division's Executive Assistant Director approves and forwards an application for a warrant to the 11-judge FISC. The court reviews the application and asks for clarification on a detail that the Counterterrorism Division promptly provides. When they're confident they've adhered to all aspects of the Foreign Intelligence Surveillance Act, they submit the final application to the judge designated to review the warrant.

The approved warrant authorizes FBI agents to conduct further investigations into idents [named U.S. citizens or corporations] discovered in the case, now named OSTRICH POKER. The Bureau's Counterterrorism Division Chief establishes and leads a joint interagency task force with imbeds from the NSA, Secret Service, and the Department of Commerce. They will meet periodically to assess the situation and its potential threat to American interests and recommend appropriate responses across the federal departments.

The FBI Headquarters notifies the Columbia, South Carolina Field Office, which copies Special Agent Wilbert Haskell at the Charleston office in adjacent Mount Pleasant.

Chapter 21

Too Close for Comfort

"**S**ir, I just got some new polling numbers you need to see," Luther tells Congressman Butler. He wasn't looking forward to Sonny's explosive reaction, but knew that bad news doesn't improve with age.

"Bring it," Sonny replies over the intercom, embittered at what he knows he's about to hear.

Butler pores over the summary of 6th District voter preference trends, "Jesus Christ, Luther, this is exactly the *opposite* of where we were going just last week; what the hell's going on down there?" His body tenses and his voice hardens. He slowly turns around in his swivel chair, stands up, and gazes out the window of the office assigned to a freshman Representative.

"I've already asked the pollsters, Sir. They're saying Mark Chambers is holding events every day because he doesn't have to work out of state like you do. They said he's also got some good name recognition as a state senator."

Sonny looks over his shoulder and glares at Luther, "Well I don't care if he's got better name recognition than the *goddamned governor!* We've got to derail that phony Boy Scout before this gets out of hand. These numbers are a real threat to my reelection."

"One more campaign item, sir, the estimate came in for the TV spots and they haven't gotten any cheaper."

Sonny looks at the budget summary and projected expenses.

"Damn it, that's going to put another big hole in the campaign budget. This is when I need to be on the Communications Committee. I'd show those robbing asshole media types a thing or two for sticking it to me. Don't they have any sense of responsibility towards good government? They ought to be giving me a discount! Hell, They ought to be running my spots as public service announcements! All they ever think about is their blood-sucking fees and themselves while I bend over backwards for the district. Goddamn low-life leeches."

"Yes sir. Just don't have any team loyalty."

"What's Harry saying about contributions?"

"He says it's time to start squeezing."

"Well, time's running out. Did Ripp sell all the seats for the fundraiser at the end of the month?"

"If not, he's sold *just* about all of them. At $10k a pop, that'll bring in a nice chunk of change, too. I've also got messages from a couple of big donors asking what you've found out for them about some federal construction contract they're going to bid on."

"That sounds like Everett and Davey. Yeah, sure, it shouldn't be too hard to help them out. My old friend over in the Defense Department can help tilt the contract specifications in their favor a little and those contracts are worth some really big bucks. We can hit Everett up for a nice donation to my charitable trust."

Luther sees that Sonny's calming down just a little, "I'll call his secretary to see when you can meet him, maybe when you're down in the district for the fundraiser."

"Good, thanks, Luther. We don't need any phone records on that one. By the way, we haven't got Boggs Colman's check, have we? And has he donated to the PAC yet? That's where the big money goes. He told me it was in the works, and I want it well before the union election. If someone takes him out then, I'll have to start all over with the new guy, and I don't have time for it now. Get him on the phone." *There's no end to what I have to do for money – just so I can serve the people.*

Chapter 22

Coffee?

P rofessor Hartman looks up from his cell phone to see curvaceous Dr. Robin Cochran walking towards him in the hall of a classroom building.

Balls! I'm just going to do it. "Professor Cochran, Dale Hartman, so nice to see you again."

"Oh, hello there. Yes, I haven't even had a chance to properly introduce myself." She extends her hand with a much firmer grip than Hartman's dead-fish response. "I'm Dr. Cochran, please call me Robin."

"Believe me, Robin, the pleasure's all mine. Listen, if you've got a few minutes, let's get to know each other over a coffee or hot chocolate in the lounge?" *Dale, you amorous rogue, you!* he thinks as his pulse rockets up.

"I'd really love to, but I'm giving a new lecture this afternoon and I really have to review my material... got to give the department and students everything they're paying for."

"Oh, sure, certainly, I understand. I'm absolutely confident they'll get more than their money's worth, though." *Crap!* "Another time, then?"

"Oh, of course, another time, for sure," she says while continuing to walk in the opposite direction of Hartman.

That's just great, I'm upstaged by a classroom full of grad students. She's a very smart lady and I can't imagine she hasn't heard of my work. She ought to be asking me to coffee, or even over for dinner.

Hartman turns around to briefly ogle Robin's tight, shapely buttocks, only to see her stop and eagerly talk to some other faculty member for several minutes - one younger and certainly more appealing than himself. *Goddamn it! And that guy hasn't published anything worthwhile in years. I've got to get that document from the kids so I can get on with my constitutional opus. Then no one, especially Robin Cochran, will pass up a chance to spend time with Professor Dale Hartman.*

He enters his office, closes the door, and sits at his standard university issued desk when his assistant knocks on the door and sticks her head in, "Professor, there's someone here to see you."

"Can't be, I don't have any appointments unless you neglected to put one on my calendar again," he says accusingly.

"He doesn't have an appointment, but he's with the government."

"OK, but let him know I'm extremely busy with actual work." *Jesus, what the hell's this all about – some state hack doing an academic accreditation report?*

Hartman's attitude changes dramatically when he sees the tall visitor at the door. The man is well dressed, walks with a purpose, and exudes confidence and authority.

"Good morning, Professor, I'm FBI Special Agent Will Haskell. Thank you for seeing me unannounced, and I promise to take only a minute of your time."

The FBI? Hartman leaps out of his chair and stammers, "By all means Agent Haskell, please come in and have a seat. Whatever can I do for you?" *Holy crap! The FBI's sending someone to see me personally? What'd I do – mess up my taxes? Was it the deductions for the books and music?*

"As I said, it'll only take a minute, Professor. Are you aware of a recently discovered historical document?"

"Why yes, certainly," he replies, very much relieved, "A colleague's intern showed me a picture of it recently; is it stolen federal property?"

"Do you know where it is now?"

"I imagine the young lady and her boyfriend still have it. I told them it was important and imperative they leave it with a professional like me. I asked her to turn it over to me for safekeeping in the university's vault and that I could authenticate it, but she hasn't done so."

"How can I contact her?"

"Through my colleague, Dr. David Arkin. Let me write down his number and address at the Charleston Historical Society. I've already started researching a paper about it, why do you need it?"

"Thank you so much, Professor, you've been very helpful."

What the hell was <u>that</u> all about? I don't know what's going on, but if the FBI's got anything to do with those notes, it can only boost the prestige of my paper.

The moment Haskell leaves, Hartman reconsiders the conversation, wondering more than ever what was behind it. After several minutes, he buries his face in his hands, searching for a way to kick-start his monumental project and unequivocally make him an academic celebrity. *It's absolutely <u>essential</u> that I get that original before some undereducated pretender swoops in with a spoiler article. Let me see if David's had any luck persuading his alluring little intern to get it for me.*

Hartman reaches for his phone, "David? Hi, Dale here. Listen, about the document your intern found; she still hasn't dropped it off for safe-keeping and authentication. I don't want to be a nag, but I'd really appreciate your doing a follow-up with her. It's critical that the paper's protected and secured, don't you agree?"

"I mentioned it to her again when she was in my office this week, but she plots and follows her own course. I'll give her your contact info again and suggest she call you directly."

"Appreciate all you've done, David. Thanks" *Thanks, hell, I bet you didn't even ask her, you over-the-hill toad. You can be so damn selfish – all you're interested in is your fundraiser and donations for your precious Society.*

Frustrated, Hartman thinks for a minute, then remembers the frantic grad student begging to do anything for extra credit. Hartman pulls up his class roster and the university's secure online student database, then sends a text to William E. Jackson IV: 'Get on my calendar ASAP for an office visit'.

Founders' Intent

Chapter 23

Ours or Theirs?

"**P**atina, I'm thinking we've missed what could be the most important question of all about the document," Riggs says after dinner at his house the next week.

"What do you mean? It's secured and preserved in a bank vault, we know that a lawyer will have to tell us if it has any legal significance, and we've got to talk to an expert who can validate it. We don't have all those answers yet, but at least we're asking the right questions. What do you think we're missing?"

"Who owns it?"

"What do you mean, 'who owns it?' *We* own it, don't we? Jason gave it to us, or did the collision wipe out your memory?" Patina comes over to his side of the table and playfully puts her hand on his forehead as though she's checking his temperature.

Riggs grasps her wrist and pulls her onto his lap. They laugh and look into each other's eyes before he resumes, "Not necessarily - think about it. We have physical custody of it and we *may* own it, or we could have no standing whatsoever. Did it belong to the government committee, or to Rutledge and his heirs? Did any of them have the authority to give it away?"

"Oh my God, Riggs, I see where you're coming from - you're absolutely right! It may not be ours at all! And if it's valuable, every one of those parties could demand it. How do we find out? Defending against all those claims would cost tens of thousands in attorney fees that we don't have."

"We need to at least talk to a lawyer that specializes in this sort of thing, whoever that is."

"And do it before this whole thing goes any further."

Riggs was wary of showing the document to a lawyer. They could all talk a good game about rights, attorney-client privilege and

Founders' Intent

such, but they could also spin and catch Patina and him in a web of legalese.

If anyone used an attorney over the years, it'd be Jason. The next morning, Riggs calls him and secures contact information for a Mr. Rudy Hayes, Esquire. Riggs calls Hayes to schedule an office visit and outlines the nature of their questions.

"Thank you, Mr. Blanding, that's very helpful. I'll go ahead and do some preliminary research before we meet," Hayes says. *This is intriguing - exactly what have these two discovered?*

On the afternoon of the appointment, Patina joins Riggs at Hayes' office. The receptionist welcomes and offers them a beverage; Riggs and Patina pass, but thank her.

Minutes later, Hayes walks into the lobby and greets them with a large open hand.

"Hi, I'm Rudy Hayes, and I understand you'd like to discuss a document you've discovered."

"Good afternoon, Mr. Hayes, I'm Riggs Blanding and this is Patina Gregors. Jason recommended you, so we called last week to talk about a document we've come into possession of."

"Yes, certainly – I remember. Any friend of Jason's is certainly welcome here. I'm pleased to meet you both. You brought up a very interesting topic, so let's sit down in my office and you can tell me exactly how I can serve you."

Hayes walks them the short distance to his well-appointed office where he's arranged several documents on a small conference table.

Unlike Professor Hartman's cluttered, self-promoting space, Hayes' walls display only his undergraduate degree in political science form Morehouse College, his law degree from Columbia Law School, and a signed picture of him with U.S. Supreme Court Justice Clarence Thomas.

There's an authentic looking framed reproduction of the U.S. Constitution displayed prominently on the wall to the right of Hayes' teak desk. Riggs thinks about the possible connection between what Riggs and Patina now possess and that framed document - the foundation for all federal laws. *Well, that's what we're here to find out.*

"OK, you two, tell me exactly what we're looking at," Hayes says.

Patina begins, "Thank you, Mr. Hayes. Jason gave us an old desk with some files and an even older envelope with a document in it. It has signatures of five states' delegates to the 1787 Constitutional Convention in Philadelphia."

Hayes listens much more intently when Patina mentions the date, the Convention, and that the document bears the names of John Rutledge and four other Founding Fathers.

After Patina explains Professors Arkin's and Hartman's assessments, Riggs asks, "First of all, Mr. Hayes, we'd like to know what our ownership rights are and how vulnerable we are to challenges. It seems like there're a number of parties, including the federal government, who could make a case for ownership."

"Well, we'd have to determine if they're simply Rutledge's personal notes or an official government record of the Convention's committee proceedings. Assuming it doesn't belong to the federal government, we'd have to establish the chain of ownership from the time it was written through the present to know how many other fingers may be in the pie. That could be extremely difficult to do over such a long period of unknown ownership."

Patina chimes in, "We believe Rutledge hid it in his mahogany desk when he returned to Charleston, and moved that desk to Hampton Plantation when daughter-in-law Harriott Pinckney Horry inherited the property. There was a lot of storage space in the attic and a ground-level basement, and it actually appears on a 1786 inventory of plantation property."

Riggs adds, "My father bought and sold antiques, and he remembers buying a desk there at an auction in 1970, which he traded to Jason's dad for a recliner that he still uses."

"That's all very useful, and can limit the number of possible claimants somewhat. We'll have to document those transfers as best we can. I know Jason's parents are deceased and I'm going to assume your father isn't going to try to claim it, Mr. Blanding. That still leaves the descendants of Harriott Horry who could also argue ownership, possibly successfully. Just realize that when money and/or notoriety are involved, it brings people out of the woodwork."

Riggs hands Hayes a transcript of the document. "We'd also like to hear your opinion about its impact on the legitimacy of a federal imposed minimum wage. I suspect that would increase its interest even more."

"Oh yes, it certainly would, no doubt about it." Hayes sits down and reads the transcript, his mind racing through the complex tangle of implications that an authentic document would exert on decades of lower federal and Supreme Court decisions. He also considers a whole new dimension of legal claims in federal courts.

As Hayes re-reads the page, he's astounded at the specificity of the notes' clear separation of federal and state authorities, the expressed unanimity of the convention delegates' position, and the potential implications on liberal SCOTUS decisions. "Providing it's an authentic document, you've asked the 64 million-dollar question, and the only definitive answer will have to come from the Supreme Court, after brutal legal battles that could take years."

Riggs and Patina both look dismayed, and try to digest everything Hayes is telling them, along with the potential impacts on their lives.

Hayes refers to several pages on the table, "These are some notes from cases relevant to your question about rulings on the commerce clause. Such decisions as the 1895 *U.S. v E.C. Knight Co.* rejected federal involvement in economic matters. Then in 1929, the stock market crashed and the U.S. became mired in the Great Depression."

"I remember my grandparents talking about those tough times," Riggs says.

"Franklin Roosevelt ran for president in 1932 on a "New Deal" platform that would get the federal government much more involved in the economy and voters elected him in a landslide. Opponents challenged his new programs in court and FDR quickly concluded that the Supreme Court would play the critical role."

"Did the court uphold his programs?" Patina asks.

"No, so during his second term FDR supported a bill that would've authorized him to appoint an additional SCOTUS justice when a sitting member turned 70½ years old. If an aging justice approved his programs, he'd withhold an appointment and use it later to dilute votes of aging judges who opposed his programs."

"That's amazing! Obviously, his scheme didn't work because we still have just nine Supreme Court justices, what happened?"

"Even the Democratically controlled Senate found it an over-reach and the bill sat in committee for 165 days as the chairman of the Senate Judiciary Committee said, "No haste, no hurry, no waste, no worry - that is the motto of this committee."

"Well good for him, I guess the separation of powers prevailed then," Riggs says.

"Well, yes and no. The threat to judicial independence was apparently enough that in 1937 former anti-New Deal Justice Owen Roberts decided to uphold a Washington State law imposing minimum wages. With that precedent, Congress passed an Act a year later that established a federal minimum wage that the Supreme Court upheld in 1941."

"So that's how we got to where we are?" Patina asks.

"Yes, Ma'am, and with the door cracked open, future decisions expanded it more and more. In the *Filburn* decision, the high court ruled in late 1942 that the Constitution allowed the federal government to regulate economic activity that was only *indirectly* related to interstate commerce. In fact, the product in the case wasn't even being sold – it was wheat grown by a farmer for his personal use. A similar argument brought us the federal minimum wage. Your document, of course, directly opposes such broad and indirect interpretations related to any federally imposed minimum."

Patina sighed, "Where there's a will, there's a way – regardless of the Constitution."

"Well remember, the US just entered WWII ten months before, so most citizens were inclined to support the Commander in Chief when they may not have done so otherwise. At any rate, the door was now ajar, and each subsequent SCOTUS decision pushed it open a little further."

"Where are we now with federal involvement?" Riggs asks.

"Well, a 1995 decision was probably the most sweeping in its impact and potential for further federal meddling in states' business. That year it ruled that congress could Constitutionally regulate, under the Commerce Clause, *instrumentalities* of commerce, the use of channels of commerce, and activities that they say may substantially affect interstate commerce."

"That sounds like a virtual antithesis of limited federal authority," Riggs says.

"You're exactly right, but that's the kind of justification they used to skirt the constitutional intent that's detailed in your document. Given the diametrically opposed positions, I wouldn't be surprised that any number of parties will challenge prior SCOTUS decisions and the Justices will eventually have to make a new ruling regarding Commerce Clause authority. That also includes the imposition of a federal minimum wage."

"Mr. Hayes, it looks like a lot of states, some cities, and some companies already have wages that're higher than the federal minimum, so why are they so anxious to preserve a federal $7.25 an hour wage?" Riggs asks.

"Reasonable question, Mr. Blanding. The actual $7.25 amount is vital to those who'd be forced to take less if the federal minimum didn't exist. But a lot of union contracts, like in the food industry, set their baseline wages as a percentage *above* the state or federal minimum wage, or they mandate a flat wage premium above the minimum wage."

"I see – that raises the stakes considerably, doesn't it?"

"Absolutely, no question about it. Without a universally established federal baseline, unions would find it very difficult to pin managements down on another acceptable national baseline. Just think about it – every city and state could have their own standard, a negotiating nightmare. There's a terrific amount of money and power in play, and your document can clearly move the pendulum one way or the other… depending upon who gains possession of it, legally or otherwise. There's no limit to what some parties would do for that kind of influence."

Hayes returns to the matter of authenticity, launching into his courtroom mode, quizzing Riggs on the source, discovery, and prior chain of ownership. Riggs reiterates how they came by the document, adding a few details, and admits that he's now as curious as Hayes regarding its authenticity.

"Who can determine if it's genuine to court-accepted standards?" he asks Hayes.

"Sorry, Mr. Blanding, but that's not my area of expertise. You'd need a well-established Forensic Document Examiner - an FDE - to do that."

Founders' Intent

Founders' Intent

Founders' Intent

Founders' Intent

108

Chapter 24

Chinese

R iggs drives back to his house with Patina, picking up some Chinese takeout along the way. "An 'FDE', huh? I guess we'll need to find one of those."

"Yep, never even heard of them before, and now we can't do without one."

They arrive at the house and set the food and chop sticks on the coffee table.

"Do you want to watch anything on TV, Patina, maybe another episode of *Justified* to see which crooks Marshal Givens is putting away?"

"Not really, not tonight. How about just listening to some tunes, OK?"

"You got it. Here're the plates – I'm famished."

"Me too, although I don't know if I can pick up enough food with these chopsticks before I starve."

"Oh, let me show you my technique, you'll be a pro in no time." Riggs stands behind her with his left hand on her hip and demonstrates his deft use of chopsticks with his right.

"Hey, you're pretty good with *both* of those hands," she laughs and leans back into him.

They sit down at the kitchen table as Riggs plays *The Phantom of the Opera* soundtrack over a wireless speaker.

"Patina, I'm not sure we know any more now than we did before we talked to Hayes."

"You're right. We heard some background on a few Supreme Court decisions, but he didn't say any more than you did about ownership. And it doesn't surprise me that its impact on prior decisions could take years to resolve – too many groups involved for anything to happen faster than that."

After dinner Riggs opens his fortune cookie and smiles.

Patina leans across the table and looks at him, "Well that's quite a grin - what's it say, what's your official fortune? They do come true, you know."

Riggs looks back at her, absolutely captivated by her large brown eyes, "I believe you, Patina, at least you're right on the money with this one."

"It must be something good, then – is it about us?" She anxiously leans farther towards him.

"It says 'Your best days are ahead', but I already knew that the day I ran into you – literally."

That's so sweet, what a thoughtful thing to say. She beams her hypnotic smile and reaches across the table to hold his hands, "I can identify with that, Mister, you're pretty special yourself."

They become lost in each other's gaze for several moments, then clear the table, put the leftovers in the refrigerator, and walk into the den and sit on the sofa. The current selection of oldies is mellow and the lights are faint.

Riggs slowly runs his fingers through her flowing hair, luxuriating in its soft tactile feel. His other hand softly glides down her toned shoulder and arm. *She has the most sensuous skin.*

Her breathing becomes more shallow and rapid. She slowly tilts her head back, opens her eyes, and looks into his. *He makes me feel so secure and cared for, so... completely loved.*

Riggs lays down and rests his head on a cushion that's propped against the arm of the sofa. Patina looks at him, closes her eyes, and lays down facing him. She pulls his arm around her and gently strokes it – lightly at first, now more firmly, pressing it against her. She slides her leg over his and softly rubs it against him. Riggs relishes her loving attention.

Patina rests her head against his chest, feeling it rise and fall. She can't remember ever having felt so warm, so protected, and cherished.

With a finger against her chin, Riggs turns her face towards his and savors these moments of her loving presence. She closes her eyes, pulls him closer and they kiss. Lightly at first, then more intensely, more passionately, feeling the weeks of pent-up emotion and growing feelings for each other.

Pausing, they look longingly at one another and sense their own and each other's inner, primal impulses to be even closer, to be unified. Intense, deep-seated feelings erupt – physical and emotional cravings to satisfy both themselves and each other.

As Riggs looks admiringly at her, Patina presses his arm, "Riggs, I've got to confess…" she begins softly, "I'm not very experienced and… I… I don't want to be a disappointment."

He looks directly into her eyes and tells her with deep-seated conviction, "Patina, you couldn't be – not ever."

She closes her eyelids and smiles, then kisses him on the forehead, the tip of his nose, and lips.

"It's been awhile for me, too, Patina, but tonight it's just us – you and me in a world of our own. There's no script, there're no roles or presumptions - just us and our feelings for each other. And here, right now with you, I've never felt closer to anyone."

I hoped, but didn't really realize someone could be so… loving.

They slowly get up from the sofa and walk into the bedroom, playfully beginning to undress each other there.

As he slowly unbuttons her shirt, Patina shyly looks up at him, "Riggs, on the off chance you haven't noticed, I've got to tell you that I'm not overly heavy up top."

Riggs pauses, pulls her closer to him and looks directly into her large brown eyes, "On the off chance *you* haven't noticed, Patina Gregors, I think you're absolutely perfect exactly the way you are."

Founders' Intent

Chapter 25

Conspiracy

S onny's blood pressure rises with every new poll - he absolutely *cannot abide* the idea of losing to Mark Chambers and returning to Charleston without his federal clout. He revels in the roles of king maker and annihilator, and knows he'd never be able to face his old cronies after a defeat by the young state senator. They'd put on a good show to his face, of course, but he'd know all too well that they were telling stories behind his back, unanimously agreeing that he was nothing but a washed-up loser.

"Luther, would you come into the office," he directs through the intercom. Moments later, Luther appears, ready to do whatever bidding his boss directs.

"Luther, I'm getting even more concerned with what I'm seeing and hearing about Chambers' poll numbers. I thought a few well-timed actions in the district would keep him from mounting any real threat, but I can't leave anything to chance."

"Do you think he could really pull off an upset?"

Brooding, Sonny slowly swivels his chair to look out the window, surveys the bleak October landscape, and ponders the very same question. *Just like this enduring government, those magnificent trees, the elms, have survived countless challenges. But their individual leaves blow into obscurity, to be replaced next year - like me?*

Still looking out after another minute, he says, "Luther, we don't hold positions of leadership and authority without knowing the risks and taking bold measures to eliminate them."

Where's the boss going with this one?

"We've got friends manning the first lines of defense – contributions, news feeds, planted stories, as well as some back-up defenses like a little voter suppression here and there. What's missing is a final, failsafe measure. This is one of those times when the past talks to us. If my WWII history is correct, the Russian Army had eight lines of resistance at the battle of Kursk, which ultimately stopped two entire Nazi Army Groups in their tracks."

Sonny spins back around to face Luther and pauses for emphasis before continuing. "Our strategy needs that kind of certain failsafe, an infallible action that absolutely precludes him from taking my rightful office - a knockout blow, Luther." He emphasizes the words 'knockout blow' by striking his right fist into his opened left hand.

"Yes Sir." Luther focuses more acutely on Sonny's words, knowing his boss's mental gears are rapidly developing a strategy.

"This office - the people's representative to the highest government in this great land - is a revered position that cannot be sullied or abused by the likes of Chambers. I simply cannot allow it to be occupied by someone who doesn't put the good voters of the 6th District first. That is my foremost obligation and I intend to fulfill it to the utmost of my ability. Besides, Chambers is untested at this level of responsibility, with no assurance he could ever deliver results to the worthy voters of the District."

Sonny speaks with practiced conviction, like someone who believes his own lofty, virtuous words. Self-delusion's become such a part of his thoughts, speech, and actions that he doesn't, he can't, recognize that it's become a fundamental dimension of his character.

Luther slowly nods and remains completely focused on Sonny's eloquent rhetoric. *If only it was genuine.*

"Luther, they're looking for a leader, someone they can elect who'll do what's right for them and faithfully carry out those 18 enumerated legislative authorities in our great Constitution. They need someone with values, virtue, and principles. Then they want to forget about the nasty confrontations, complications, and intricacies of politics and go about their own business. They were born to elect me, and I was born to lead them."

"I'm with you, Sir. What kind of last defense do you have in mind?"

Sonny looks out the window again, "Like great generals, I conceive the strategy, the broad strokes necessary to achieve a grand purpose. I relegate the implementing details to a trusted lieutenant - to you, Luther. I'm absolutely confident you'll come up with the tactics for a rather... permanent solution. You've never let me down."

"Thank you, sir, and you know I never will."

Sonny turns back towards Luther and nods in agreement. "I need you to fly down to the district as soon as you can, look around, and make something happen – something permanent. The more incidental it appears, the better, of course.

"Certainly, sir."

"Oh, and Luther, maybe add just a little southern flair to make it ever so much more poetic."

Luther returns to his office, immediately books a flight for Charleston and reserves a car. He also smiles at the prospect of conducting sanctioned violence in the name of the 6th District and the Constitution.

Founders' Intent

Chapter 26

Battle Plan

L uther Phillips assumes complete freedom of action and is well aware of the need to avoid even a hint of Sonny's involvement. That shouldn't be a problem because as they say, this ain't his first rodeo.

After a 45-minute drive west from Charleston International Airport, Luther arrives at Sonny's property, where he'll stay to minimize his visibility. If anyone asks about the trip, he's just there to coordinate the congressman's final $10k per plate fundraiser.

True to form, Sonny's loyal house manager meets Luther on the front steps leading up from the circular driveway.

"Welcome back to *Waterside*, Mistuh Luther, let me get yuh bags."

Waterside describes both the house and its surrounding 96 acres on Little Britton Island, 22 miles west of downtown Charleston. The main house's expansive covered porch overlooks the Lower Toogoodoo Creek, which flows sequentially into the Wadmalaw, the Dawho, and the Edisto Rivers before emptying into the Atlantic Ocean between Edisto and Seabrook Islands. Luther takes in a satisfyingly deep breath and relishes the island's salty breeze, lazy pace, and solitude – a complete contrast from the crushing tempo of Washington D.C.

"Thanks, Jasper, I'm only here for a day or two, so I didn't bring much with me. The back bedroom?"

"That one's all made up, Mistuh Luther, but no one else here now, you can use anyones you want."

"Place looks the same – nice and quiet and away from neighbors."

"Yessuh, it pretty much always be the same. But we been havin' lots of weather and that brings out the snakes, gators, skeeters, and roaches."

"Hate 'em, Jasper, hate 'em all. Just make sure they're all *outside* the house!"

"Oh, yessuh, Mistuh Luther," he laughs. "Mistuh Sonny and his lady hates 'em all too, every one of 'em. The screens on the porch is all good, and I catched two water moccasins outta da yard this morning – got 'em in a croker sack in the shed to sell to the reptile farm."

Jasper carries Luther's small duffle bag into the house and sets it on the bed in the back guestroom. Luther grabs a beer from the kitchen and walks out the back door, down the porch steps, and across the lawn to the dock. He casts an admiring eye on Sonny's high-end bass boat, raised out of the water by a lift.

Luther sits down at the end of the dock, nurses his beer, and gazes across the tidal flats at herons and the virgin forests. It's so undisturbed, serene, and soothing. Tomorrow morning he'll scout Mark Chambers' house and who's in it. He'll also track Chambers' route to work, campaign headquarters, and where he hangs out. *Let's see where he's most vulnerable,* Luther reflects with a widening grin.

At 5:00 the next morning, Luther drives towards Charleston and Chambers' middle-class neighborhood with its neatly cut grass and regularly pruned shrubs. Following his phone's GPS, he cruises past Chambers' house, ensuring no one's coming out the door or garage. Satisfied, he makes another pass to take a video, then parks two houses away and watches.

After a full hour, Mark Chambers comes out of the house and gets into his Ford F-150 pickup truck for the brief ride to his campaign headquarters. Luther slides down in the seat as Chambers drives past him, then looks for signs of any other occupants. Seeing none after 15 minutes, he approaches the house on foot, and knocks on the door.

He's not altogether surprised when a woman opens the door and asks through the storm door, "May I help you?"

"Good morning, Mrs. Truett?" Luther inquires.

"No, I'm sorry. No one named Truett lives here – you must have the wrong address."

Luther pretends to check his phone, "Oh, gee, I'm so sorry to have disturbed you, Ma'am. I obviously do have the wrong house,

I'll double check Matt's address. Sorry to have bothered you." *I guess the misses isn't such an early riser.*

Luther walks back to the car and waits inside until Sheila Chambers leaves for work at the campaign office.

From inside the car, Luther checks both ends of the street for activity and scans nearby house windows for any curious neighbors. He drives to the corner of Chambers' property, gets out, and briskly walks up the driveway and around the side of the house. In the back yard, he surveys a freshly mown lawn surrounding a patio and pool. A single set of large, wet footprints shows him that the senator used the pool this morning.

Late the following morning, Luther relaxes at *Waterside* on Sonny's big leather recliner and notices Jasper walking by in a huff.

"Something wrong, Jasper?"

"The snakes is gone - the ones I wuz gonna sell to the reptile farm. Bag gone too, so I knows they didn't just crawl off. Who'd wanna take those nasty critters?"

"That *is* terrible, Jasper. Must have been some real low-life son of a bitch to do that."

"Yessuh, lower than scales on a snake's belly. I just don't know about some people, Mr. Luther. You and Mr. Sonny are always so kind to me and everyone else, but other peoples... "

"I hear you, Jasper, you just don't know who you can trust any more. There's nothing that some people won't do to get their way – but taking a man's snakes, well that's the worst. Hey, let me help make this one up to you." He peels a $20 from his wallet and hands it to Jasper.

"Oh, you don't have to do that Mistuh Luther, it wasn't yer doing they be missin."

"Just trying to help out, Jasper, just trying to help a good man out." *Best $20 I ever spent on an election!* Luther makes a mental note to claim the amount as a miscellaneous campaign expense.

Founders' Intent

Chapter 27

The Last Dip?

W hile Luther's flying back from Charleston, Sonny Butler is resplendently sequestered in the Longworth House Office Building on Independence Avenue. He's shocked at the Charleston Gazette's on-line headline,

Wife of Congressional Candidate Mark Chambers
Suffers Potentially Lethal Snake Bites!

"Wife? Jesus Christ, is this some kind of coincidence or Luther's doing? Instead of some damn snake story about his wife, I should be reading that son of a bitch's obituary!"

Sheila Chambers was the victim of an undisclosed number of venomous cottonmouth water moccasin bites while swimming in the family's backyard pool this morning. Rescue crews rendered first aid to Chambers before rushing her to the emergency room at Tidewater Memorial Hospital.

Moccasins are common around wetlands and are one of the two most common pit vipers in South Carolina's coastal region. Like people, moccasins can tolerate pool chlorine.

Chambers is being treated with antivenom and is in guarded condition. A spokesman says it is too early to determine the effect of the tragedy on her husband's ongoing campaign to unseat incumbent 6th District Congressman Sonny Butler. State Senator Chambers' standing in polls has been rising steadily.

The second Luther pushes his way off his flight at Reagan National Airport and switches his phone off airplane mode, he instantly spots a number of calls and texts from Sonny. *Hope he's giving me the rest of the day off for taking care of business, but he'll probably want to hear all the details... personally.*

Luther steps away from the throng of passengers and immediately calls the office. "Sorry I've been out of touch, Sir, just got off the plane and turned the phone back on; saw you'd called..."

"What the *hell* happened down there? What am I reading all over the Gazette's front page? No, don't say a word, just get back to the office, NOW."

A stunned Luther looks up at a television newscast to see the breaking story about Sheila Chambers. *What the hell, her?*

"Close the door, then explain exactly what happened down there. Tell me this story about his wife is a coincidence; do we still have a problem with Chambers?"

"Sir, at this point, I can only tell you what I did. I cased his place yesterday and found out that he jumped in the pool before work. This morning, I tossed the snakes in before he woke up, then left. I guess they changed their routine and *she* took a dip this time."

"Oh, that's great, *just fucking great!* Now he's still going to be on the campaign trail and breathing down my neck. And the SOB'll get the sympathy vote too. Shit!"

"There may be some silver lining in all this," Luther cautiously offers. "As long as she's in the hospital, he can't appear to be *too* caught up in politickin'; it'd make him look like he only cared about himself and the election... family values be damned. He'll have to curtail his personal appearances - like Jimmy Carter staying in Washington instead of hitting the campaign trail during the Iran hostage crisis."

Sonny ponders, "You may have something there, Luther. As I recall from the pollsters, his personal appearances were jacking up his numbers. Let's hope she's got a real slow recovery – at least until the election's over." *Next time, don't send a boy to do a man's job.*

Sonny leans back in his overstuffed chair, only a little less worried about the election. *It's all for the citizens, especially the next generation* he assures himself.

He and Dana have no room in their lives for children of their own, but he dotes on his niece whenever he's back home and relishes opportunities to support her interests. Helping affiliated organizations while he's in Washington helps fill some of the many voids in his life, too. He turns to his intercom, "Angel, what time do I talk to the Girl Scout Council today about the duties of public officials?" Butler asks his secretary before turning to the phone to raise more campaign money.

Outside the Intensive Care Unit, Mark Chambers asks, "How's she doing, doctor?"

"She's stable, but still in very guarded condition. Without your quick 911 call, we'd be having an entirely different conversation."

Mark trembles when he contemplates what 'an entirely different conversation' meant. "I called as soon as I could."

"Most snake bites occur on people's extremities - their legs, hands, and arms. In this case, though, your wife was swimming, so the snakes were able to bite her on her shoulders four times. That means the venom was injected much closer to her heart and head – significantly increasing the potential for greater damage."

"Oh my god," Mark says as he considers the severity of the morning's event.

"Moccasin venom coagulates victims' blood – creating globules that block small vessels. It also increases vascular permeability and degrades capillary membranes, which results in reduced blood pressure. We've administered antivenom to counteract it, and have additional blood on hand in the event it's needed. For now, we just have to closely monitor her condition."

"Thank you, Doctor, and please keep me informed, for better or worse."

"Of course, Senator"

Founders' Intent

Chapter 28

A Grand Hoax?

T
he morning after they consulted attorney Hayes, Riggs
and Patina wake up from their intimate night together
and simply gaze at one another for several magical
minutes. Riggs pulls a hand out from under the sheet and gently
brushes her hair aside. She strokes his arm and smiles.

"How'd you sleep?" he asks.

"You mean for the couple of hours we actually *did* sleep?"

"Yeah, you're right," he laughs back at her. "It was the most in-
credible night of my life."

Riggs savored every possible moment of their just-shared experience. He found Patina more graceful and attractive than any statue,
portrait, or other art he'd ever admired. Every visceral fiber of his
being was completely gratified, a pleasure that was immeasurably
heightened by Patina's simultaneous and equally intense rapture. The
experience, though, was much more memorable, much more pro-
found emotionally. It'd been thoroughly exhilarating to be *the* person
with whom this amazing woman attained her deepest satisfaction, and
who found him so completely desirable that she unreservedly strived
to please him just as fully. *I've never had such deep feelings... about
anyone,* he wondrously reflects.

They slowly run their open hands over each other's shoulders,
arms, and torsos.

Suddenly, Patina sits upright, "Riggs, I just remembered – we've
got to take your document stand to the Society before Dr. Arkin goes
off to meetings today."

Riggs looks confused and tries to pull her back beside him.

"Can't now, big guy." She tickles his chest, "To be continued?"

Riggs sits up and kisses her, and reluctantly throws the covers
back. They get out of bed, turn on the shower, and playfully wash
each other under the rainwater showerhead. Patina turns around, facing Riggs, and looks into his eyes, "Last night was... absolutely

sensational. I've never felt so fulfilled, more alive, closer, or more special."

"Since the day I met you I knew we'd be amazing together… in every possible way." He smiles down at her as they tightly embrace each other.

"If we make a habit out of this, I'm going to have to bring a couple of more things over," she tells him.

Riggs smiles, "I think we could find some room in the closet and bathroom, and maybe even space in the driveway for your Honda if you're not afraid of being rammed from behind."

"Hey, cowboy, are you talking about my Honda or me?" she asks with a flirtatious smile.

They towel each other dry, get dressed, and quickly eat a light breakfast before taking separate vehicles to Dr. Arkin's office.

"Good morning, Dr. Arkin – Riggs brought the display in for you," Patina says, noticing an early unscheduled guest in his office.

"Ah, so good to see you this morning, Ms. Gregors. May I presume you have the original document with you for Dr. Hartman, the one that was in your pictures?"

"Not yet Sir. You remember my friend Riggs Blanding? Since we're joint owners, we thought it'd be smart to discuss the next steps together. But we did bring the display stand in for you to check out, it'll look great in the Rutledge Room."

"Good morning, Sir," Riggs says with an extended hand. Here's the stand – I still have to get the plexiglass for the document cover."

"A pleasure to meet any friend of Ms. Gregors. And thank you so much for lending us your woodworking talents," Arkin responds with a firm handshake.

Riggs concludes that he's dealing with a professor who's the antithesis of Dr. Hartman. *I can already tell this guy's so much more genuine that narcissist Hartman.*

"Ms. Gregors, may I introduce FBI Special Agent Will Haskell. He's inquiring about the paper you photographed."

"The FBI? Why, is it a missing government document?"

Haskell steps forward, "Neither one of you are under investigation of any kind, I'm simply trying to determine where it is and, if possible, *what* it is."

Patina recounts how she and Riggs found the document, their conversation with Professor Hartman, and his speculation about its potential impact. "We've secured it in a bank safety deposit box for now."

"Sounds like you're taking all the right steps, ma'am. I need to tell you that we've recently become aware of some foreign interest in the paper, so please exercise proper precautions."

Riggs asks, "*Foreign* interest? Well you've certainly got my attention, Agent Haskell. What kind of foreign interest are you talking about? I thought there were just a few of us here in Charleston that were even aware of it. Are we in danger, I mean we *are* talking to an FBI agent?"

"I don't believe you're in any immediate danger, but I would recommend you consider relinquishing physical custody of it to a federal office such as the NARA or Library of Congress. I can't really tell you any more than that right now since it's an open matter. Here's my business card, and I'll keep you posted if you'll give me your contact information." After answering a few more questions as completely as possible, Haskell thanks everyone and takes his leave.

Patina adds, "Dr. Arkin, if the document has some historical importance, we're concerned about its security too, especially if it's genuine."

"And there may be some questions about ownership," Riggs adds.

Dr. Arkin weighs in, "Yes, yes, my dear, that's all very prudent and necessary. But you realize that experts will have to access the original to determine its authenticity, don't you? We certainly wouldn't want to announce the discovery and later learn that it was a grand hoax. Oh, and Professor Hartman's urged me to remind you that he'd like it as soon as possible for that very purpose. He could secure it at the university, away from any curious foreign interests as well – after the donors' event, of course."

Oh, I bet that little weasel asked for it again, Riggs thinks.

"Certainly, Dr. Arkin. We just want to understand who can determine its authenticity, the steps involved, and timetable," Patina adds.

"And what authentication would cost," Riggs says. "After seeing the pictures, do *you* think it's real?"

"Mr. Blanding, I haven't done any detailed research on it, and don't have the means nor training for the required technical tests to answer that question."

"I understand, sir."

"But not to leave the matter on a completely negative note, Dr. Hartman and I have agreed so far that the dates, names, and subject matter are all in accord with what we know of the Convention."

"That's good enough for now," Patina says.

"Ms. Gregors, to learn more about it, I'd ask the NARA's Chief Operating Office which experts have certified the most recent documents they've accepted for archival. And perhaps ask the same question to the Library Services Office at the Library of Congress."

"And then contact those people…?"

"Yes, exactly. Then you'd know you were dealing with someone whose opinion was highly respected and was accepted by authoritative federal government offices. Their collective support will be most meaningful in any academic or court arguments that may arise."

"Thank you, Dr. Arkin, thanks for that information; I'll get right on it."

Patina walks Riggs out the Society's rear door to the small parking lot.

"That's the second professor and first agent to recommend the NARA, Patina, have you ever heard of it?"

"Yes, when I did some research on my family tree. The NARA stores all the U.S. census records among tons of other federal documents. I'll call them this morning to see what they can do for us."

"Good luck, I'll bet it and the Library of Congress are two government offices with organization charts that look like rats' mazes."

He puts his arms around her and they lean in to kiss each other goodbye; she pats him on the butt when he turns to walk to his car.

Patina returns to her cubicle in the Society building and calls what she hopes is a promising number on the NARA's web site. Each person she talks to refers her to someone in another office.

"Good morning, Juanita Menendez? Do you handle the authentication of documents accepted by the NARA?"

"Hello, yes, this is Juanita. No, not really, Ma'am. Federal agencies submit documents to us for archival, but we don't do any authentication here. It's up to those agencies to validate their submissions to whatever extent they think is required."

"Oh, OK, well thank you. Oh wait a minute, what agency would likely submit a historical document for archival at the NARA?"

"There're any number of them, as you can well imagine – the federal government's a very large organization. But we do a lot of storage for the Library of Congress, have you tried them?" Juanita asks.

Patina, a little frustrated with the federal government's labyrinth of offices and hierarchies, repeats the process with the Library of Congress. In turn, the Library staff refer her to the Office of the Associate Librarian for Library Services, and then to that office's Acquisitions and Bibliographic Access Directorate.

"Good morning, this is Marjorie, may I help you?"

"I sure hope so, Marjorie, I feel like I've talked to half the federal government today. My name is Patina Gregors and we've found what we think are original notes by five Founding Fathers from the Constitutional Convention."

"Well that certainly sounds intriguing. How may I help you with the notes?"

"I'd like to know about your authentication process, how you know if a document is the real deal or not."

"I see. Well, if we're interested in a document that is offered to the Library, we generally refer it to a highly-qualified Forensic Document Examiner, or FDE. Is there anything more you tell can me about it?"

"I can do better than that. Let me email you a detailed digital image of it."

"Sure, that'd be very helpful. I'm going to give you the office email address of one of our interns. Send her the files and your contact information; she can print copies that I'll be happy to look at."

"Thank you so much, Marjorie. Two history professors have already expressed considerable interest in it because they say it provides background information about the U.S. Constitution's commerce clause, information that could possibly even affect Supreme Court rulings on the clause. That'd be huge!"

"I imagine it would be," Marjorie says, not knowing what the commerce clause is, much less any Supreme Court decisions related to it.

"Can you refer me to an FDE whose opinion you'd accept at the Library?"

"I really can't promote or recommend any specific business or person. I'm sure you understand the government's need to avoid even the appearance of playing favorites."

"Oh, sure, I guess you're right about that. Let me ask this then, which contract-examiners' opinions have you accepted for the last half-dozen or so documents?"

"Yes, I can respond to that question, that's an easy one. Janet Lewis authenticated our last four historical documents. We assessed the education, training, experience, professional affiliations, publications, and performance of a number of FDEs, and Janet's always been on the A-team. Would you like me to email her contact information to you?"

Chapter 29

Extra Credit

"**W**hat the hell is this? A text from Hartman? What's he want to do – rub some of his BS in my face again?"

Billy Jackson's more confused than ever, but faintly hopeful that Hartman's short notice shout-out may be a good omen. Uncharacteristically, he's been hitting the books, but he's also too far into the term to salvage his Constitutional History grade... without some help from on high.

Billy is outside Hartman's office seven minutes before his 4:00 PM appointment – unheard of punctuality for him. Hartman returns from a lecture and invites him inside.

"Mr. ... Jackson, right? Take a seat."

"Yes sir, thank you."

"I've been thinking about the hopeless situation you've got yourself into and was moved by the passion you expressed to rectify your constitutional course shortcomings. I may have been a bit hasty in denying your request for extra credit, and have a short-term project, that, if successfully accomplished, would make up for past deficiencies. I've got to tell you, though, it's a bit unusual."

"Sir, as I said last time, I'm willing to do whatever it takes."
Holy crap, I hope to hell the old bugger isn't coming on to me!

"Splendid. I need you to do some field research, as it were. It involves some literal leg work that I'd be happy to do myself if my academic load wasn't so heavy." *That and the fact the tart of an intern has already avoided all of my requests.*

"I understand, you must be awfully busy, Sir."

"Why, yes, I am. I'm preparing a large, intricate analysis that relies heavily on a document that a young lady has. Of course, she has no earthly idea what it is or its potential basis for a scholarly article on the Constitution. I need you to recover that page for me to analyze and reference for my article."

"Do you mean steal it?"

Hartman reels back in feigned shock, "Oh, heavens no, Mr. Jackson, not at all, I'd never suggest any such thing - that'd be illegal, wouldn't it? I'm simply offering you an opportunity to do some 'field research' to ensure your passing this semester. I'm sure you're a clever fellow, so I'll leave the specific method up to you."

Cagey old fart. He won't <u>tell</u> me to swipe it, but I bet he won't object one bit if that's what it takes to get it.

"I guess so, Professor Hartman, if it's for your academic research. Who's got it and, where are they?"

"Her name is Patina Gregors, here's her address."

Billy walks out of Professor Hartman's office, surprised by both the assignment and the realization he'll pass Hartman's course in time to withdraw money from his trust next year. Now, how to do it?

Maybe I should just find out where the page is and take it? No, it has to be crucial to Hartman's research, otherwise he wouldn't have me going after it. And if it's that important to his big article, he'll list it as a reference – which the public will see. Someone will look for the link between Hartman and this Patina lady's missing document ... and they'll end up with me.

He strains to find another approach.

Wait a sec. I stand to get some big-time bucks from the trust, why don't I just make her a cash offer, a big enough one to seal the deal? Hartman already said she doesn't know what the page is, what it may be worth, and she certainly can't write an article herself. Besides, everyone could use a couple of grand, right?

A day later, Billy knocks on the door to Patina's apartment, "Hello, Ms. Gregors?"

"Yes, may I help you?"

"I think so, and I think I can help *you*, considerably. My name's Billy. I'm taking a history course at the university that I have to write a paper for. I really want to ace the course, so I'm looking for a unique angle for my project - it's going to be on the U.S. Constitution."

Where did this guy come from, and how does he know my name and address? "I enjoy history, too, but I don't know how I could possibly help, unless you need an introduction at the Charleston Historical Society where I intern."

"Thanks, I may take you up on that later. For the paper, though, I want to go with something very original, something with a new slant to it. Someone at the college said you may have a page that could be useful for what I'm planning to write."

Now this is strange, very strange. Is this a coincidence? Riggs and I haven't spoken to anyone at the university about the document... except Professor Hartman.

"Billy, was Professor Hartman the 'someone' at the college?"

"It's been a while and I've been really busy with school work, I don't recall Ms. Gregors. But as I was saying, I'd be willing to compensate you for the page – it'd be exactly what I need for the paper."

"I have no idea how relevant it is or its possible value. Professor Hartman also said it'd have to be authenticated to be of any real use."

"Sure, I understand, but even if it isn't real, I'll use it to do a 'what if' kind of essay. This is important enough to me that I'm willing to give you $2,500 cash for it right now." Billy pulls a roll of $100 bills out of his pocket and holds them up to tempt Patina.

Patina's shocked at such a substantial offer from a stranger – a graduate student, no less. *Hmm, a very nice chunk of change. But I've never seen a grad student with $2,500 in cash for a page of research material. Especially unauthenticated material. What's really going on here?*

"Billy, I'm sorry, I really can't right now. And besides, it's jointly owned by me and my boyfriend."

Billy looks down for a few seconds, seeing his passing grade evaporate and early trust withdrawals kicked down the road another five years.

"Oh, I didn't know someone else was involved. To keep things fair, I'll extend the offer to him too - $2,500 apiece, $5,000 to the both of you."

"That's extremely generous, Billy, but I can't speak for him; why don't you leave a phone number and I'll talk to him."

Dejectedly, Billy knows she isn't going to deal today.

"Sure, let me write it down for you." *Crap, Hartman's going to stick it to me for spite, if nothing else.*

A very despondent Billy calls his task-master, "Dr. Hartman, this is Billy Jackson - you asked me to help you get that document for your article?"

"Yes, of course, Mr. Jackson, when can you drop it off? I'm happy to wait here at the office for you." *Oh happy days! Dale, you're on your way! Chairman Bentson's on the short path to retirement and I'll be his shoe-in successor with the notoriety my article brings to the university.*

"Yeah, about that, Doctor Hartman. She wouldn't give it up. I told her I needed some new kind of material for a paper and she said 'no'. I even said I'd buy it from her, offered her $5,000 and she still kept it. I'm really sorry, but I gave it my best shot."

Hartman's elation instantly reverts to depression and veiled rage, "I see, so there's no possibility you can obtain it any other way?" *Why didn't you just steal the damn thing, you idiot? How could I have been so naive as to even imagine dimwitted 'Mr. Stud' would get it. What was I thinking?*

"No sir." *There's no way I'm breaking in to get a paper for you, you asshole.*

"Well, it's very unfortunate that you weren't able to fulfill your part of the extra credit agreement. Perhaps I'll see you in my class next term."

"But Dr. Hartman, I was going to give them five thousand dollars for your paper, doesn't that count for anything?"

"The world is a cruel place, young man, a place where agreements made must be kept if you expect to reap the rewards. Have a nice day."

That son of a bitch! He didn't so much as offer me another project. But if I'd stolen the paper, he'd have gladly taken it... after I took all the risk. That worthless loser hasn't seen the end of Billy Jackson!

Chapter 30

Transfer

B illy Jackson is brooding in his fraternity room, again. He re-reads the note from his parent's attorneys just like he'd done ever since he'd received it - focusing on the single line, *Failure to meet either of these conditions shall advance the date you may withdraw any amount of the principle until age 30.*

He's convinced Hartman will grade his remaining papers with an eye to failing him, no matter how much he studies. And studying was a steep uphill climb for Billy, especially to start this late in the course. Then, another thought crossed his desperate mind, *What if I could transfer out of Hartman's class? The normal add-drop period's over, but I could probably come up with some kind of excuse. Hell, I'm Billy Jackson, right?*

The next morning, Billy's in the Registrar's office talking to an administrator, "Well, I've laid it all out and you can see what a bind I'm in. I've got one term before graduation, and it'll be filled with mandatory courses. I've *got* to graduate on time."

"Have you talked to your professor?"

"Yes Ma'am, absolutely. I asked Dr. Hartman about doing something, anything, to demonstrate at least a passing understanding of the material. Something like research, or writing additional papers, and he said he didn't do that sort of thing."

That sounds about right for Dale Hartman, the administrator reflects.

As an afterthought, Billy adds, "He did call me back later with one project, though – he wanted me to get a paper from someone – a paper he needed for an article he said he's going to write."

"Why didn't he just get the paper himself?"

"I think he'd already tried and they wouldn't do it, but I really don't know. He seemed to know everything about it, exactly who had it, and where she lived – some grad student in the computer department, from the sticker I saw on her car."

"Wait a minute, you're saying Dr. Hartman disclosed personal information to you about another student? And how were you supposed to get the paper if he couldn't?"

"He didn't really *care* how I did it. I think he was hinting that I just take it if I had to, so long as I got it for him."

"*Did* you try to take it?"

"Oh, no, not at all. I went to the home address he gave me and asked the other student if I could have it for research and she said 'no'. Then I offered to buy it – even offered her $5,000, but she wouldn't sell it. When I told Professor Hartman, he basically said 'tough luck - too bad, so sad'; wouldn't even offer me another kind of project or anything, just the one to get the paper from the other student."

"Wait a sec, you were going to pay someone *$5,000* of your own money to get a piece of paper for Professor Hartman's project?"

"Yes ma'am. I know it's a lot of money and sounds kind of stupid at first. But missing my graduation date and having to pay living expenses and tuition for another term would be too. Plus, I wouldn't be able to start drawing a paycheck for those months."

"Mr. Jackson, this all sounds highly irregular. Our university clearly prohibits sharing students' personal information, and the university certainly doesn't condone doing business with students the way you've described. Would you be willing to write down everything you just told me, starting with your initial conversation with Dr. Hartman?"

"Sure, I guess so. Then can we do a transfer to another class?"

"In light of the improper conduct you've described and the potential for unfair treatment during the rest of the term, I believe that's most appropriate."

Billy beams with delight, *I'd give just about anything to see the look on that clown's face when he finds out he can't crap all over me anymore!*

Chapter 31

Document? What Document?

I n Silver Spring, MD, Food Service Employees International Union President Boggs Colman is ranting (again) in a breakout room during contract negotiations.

"Goddamn suits have no respect at all for working stiffs - absolutely none at all. The rank and file *work* their asses off while the suits just *sit* on theirs - especially the fast food joints. Listening to those overpaid stuffed shirts, you'd think they actually *did* something a day or two a week. What a goddamn joke! And now, again, they're trying to buy their next Mercedes by screwing us! I'm fed up with it!"

No one dares challenge Colman during a rant.

Boggs stares menacingly at his lead negotiator, "Donnie, you're heading the team, and we *will* bring the health package back from the table." he orders with a scowl. "Keep throwing wages up there too to keep 'em off balance, but we all know we won't even *think* about fiddling with wages - the members would crucify us if we botched wages. With all of them based on the fed's minimum, we really need the damn Secretary of Labor to grow a pair and index the rate for inflation. *Raising* it would be a plus, too, but the damn Republicans aren't about to even consider that. Manny, how long's it been since the feds raised the minimum?"

"Hasn't been touched since 2009, Boss – ten stinking years."

"Ten years! You can bet your asses the suits haven't frozen *their* paychecks for ten years. Well, we're not going to get anything like that done for this contract, but maybe we and the other unions can buy enough congressmen to get it done long term. So much would automatically go right if the fed wage was changed, and we'd be in some *really* deep shit if anything bad happened to it. Christ, I don't even want to *think* about that."

"That'd sink us for sure, Boss – all of us, and I just don't mean everyone in *this* room," Manny adds.

Boggs continues his tirade another three minutes, a lopsided mix of genuine disgust and a profusion of pure showmanship – knowing that union elections are now only a month away. Boggs is acutely aware that a negotiating coup would keep him in his very well-compensated office for another four years, and failure would put him out on the street, without any of his many perks or his substantial paycheck.

The American Association of Restauranteurs' negotiating team isn't making it easy for Colman, either. Health care is expensive and Colman's team hasn't indicated any willingness to budge on any other contract provisions in exchange for increased health provisions.

At 5:00 that afternoon, the two sides call it a day and after plotting more strategies for 30 final minutes at the office, Boggs Colman heads home.

By 6:30, he plods through his front door and gives his wife a warm hug and an extended kiss.

"Well that's always a nice way for you to come home, Dear - and just in time for dinner, what would you like to drink… tea?"

"Nope, need a bourbon tonight, Babe, maybe two of 'em" he answers while affectionately patting her buttocks.

He, Dianne, and their 19-year old daughter Maddy sit down to eat, about the only time they have together.

"How was your internship today, Maddy? The Library doing anything new?" Most days sounded pretty dull to Boggs, but he dutifully asks the same question every night. He's counting the months until she graduates and loosens up the strained family budget.

"Pretty much the same old stuff, Daddy. They're getting ready to upgrade the software I use, so next week will probably be a mess."

"Yeah, that's always a problem. I guess they pull all the engineers who're supposed to make programs actually work and put 'em in some fruitcake office that dreams up new kumquat emojis or other equally frivolous crap," he mutters contemptuously.

"Dear, will you be off this weekend so we can go to our shore condo?" Dianne asks.

Jesus, there's another expense! "I'll know by Wednesday; we're working the contract with those damn Association suits. Can you believe they're still pushing back on health care?"

"No wage increases this time?" she asks.

"Not this time; leaders' wages are already indexed, with automatic cost-of-living increases tacked on to that."

"Well, that should be a relief."

"That federal minimum's a joke anyway; thank God most states have a higher one, but still, we need to ramp it up to at least two times the current fed level over the next five years."

"Just try to relax for dinner," Dianne pleads, tired of shop talk already.

"Yeah, you're right, Hon. This meatloaf and potatoes look great, we ought to have them more often."

"I'm glad you like them, Dear."

"That's just one of the reasons why you're my one and only, Di."

"I'm glad you feel that way, Boggs. Now, about this weekend?"

"I'd love to sneak away with my special girl, seems like all my trips lately have been business."

"Didn't you and Sonny get to play a little golf last time you were in Charleston?"

"A little, but even on the links I had to talk business. And to top it off, my caddy left most of the decisions to me; *I* had to figure out what to use for every hole," he happily and secretly reflects on the comment.

"I'm sorry, dear. But maybe that's even more reason to take off this weekend."

"Anything to make my sweet bride happy, Dianne," he says while stretching over the table to kiss her.

"Oh, Daddy, what you said about the government wages reminds me, we had some people send in a picture of an old document they wanted to get checked. I made a transcript of it for my boss, and it said something about wages."

"What do you mean? The fed's been involved in wages for 80 years and the Court's upheld their minimums a couple of times since then. What kind of old document would the Library possibly care about?"

"I don't know, Daddy, I just got a picture of it in my email with instructions to print it for my boss. The person said they found it somewhere and it explained more about something in the Constitution," Maddy said, not really knowing what she was talking about.

Boggs thinks about it for a minute before helping himself to some more meatloaf. *The Library of Congress is interested in some old piece of paper about wages? What the hell is this all about? It's probably some garden-variety attic relic that someone wants to sell on eBay for a couple of bucks. I'll give Sonny a buzz in the morning, maybe his guys can see if there's anything to it.*

Chapter 32

We May Have A Problem

The next morning before contract negotiations get underway, Boggs is on the phone to Sonny Butler.

"Good morning to ya, Sonny, got a quick second?"

"Well, if it isn't my number one supporter, bright and early. I'm about to head over to the Hill for a caucus meeting, but I've always got time for you, Boggs. What's up?"

"It's probably nothing, but last night Maddy told me someone sent a picture of an old document to the Library of Congress yesterday, and she thought it had something to do with federal wages. I don't know if it's dealing with the wages of congressmen, the president, or the minimum. I really doubt if there's anything to it, but we're in the middle of some touchy negotiations and I don't need the suits trying to stall things with some kind of red herring. I know it's a long shot, but I'm just making sure I cover all the bases."

"That's smart, Boggs. I don't have any idea what we're really talking about, either, but they could try making a play out of *anything* to sidestep a fair deal with your guys. Even if something doesn't have any real legs, they'll throw it on the wall just as an excuse to stonewall you." *Always something... I really don't need the suits gumming up his negotiations and stalling his contributions.*

"Yep, that's what I was thinking. I may sound a little paranoid about this, but I've *got* to have a solid contract when the dust settles. Of course, if there *is* anything to it, it could affect a lot more of your other contributors and voters too. I can't imagine any of the suits have even heard about it; hell, I just heard it last night from Maddy."

"OK, fine, happy to make a couple of calls. I'll keep it below the radar, of course."

"Thanks, Sonny. And just thought you'd want to know that the Board approved my recommended campaign donation plan. It's got you and your PACs in the top tier again." *Christ, what I have to do just to get a congressman to do his damn job!*

"Well, I hope you know how much I appreciate the support you and all your hard-working members provide. I'll get back to you with whatever I find." *Jesus, chasing his intern daughter's rumor? The bullshit I have to put up with for campaign money to do my job.*

Sonny leans towards his desk and presses the intercom button for his Chief of Staff.

"Luther, see if we know anybody at the Library of Congress, preferably in the office that checks if documents are real or not."

Ever obedient, Luther immediately complies, "Yes sir, I'll get right on it."

Luther's been on Sonny's staff for over 15 years, ever since Sonny was a Councilman in Charleston County and then a State Senator. Luther knows all of Sonny's above and below-the-table dealings except maybe a few of the most intimate ones. Luther survives, even thrives, by knowing when to keep his mouth shut and when to raise a point that Sonny overlooked.

"Are you looking for anything in particular, Sir?" Luther asks in hopes of narrowing the search.

"I'm not really sure. I'd just like to know if a couple of people sent in an old document yesterday for authentication, a document that was related to the Constitution in some way."

"The U.S. Constitution?" Luther asks. It'd be very unusual to find anything new with meaningful ties to the Constitution. After the Bible, it's probably the most studied writing there is.

"Yep, you got it, the U.S. Constitution. Thanks, Luther."

Luther looks up the Library's Congressional Relations Office, calls it, and passes on the information request. It was a relatively simple one that didn't entail the usual research and digging through racks of dusty material or digital records.

The Congressional Relations Office expeditiously prepares and forwards a Congressional Inquiry to the Office of the Associate Librarian for Library Services. That office isn't sure, of course, which subordinate office the two customers spoke with, but takes a chance the reception desk directed them to the Acquisition and Bibliography Access Directorate. Yep, this was the federal government, with all of its glorious levels and offices.

As luck would have it, this directorate was the very office that Patina contacted and emailed a photograph to the day before.

Director Marjorie Tanner receives the congressional inquiry just before walking to her weekly meeting with her Division chiefs. After tackling the regular staff business, she asks Team Chief Piper Lawrence to prepare a transcript from the picture Maddy received and return it and the picture to her office before noon.

As soon as Piper delivers the picture and transcript, Marjorie prepares an official written response to the congressional inquiry. She includes a copy of the picture and the one-page typed transcript, then asks Maddy to hand carry it back up the chain of authority to the Congressional Relations Office. Luther has an emailed version by mid-afternoon.

During his daily update to Sonny Butler the following morning, Luther includes the response. "Sir, the Library of Congress responded with a picture and a transcript of the document the people asked them about day before yesterday."

"Picture? Transcript? Let me see them," Sonny dismissed the picture - too difficult to read the elegant cursive writing. He scans the transcript and re-reads the 4th and 5th paragraphs. As a member of the Committee on Education and Labor, his attention is riveted on one passage:

> "It shall be the sole purview of the several states to establish and enforce all manner of labor wages within their boundaries as they may decide."

"*Sole* purview of the *states*? What the *hell* is this, Luther?" he bellows. "Is this supposed to mean the federal government doesn't have any authority to set a minimum wage? Says who? What is this paper, and who wrote this crap? Where'd it come from, and why hasn't anyone seen it before? This is absolute bullshit! How can it have any relevance or standing?"

"Not sure sir, this is all we got. The Library accepted the picture for study and possible authentication if it seems relevant," Luther responded, knowing this wasn't the end of the matter.

"Well, as a member of the Committee on Education and Labor, tell 'em I'm *damn well* interested whether they are or not. If it amounts to anything, anything at all, we need to get in front of it right now. And Luther, find who has the real document, not just this picture."

"Yes Sir."

"And get Boggs Colman on the phone for me."

Boggs is a little surprised to hear from Sonny so quickly, and suspects he'll be squeezed to speed up the campaign donations. "Hello there, Sonny, what can I do for you?" Boggs asks as innocently as he can while waiting for the expected request.

"That document you heard about... I got a transcript of it. I don't know if there's anything to it or not, but here's the thing. It has an old date on it, signatures of some members of some kind of committee, and it says the federal government can't establish a minimum wage."

"*Can't* establish?" Boggs asks, shocked.

"Yep, *cannot*; only the states can. That's bullshit, of course. But like I say, I don't know if it's nothing at all or a big, stinking pile of crap for us."

"Jesus, if it has any relevance at all, that's all the suits would need to start a shit storm. They and the Republicans would love to use something like this to stall or screw up negotiations. We've been pushing for health because we assumed wages were solid and would only get better with hikes in the federal minimum. Is it real? It could be a real game-changer; damn it! We'd have to turn everything around at the table and completely shift our focus back to fighting for wages all over again. Holy shit, Sonny, this'll be an absolute disaster!"

"I already asked Luther if it amounts to anything, but no one knows... it just popped up a couple of days ago."

"Goddamn, if the suits, and not just the ones we're dealing with, got this into the courts, we'd probably be dealing with the case and challenges for years. This would screw the entire labor movement for a decade… hell, maybe forever! What can you do in the Ed & Labor Committee?"

"First, let's see if we even need to go that route. It could be a fake, or the legal eagles could tell us that old papers like this one became irrelevant as soon as the actual Constitution was ratified. Hell, I don't know - nobody does at this point."

Boggs calms down, but just a little, "Yeah, I guess you're right, Sonny."

"Right now, we can't have any more people knowing about this than absolutely necessary. Luther will send you a copy of the transcript."

Sonny doesn't bore Boggs with the details of Constitutional authority – that the federal government was limited to only those powers enumerated in the Constitution: if the Constitution didn't provide the authority, the feds couldn't legally do it. Even if Sonny, the entire Education and Labor Committee, the House, Senate, and President wanted to approve minimum wage legislation, they couldn't do so unless it was somehow interpreted as authorized under the Constitution. As Sonny also knew, all matters of government not enumerated for the federal government were reserved for the states.

Attorneys had argued before the eight sympathetic FDR appointed Supreme Court justices that lower wages in one state would reduce product costs there and disrupt commerce of similar products in higher wage states. Even though that's exactly how open markets were designed to operate in the new republic, the ensuing passage of The Fair Labor Standards Act of 1938 initially set a U.S. minimum wage of $0.25 per hour for covered workers.

Sonny was impressed with the ability of his legislatively creative liberal predecessors to link regulation of commerce among the states with a federally imposed minimum wage. As a politician, Sonny smiled at maneuvers that successfully bent or outflanked laws in order to achieve one's ends. *I wish we had some of that creative logic nowadays when the damned Constitution blocks so much of what we want to do.*

The Founders believed competition among states would drive more innovation, effective distribution, and efficient governance – a theme that Supreme Court Justice Brandeis echoed in his 1932 position that the different states could exist as 'laboratories of democracy': better solutions in one state could be emulated in others, while a failure wouldn't directly affect the rest of the states. This freedom to innovate would be a key element in the security and economic lot of all citizens. The newly-discovered document conclusively reaffirmed that principle as it related to wages.

Those years of legal jousting, however, were carried out in the absence of any documentation elaborating the Founders' intent to prohibit the feds from establishing a minimum wage. Could the document that Patina and Riggs found change all that? This was uncharted territory... if the document was legitimate and survived.

"Sonny, do we know who's got the actual paper and where it is? Be a crying shame if something happened to it, and the whole mess went away before it even got started."

Sonny avoided answering the question over the phone, "We haven't eaten lunch together for some time, my friend. Let's fix that as soon as we can. How about Thursday?"

He was a wary old southern fox who assiduously avoided passing sensitive information over a phone, email, or text message just to have it come back and bite him. There were just too many political enemies, young bucks, and reporters trying to topple those in power to attain it for themselves.

He hung up the phone and punched the intercom button for Luther, "See who has that damn document, where it is, and how we get it."

Chapter 33

How We Do It

With the name of a trusted forensic document examiner in hand, Patina makes a call, "Hello, this is Patina Gregors, may I speak with Janet Lewis?"

"Yes, good morning Miss Gregors, this is Janet, how may I help you?"

"Ms. Lewis, my friend and I think we've got a very old document we'd like authenticated, and I understand you're an expert at doing that."

"Thank you for the compliment, what can you tell me about it?"

"We discovered a page that was in an old desk here in Charleston, South Carolina. According to the date on it, it's over 230 years old. Two professors have already said the five signatures at the bottom are Founding Fathers. I've taken high resolution digital pictures that I could send you."

"It sounds very interesting, and digitals would be useful for initial familiarity. Of course I'd need the original in order to examine the paper and ink, though."

"Sure, that makes sense. How long would it take and what would something like this cost?"

Janet thinks for several moments, then responds, "You're in the range of $15 - $20,000 in professional fees and the appropriate tests required for the paper, ink, and authenticating five signatures. In a matter like this, a questioned signature is generally compared to as many as 30 known signatures. This sounds like a significant find, so you'd want to be absolutely sure of the opinion. Oh, and I ask that clients please provide just the questionable document, without any other contextual material. We do that to maintain utmost impartiality."

"I understand. And how long would something like this take?"

"I'd allow two weeks. Much of it will depend upon the availability of known signatures. All of the Founding Fathers were prominent before, during, and after the Convention, so I should be able to find authentic signatures without undue difficulty."

"Should we mail or FedEx the document to you?"

"You could do either, but given its potential importance, I'd suggest you consider a courier service. Would you like me to email you a work agreement to review?"

"Yes, that'd be great. Thank you."

After finishing her intern duties for the morning, Patina meets Riggs at Ahab's restaurant for lunch to tell him what she's learned.

"$15,000 - $20,000? That's a lot, and a lot more than we'd figured."

"Yeah, it is, but I called a couple of other FDEs from the internet and they were all in the same ballpark. There was one exception, but he didn't have any FBI or Secret Service experience, no record of a two-year training program, and no court testimony."

"I wonder if Hartman could get us an educational discount," Riggs jokes.

"Jason's attorney, Rudy Hayes, seemed pretty interested in this project, maybe he'd throw some money at it," Patina suggests.

"He might, but he'd want something in return - something that would probably be bigger than his contribution. I've got about $15k."

"I have about $20,000 left from my part of Richard's life insurance payout. Should we split the cost down the middle?"

"Yep, let's split the costs and whatever benefits come out of it. It's a deal," Riggs agrees.

Chapter 34

Examinations

L ater that week, Riggs and Patina call Janet Lewis again at her Springfield, VA office.

"Good morning, Ms. Lewis, this is Patina Gregors – I called you earlier about the paper with the Founding Fathers."

"Of course, Patina. How may I serve you today?"

Riggs already perused Janet's web site and reviewed her education, experience, and credentials: she was currently certified by the American Board of Forensic Document Examiners, a member of the American Society of Questioned Document Examiners, and a former employee of the U.S. Secret Service and FBI. She worked at a lab accredited by the ANSI-ASQ National Accreditation Board, *I'm not sure what all of that means, but it certainly looks impressive to me.*

"We signed the agreement and couriered the document with a retainer check to your office this morning, can you tell us what happens next?" Riggs asks over Patina's phone speaker.

"Certainly. The process has come a long way since Albert Osborn first applied the scientific approach to examinations a century ago. For this document, my associate and I'll examine the paper, ink, and what's written on it. We'll compare those results with known examples from the period and form our conclusions accordingly. Most of what I'll do is non-destructive, but this project may call for a test that requires the removal of a small amount of ink. Is that something you're comfortable with?"

"Yes, if it becomes necessary," Patina says, glancing at Riggs for concurrence.

Janet and her associate begin their methodical examination as soon as the document arrives. Janet starts with the paper, which is relatively easy to authenticate. If it proves to be counterfeit, it negates the need for further and more complex examinations of the ink and writing. From her Secret Service experience, she's well versed in the techniques forgers use to create what they hope will pass for old paper. Sometimes it's as crude as soaking it in tea and drying it out in a warm oven. Other con artists are much more ingenious.

Paper was an uncommon commodity in colonial America – treasured documents like the Constitution were recorded with iron gall ink on animal skins, usually sheepskin. For purposes such as John Rutledge's committee notes, paper made from reclaimed household cloth, sails, or rope would have been used. Wood pulp-based paper wouldn't appear for another 100 years.

Thomas Willcox was a key paper supplier during the time of the Constitutional convention and built the colonies' third paper mill, known as Ivy Mills, in Chester County, PA - a scant 20 miles southeast of Independence Hall. Janet recalls that Ivy Mills filled the first orders for continental currency paper and provided paper to Benjamin Franklin.

The cream-colored page is a lesser grade than high-quality white paper of the era, which is consistent with Janet's expectations. She carefully places each page under a microscope and finds the watermark "MW" – further corroborating the paper as coming from Mark Wilcox, son of the Ivy Mill's founder. Janet goes on to examine the paper fibers, meticulously noting their types, diameter, length, and how coarse or smooth they are. Janet then compares each characteristic with data bases of known papers available in Philadelphia in the late 1780s to confirm her initial assessment.

The next target is the ink. "Janet, do you want me to prepare ink samples for a TLC?" Regina asks.

"Not yet," knowing that she'll have to physically remove small ink samples from the document for the destructive Thin-Layer Chromatography Test. If other tests support the document's authenticity, she'll do it later as a confirmation.

"But I would like you to prepare the VSC, though." Her Regula 4307 Video Spectral Comparator helps discriminate between different inks by using combinations of light sources and filters under various wavelengths of radiation.

Regina does so and helps Janet examine the ink on the page, "It looks like the ink is authentic for the period."

"Yes, it does. The ink is consistent throughout the note and three of the signatures. The other two signatures are different inks, but not unusual if those men favored a different writing instrument they dipped in different ink wells."

Janet and Regina now turn to the more time-consuming task of handwriting analysis, beginning with enlarged scans of the page. Knowing that no two writers exhibit identical features in their handwriting, Janet turns her attention to the enlargements, looking very closely at words, sentence structure, and paragraphing that she'll compare to Rutledge's known works during the time of the Convention.

Janet knows that everyone has a normal variation in their writing, so any words that are exactly alike signal a likely forgery. She's also well aware that people cannot exceed their skill as a writer, that is, using words, style, and grammar that is beyond their education and experience. That's not an issue with these gentlemen, as they were all very accomplished in their own right.

Both she and Regina look for similarities and differences in letter spacing, slope, embellishments, and capitalization. Even letter proportions and punctuation come under their perceptive analytical scrutiny. Were strokes made upwards or downwards? Are any letters re-touched? If so, was it consistent? How heavy were the pen strokes? They compare all of these characteristics with those in the known samples they've collected from the same time-period.

Next, they begin confirming or challenging a single examined signature by comparing it to authentic known samples they've collected – starting with the presumed John Rutledge signature. Since he held a number of senior government positions, it was relatively easy to find known specimens near the year this document was presumably written.

Janet continues with a computer search for collected known specimens of the other four signatures. They also locate several original specimens at various Revolutionary era museums, state archives, court records, the Smithsonian, and the Library of Congress. They have to receive special permission before taking non-flash images to document their examination.

By the end of the next week, Janet and Regina have found sufficient specimens to begin comparative analysis of the handwritings in greater detail.

"How do you want to do it, divide the note and the signatures?" Regina asks.

"You start with the note, and then John Rutledge's signature since we think he wrote it. I'll examine the other four signatures. Then, just to double check, we can swap and independently compare our findings."

By the end of the week, they've completed their examinations, swapped key tasks with each other, and re-examined key material. Throughout the process, Janet and Regina maintain meticulous records of sources, processes, test results, and conclusions, since their final opinions will no doubt be challenged from every conceivable angle if the document proves to be authentic.

"If nothing else, I think I've got an excellent understanding of their intent of the commerce clause," Janet quips.

"Agreed," Regina laughs. "Didn't know a thing about it two weeks ago, and now I feel like an expert. What'd you conclude?" Regina asks her mentor.

"My opinion, after examining the ink, paper, and handwriting, is that the document is the original writing of John Rutledge and is co-signed by the other four Founders. What about you?"

"I'm of the same opinion. I didn't see any markers that lead me to suspect the originality of the paper, writings, or signatures. Shall I draft the opinion?"

"Not quite yet. Since all the analyses so far confirm the document's authenticity, I think it's time to run a confirmatory TLC. I'll collect the sample from a flourish or serif to minimize the impact on the actual page."

TLC is a very sensitive analytical technique for separating compounds of mixtures, like those found in inks. It can help determine the number, identity, and purity of each compound. A significant benefit is Janet's ability to run the analysis in 10 – 20 minutes.

"Regina, the TLC results support all our other findings that the document is authentic; will you put the formal report together while I call the clients with the good news."

Regina adds a comprehensive array of detailed attachments to their report, listing every item's name, source, and its relevance to comparisons on the questionable document. That will facilitate any future explanation to a court on how they analyzed the page and formed their conclusions.

> "Based upon a thorough forensic examination of the paper, inks, and handwriting as shown in exhibits 1 - 171, it is my professional finding that the document dated August 6, 1787 (copy attached) is an authentic product of John Rutledge, SC delegate to the U.S. Constitutional Convention. It is my further finding that the signatures of said document by Convention delegates Oliver Ellsworth of CT, Nathaniel Gorham of MA, Edmund Randolph of VA, and James Wilson of PA are also authentic and written by their hands."

Regina makes copies of the report and places the original in a large reinforced envelope that a courier will return to Riggs and Patina.

Founders' Intent

Chapter 35

Plan A

A fter Luther's mishandled effort to derail Senator Chambers' campaign, he works through today's task list with renewed vigor: squeeze key labor movements for donations and voter turnout plans, tally committee and floor votes for Sonny's new labor bill, gather background information on candidates seeking Sonny's support (particularly if it's personal and sensitive), and reach out to the Library of Congress again.

This time Luther bypasses their Congressional Relations Office to speak directly with Mrs. Tanner. She'd written the response to his original inquiry and she probably didn't speak with Congressional Chiefs of Staff very often. He was confident he could smooth-talk her into providing some personal support.

"Hello, Marjorie, this is Congressman Sonny Butler's Chief of Staff. I wanted to thank you for the very prompt, comprehensive, and professional response you provided to the Congressman's request this week."

"Why thank you, Mr. ---, I'm sorry I didn't catch your name..."

"Oh, my mistake, please forgive me, it's Luther Phillips. Listen, as a key member of the House Committee on Education and Labor, the Congressman asked me to follow up with you personally to see the actual document that was in the picture."

"I'm so sorry, Mr. Phillips, but the owners communicated with my staff by phone and email, so we don't have the actual document – they simply emailed the photo that was included in my response to the congressman."

"Oh, I see. Well, maybe it'd be simpler all the way around if I just coordinated directly with them."

"If you'll hold on a minute, I'll check with our intern to see what contact information they may have left her."

"You're too kind," he said, grinning with satisfaction. *Everyone wants to be relevant, to feel special; amazing what they'll do for a congressman's praise, or even his chief's!*

Luther copied the mobile numbers of Riggs Blanding and Patina Gregors, along with Riggs' address in Charleston.

With a partial victory under his belt, Luther turned to other equally important matters. It wasn't until late that afternoon when Congressman Butler left for a cocktail fund-raiser that Luther returned to the document chase and called Riggs.

"Good evening, Mr. Blanding, Riggs Blanding?"

"Yes, this is Riggs Blanding, what're you selling?"

"Oh no, nothing of the sort, sir. I'm with the federal government here in Washington D.C. and would very much like to follow-up on the newly discovered document you discussed with someone at the Library of Congress this week. We think it may be a vital contribution to our body of knowledge about the U.S. Constitution."

Riggs is surprised and suspicious. *Who is this? What office is he with, and why's he calling after hours? Nobody at the Library of Congress stays late just to ask about a paper they don't even know is real.*

"And you are...?" Riggs inquires.

"I apologize, my name is Tom Edwards," Luther lies, "and I'd really like a chance to see your discovery – they don't come along all that often, as I'm sure you know. If it's significant to our understanding of the Constitution, we'd certainly like to add it to the nation's historical records. And of course, there'd be a handsome finder's fee of up to $10,000 for you. Can we get together when I'm in Charleston next week?"

Luther knows he's pushing it, but wants to find out if Riggs is going to be an easy case or not.

Riggs feels uneasy with the stranger on the phone. *He never did say what office he worked for.* "Tom, I haven't seen a report on it to know if it's real or just another old piece of paper – could be a complete fake. Until I know more, I'm really not comfortable doing anything with it."

"Well, you know that we could determine whether it's real or not, and it wouldn't cost you anything – those examinations can run as high as $25,000. For history's sake, though, please consider letting me arrange for checking the document for you. In the meantime, I know you're responsible enough to properly preserve it and protect it somewhere safe so it doesn't get lost again? We also provide secure storage for a number of historically significant government papers."

"Yes, I'm exercising every precaution with it. It's in a very secure place."

Luther thanks him and reluctantly hangs up. *Taking every precaution, huh? Sounds like the little pecker's storing it off-site - that rules out a simple smash-and-grab. Going to have to up the ante on this one.*

The next morning, he briefs Sonny as part of the morning update. Sonny listens intently, then says, "Let's see what the Library people say, whether it's real or some fake, and if it could have any real impact on anything in the Constitution. I don't want to stir up a hornet's nest if I don't have to, but I don't want to miss the chance to nip it in the bud if I have to, either."

At the Library of Congress, Maddy Colman wasn't the only person who shared information about the newly discovered document.

Founders' Intent

Chapter 36

Outside-the-Box

L ibrary of Congress' Acquisitions and Bibliographic Access Director Marjorie Tanner arrives home just before her husband Neal finished contract negotiations, and starts dinner. They both work full-time jobs - all too aware that Washington D.C. is very expensive and they have three children who they're grooming for ivy league schools. Losing either of their jobs, especially Neal's, would be a financial catastrophe.

Twenty minutes later, Neal pulls up, exhausted from strategizing about contract negotiations. Boggs' Food Services Union of America represents about 5% of the over five million fast food workers, and Neal Tanner's National Association of American Restauranteurs represents owners of 32% of the country's 190,000 fast food establishments. With overall annual industry revenues of $200 billion, there's a tremendous amount of money and influence at stake on both sides of the negotiating table. Greed and personal egos, of course, trump all of those considerations.

Neal left all that at the office when he walked out for the day. Now he was home, could relax for a while, and enjoy dinner.

"This looks great, Hon, and I can really use a home cooked dinner tonight," he compliments Marjorie as he and the kids help with beverages, salads, and silverware. "How was your day at the Library?"

"Thanks, Dear, it was very successful – even got a call from a congressman's office thanking me for my professionalism," she beams with satisfaction.

"That's great, which one?"

"Representative Butler. He's on the Education and Labor Committee. Have you heard of him?"

"Believe me, I've heard of him, and I don't trust him any farther than I can throw him – if that far. What did you do so professionally to warrant a call from him?"

"It wasn't that much really, and it was actually his chief of staff. A young woman called earlier in the week with a picture of a document and asked about getting it authenticated. Butler's Chief of Staff wanted to know where the original paper was and who brought it in," she elaborated.

"That's a little unusual, isn't it? What was the document, and why was Butler interested in it? He never struck me as an intellectual sort."

"Well, yes, it certainly wasn't the kind of call we get very often. I'm not sure what it really is and why he wanted it. I just scanned over a transcript of it; the staff will be looking into it further. It might be notes from a committee that helped draft the Constitution, and it referred to federal authorities and how only the states could set wages."

Instantly, Neal turns around and becomes much more interested, "What? Federal minimum wages? That whole federal wage thing's been decided since FDR. Not the way the Founders intended, but we are where we are, I guess." *What the hell is Sonny Butler on to, or think he's on to? How could some recently-surfaced document affect the current status of the federal minimum wage?*

"Like I said, I didn't spend much time on it – just proof read the transcript we prepared – I can't remember the exact wording, but it did say the federal government couldn't set wages. That doesn't make any sense though. Washington *has* set a minimum wage, hasn't it?"

"*Didn't* have that authority, that's what it said? Did it seem real? Is there a link between it and the Constitution?" he asks, growing ever more anxious.

"Couldn't say yet. And I suppose it'd have to be validated before anyone would take it seriously."

"But if it *is* real, how would it relate to the Constitution? Could it?"

"If it *was* official convention notes, I imagine it could provide some additional perspectives on the meaning and intent of the authority that the Constitution gives to the federal government about commerce. But that's just me speculating now. I'm certainly no Constitutional lawyer."

"Jesus, Marjorie, this could be big, I mean HUGE. We've always known the FDR Court overstepped when it supported federal minimum wage cases. Can you get me a copy of the transcript and the pictures?"

"I suppose so. They're not classified or privileged, and they *are* a public record now. I'll email you a document request-form tomorrow. You complete and return it so I've got something on file."

Neal enjoyed his dinner even more than when he sat down just minutes ago.

The next morning, as soon as he receives Marjorie's email with the attached request form, he completes and returns it. Thirty minutes later, he's reading the transcript – very intently.

Neal punches the intercom button for the Association's Chief Council.

"George, would you come down to the office?"

George Wickley walks the short distance to Neal's office, wondering what new argument can counter the union's strident demands for increased health benefits.

"Good morning, Neal. What's up already?"

"George, every now and then even a blind squirrel finds an acorn; we may have just found ours and it could be a big one."

"OK, but I must be missing something – what's our acorn?"

"Look at this, it's a document transcript Marjorie sent over this morning that elaborates the Founders' intent of the Constitution's commerce clause. Read the fourth and fifth paragraphs."

George reads through it, raises his head, grins, and looks squarely at Neal.

"Is this real? Where did it come from? Why hasn't anyone seen this before, or has everyone just missed it? Who are these names at the bottom, and how does it relate to the Constitution?" he asks in a staccato manner.

"Can't answer any of those questions myself, but I need you to. Marjorie said the Library's working on it. She also told me that our old pal Sonny Butler got wind of it two days ago," Neal responds sarcastically.

"That *could* be in our favor," Wickley begins strategizing aloud. "Assuming he's read and shared it with the union, Boggs'll be even more anxious to wrap up negotiations. He'll be pissing in his pants worrying that we find out about this and throw some kind of Hail Mary legal challenge to the constitutionality of the whole idea of a federally-mandated minimum wage. That's the foundation of everything they ever argue for. Hell, we don't even need the case heard in court right away. Just the fact that we filed an objection will give us the rationale to stall the whole bargaining process long enough for the union to toss him out. Boggs'll be tripping over himself to give us key concessions on health to speed things up, protect wages, and save his job."

"You're singing my tune, old friend. Can you run with this one? I'll tell the negotiating team to step on the brakes. If nothing else, the union may just tip their hand on how much they know and what they're afraid we'll do. If they sense that wages are threatened in any way, they'll fall off the health demands in a second." *CEO of Burger Joints – got a really nice ring to it...*

"More than happy to dig into it – just remind Marjorie to keep me updated, OK?"

Within the week, Wickley and his assistant prepare and submit a complaint to the Eastern District of Virginia's Federal District Court in the Alexandria Division. The Clerk of Courts logs in the petition and enters it into the register. When the U.S. Attorney reviews filings with potentially broad consequences, Wickley's case, challenging previous Supreme Court decisions regarding interpretations of the commerce clause, stands out.

As a courtesy to Congress, he asks his clerk to inform the Chief Administrative Officer of the U.S. House of Representatives about the petition. The CAO forwards a copy to the Chairman of the Education and Workforce Committee, who distributes copies to each committee member.

Sonny is absolutely furious when he reads his copy of the notification, *Goddam it! They did it – those goddamn sons of bitches filed a federal suit! No matter how it turns out, it isn't going to make any difference and they know it; it's just an excuse to slow-roll negotiations until a judge tosses it or rules on it. And that'll take months, after the union election.*

"Luther, get Boggs Colman on the phone right now."

Founders' Intent

Chapter 37

Fun and Felony

"**B**oggs, Sonny here. I'm afraid the shit's about to start flying. Luther tried to work with the kids to get the document, but they wouldn't play ball – even for a nice chunk of change. And worse, I just found out the suits filed a case in federal court, which I'm sure they'll use to gum up the negotiations until after your election."

"Goddamn it! My daughter Maddy's interning at the Library of Congress and even *she* saw a picture of it – is that damned thing all over Washington!?

"It sure seems to be making the rounds."

"That's all I need right now. We just picked up some juice at the bargaining table and now those pricks are going to throw the whole federal minimum wage thing in our face. Now I'm going to have to change horses in mid-stream and defend wages instead of getting healthcare. How'd the suits even *get* the document when the kids wouldn't sell it to Luther?"

Sonny ponders. "You know, that's a great question, Boggs… let's think about this for a minute."

"What do you mean?"

"Well, the suits may not even *have* it. They didn't need to submit an original document as evidence when they filed, they probably just alluded to it in their petition. I wouldn't be surprised if they don't even know if it's real."

"But they'd need the original at the hearing, wouldn't they?"

"Oh yeah, absolutely. But if the kids still have it, the suits would have to bring them on board as parties to the lawsuit. Otherwise, the suits wouldn't have access to the original – couldn't even get a judge to subpoena it from a non-interested 3rd party. If they did get it, they'd also have to show it to your lawyer as part of his discovery. If they can't show it to him, you could request the judge dismiss the case entirely for lack of evidence."

"And then we're right back to where we were before this whole damn document thing popped up – we'd still have a better hand!"

"Listen, why don't you join me at the house in Charleston in about ten days so we can dig into this a little deeper. I just don't like planning too much over the phone. I'm hosting a very special golf game for my closest supporters and a fund-raiser two days later. I *know* you'd enjoy playing this course... with the same caddy you had last time."

"Starburst again? I can certainly add *that* to the calendar."

"We'll let the wives stay here in town to shop or something while you and I watch out for the caddies and snakes," he says only half-jokingly.

"Caddies, fine, but I've got no use for the man with no shoulders - you know that Sonny," Boggs says in reference to the area's many venomous serpents.

Sonny hangs up and punches the intercom button for his executive assistant, "Angel hon, will you please get my dear wife on the phone."

"Hello, Sonny, what a pleasant surprise to hear from you so early in the day. Is anything wrong?"

"No, not at all, Dana. Just wanted to tell you that Boggs and I have to go to one last fund raiser in the district – it's a big one, $10k a seat and I need the money for the TV ads. Chambers is still hot on my tail this time around."

"Oh Lord, another one? Still, better to spend someone else's money campaigning than ours. What should I bring to wear?"

"Why don't you and Dianne have a girl's weekend right here in Washington. I can cover this one, and it's just a quick flight down and come back a day or so later. When I get back, we can go off somewhere by ourselves."

"I guess so, Sonny, if you think that's best. You know how I dislike the heat, humidity, and all those creatures that crawl and fly around there."

"You and Dianne spend a little ladies' time together, without Boggs and me tagging along, bored with the department stores. Or maybe see if there's anything going on at the Kennedy Center."

"OK, I'll call Dianne. You two be good down there."

"You know you're my one and only, Dana – always have been and always will be."

Founders' Intent

Chapter 38

We're Here To Help

As soon as Zhu Jianjun receives Beijing's order to obtain the document, he passes the matter to his trusted collaborator at Sunrise Mechanical – CEO David Wang. David turns to his long-time executive assistant, or EA, who calls a covert contact he reserves for his most sensitive assignments.

The EA knows the operative as Jim Sparks but was never sure, nor did he ever question, if it that was his real name. Sparks was reputed to have worked an extremely critical matter for a very senior federal government official several years ago and accomplished it completely under the media's radar. The EA and Sparks mutually agreed that all payments be made in cash.

Adept at reading people, Jim Sparks is somewhat unique in his field, having extensive experience in old-school investigative and operational techniques as well as expertise with information-age resources and processes. Just as important, he knows people with specialized skills that are crucial to his special line of work.

In contrast to the coarse Ivan, Jim carefully and methodically analyzes each assignment - its objective, timing, locations, risks, and the people involved. He relies much more on his intellect and cunning than raw muscle, but has readily employed brutal force when the situation required it.

The EA asks Sparks to investigate the professors and discover which organizations may already be trying to leverage the Founding Fathers' document to support or oppose the fed's minimum wage, "We don't want wages reversed or even a serious discussion about it," the EA tells Sparks.

Jim's search, with help from contacts in labor, leads him to the National Association of American Restauranteurs, the Food Services Union of America, and that union's close relationship with U.S. Representative Sonny Butler. After doing some research on Boggs

Colman, Jim arranges a direct meeting with him at a boutique coffee shop.

"Are you Mr. Colman?" Jim Sparks asks when approaching a corner table where Boggs is sitting.

"Yes, I'm Boggs Colman, you must be... Jim ." Boggs couldn't pry much advance information out of this secretive, enigmatic caller, but he sounded both important and helpful to his cause. "Your call got my attention, tell me more," he says, getting right to the point.

"Thanks for meeting me personally, which is important because we have a shared interest in stopping a certain challenge to the federal wage. I believe I can assist your organization through some funding and by shaping public opinion via social media."

"That's a very interesting proposition, Jim. What's your interest in the matter, or maybe I should just ask who are you working for?"

"That's not really important so long as the money's green and we agree on the desired outcome, right?" He smiles, but Boggs knows Jim is dead serious.

The ever-wary Boggs becomes more curious and cautious, *It'd be great to have some outside help and he's right about the color of money, especially in the short term. Help with social media would be useful longer term if the court case gets any traction. But it's sure odd for someone out of the blue to make this generous an offer. I've got no earthly idea who this guy is... he could even be a federal investigator.*

"I suppose so, Jim. Based on the document, the Restaurant Association filed a lawsuit to slow-roll our bargaining. We need to kill that action to keep pressure on the Restaurant Association so they'll come to terms on the new contract. That way I can get reelected, for the good of the membership, of course."

"Of course, Mr. Colman, it's all for the membership." *All this chump sees is getting reelected to his overpaid, perk-laden office, but he'll be useful as the public face of the opposition. So long as the document's off the street, I could care less about his election.*

"A contract win will take away their immediate need to push the lawsuit, then we can concentrate longer term on the document they're relying on for evidence," Boggs says.

"Do the Restaurant Association people have the evidence?"

"Not sure, Jim, but we don't *think* they have the actual page; here's a photo of it you can have. And that's their Achilles heel. It looks like a couple of 30-ish kids found it and stashed it somewhere. An old friend of mine tried getting it from them with a big cash offer, but the little shits didn't bite."

"That would've been an offer by your colleague Congressman Butler?"

Boggs is shocked, and ducks the question. *Jesus, how does this guy know about Sonny? Who the hell does he work for... and what's he know about me?*

Jim sees the surprised look on Boggs' face and moves to ease his concerns, "No worries, Mr. Colman. If I didn't know how and when to be discreet I wouldn't still be in my line of work. Maybe I should get involved with the two kids."

"Let's have you hold off on that right now. Believe me, I know how to play hardball if it comes to it, but we've still got some options and you'll be the first to know if we'd like your help getting the paper from them."

Jim sits quietly, contemplating and staring across the small table. Then he leans forward with an icy stare and slowly, deliberately addresses Boggs, "I understand completely, Mr. Colman. But it's also imperative, my good friend, that you fully recognize and appreciate that I too have a stake in this matter – a very *critical* stake. I can defer to you and Sonny for now, but will insist on taking the primary role if the case moves close to a hearing date." Jim straightens back up in his chair, with his eyes still firmly fixed on Boggs before looking down at his coffee and taking a drink.

Boggs cringes uneasily at the look in Jim's eyes and the pronounced shift in his tone. Boggs has already concluded that the man, like himself, doesn't suffer fools or failure lightly.

After their meeting, Boggs immediately calls Sonny.

"Boggs, you sound a little rattled, what's up my friend, can't get a kitchen pass to see Starburst for the golf game?"

"Sonny, I don't know who the guy is or how he got my name, but I just finished a meeting about the document with someone named Jim. He knew you were involved, too, but I don't have a clue where he's getting his info. Christ, I thought all this was pretty much under wraps, and now some stranger knows as much as we do! He offered money and to run a smear campaign for us. Ever hear of him?"

Sonny pauses and reflects on all the shady characters he's dealt with in Washington and South Carolina.

"I'm afraid I'll need a little more than just a first name. You say you met with him and it was about the document? What's his angle – why does he want it?"

"It's strange, really strange. It was obvious he's working for someone, but he wouldn't tell me who – just said they're as interested as we are in getting the paper and killing the suits' case. He wasn't an amateur, either - strikes me as the kind of guy you hire when you need to get a job done absolutely right the very first time, no matter how tough it is. I'll send you his number in case you need to contact him."

"That's fine, Boggs, but keep my office at a very long arm's length from this guy. He could be anyone – even a fed with a wire."

Chapter 39

Fore!

S onny's loyal and compliant 6th District field representative Ripp Jennings assists with planning for the upcoming fund-raising events in the district. He's already reserved a private golf course for a unique best-ball tournament that Sonny's hosting for his closest friends and supporters. Ripp's also coordinating the grand dinner at the Charleston Club for especially well-heeled donors.

Several days before the golf game, Ripp talks to the greenskeeper, "Eddie, I'm sure the thunderstorms left a ton of crap on the links and greens; can I count on your crew to have the place in tournament condition by Thursday?"

Thursday morning, Sonny's at the clubhouse to greet his special guests, most of whom he's rewarded with political favors since winning his first county commission election ten years ago. They've all hosted Bacchanalian parties aboard their yachts and at their antebellum estates, and Sonny knows exactly how to reciprocate.

The event begins with a full breakfast, mimosas and stronger libations at the open bar, and raucous stories touting their successful schemes to funnel public money into private accounts. At 9:30 AM, Ripp stands up to announce that the golf match is about to get under way.

The men walk from the clubhouse to a wide tree-shaded deck and line of carts, each driven by a very attractive female caddy clad only in a visor, bikini bottom, sneakers, and small 'I Stick Up for Sonny' stickers on their nipples. Only the sneakers and visors will stay on for the entire match.

Boggs immediately spots a statuesque, well-endowed redhead pulling up next to him, "Well hey there, Starburst, so very, very good to see you again, darlin'. I've almost recovered from our last round a month ago."

"Well hey there yourself, Big Boy. Has it been a month? You *better* be ready this morning, because I'm going to give that wood of yours a workout, and I know we'll need a couple of mulligans."

Boggs grins ear-to-ear, "Now tell me Starburst, are we playing the front side or the back side today?"

"I thought you'd want to play the whole course," she replies with a devilish grin.

The bevy of girls smilingly beckon to the other players, "Hop in fellas." The donors are thrilled, and invariably ask their caddies to bend over to tee up each shot during Sonny's self-designated 'cooter ball' tournament. He leads off with his favorite caddy, shapely 28-year old Caprice Flowers.

At each green, the caddies tend the pins and obligingly bend over again to retrieve balls from the cups.

At hole #5, Boggs' drive fades into the rough and he tees off again with the same result. *Damn left shoulder!*

"Starburst, Darlin', I think I'm going to need some help with my balls over there."

Starburst smiles, *I know he doesn't want me looking for Calla-ways or Titleists, but the cash tips are fantastic.* The union accounts will simply show an expense for 'Outside Services'.

After hours of golf, drinking, and debauchery, Luther drives Sonny and Boggs back to Waterside with Starburst and Caprice, where they amble into the parlor as the phone rings.

"Mistuh Butler, it's Mizzez Butler for you."

"Thanks Jasper." Sonny covers the phone and signals the others to be quiet, "Hi Hon, how was your day with Dianne?"

Boggs and Starburst step out of the parlor; she goes to a bathroom down the hall and Boggs regales Luther with details of his day. Caprice stays in the parlor, casually catching up on text messages.

"Honey, it's been a rat-race down here, just like I figured it'd be so close to the election – hearing a lot of drivel from some people I can't stand so they'll write campaign checks. Of course, every one of them's going to remind me of it down the road."

Then he dutifully listens to details about shoes, hair, outfits they bought, who they met and what they said, where she and Dianne had lunch, and every morsel they ate. *Jesus – this is like the damn Chinese water torture.* Bored with so many inconsequential details, Sonny unzips his trousers and waves Caprice towards him. She puts her phone down, and suggestively saunters over to pleasure him. He leans against the back of a sofa and strokes her hair with his free hand.

"Open time? No, not really, hon. Had an obligatory game of golf to show the flag, that's about as close to any time off as I've had. Yes dear, I love you and miss you too. OK. Can't wait to see you as soon as Ripp gets me on the first flight back after the fund-raiser. Love you Dana."

Sonny hangs up, tells Caprice he has some urgent business, but can't wait to see her to finish in thirty minutes. He zips his trousers and points to the hall door beside him, "This way, Darlin', no need for Jasper to see you were here while I was on the phone with the misses."

As she leaves, Boggs comes back in, knowing it's time to get serious.

"Boggs, I can put some pressure on Neal Tanner and his boys through the Education and Workforce Committee, but that takes time, and that's something we simply don't have right now. We've both got elections coming up and Tanner will have a few committee members in his pocket, too. Those actions are a good strategic move, but we need something much more immediate, something effective, some hard-hitting tactics for the close battle."

"You're reading my mind Sonny. There're a couple of young bucks in the union who'd just love to see the negotiations go sideways so they could push me out. And I just gotta say it, their priorities for political donations don't include you." Both Sonny and Boggs also contemplate the personal financial disaster of losing their elections.

"Well they don't understand that my tenure brings advantages to the union they can't get anywhere else, advantages and benefits they definitely won't get if Mark Chambers takes my seat."

"You're preaching to the choir, Sonny – you've been a real friend every time we've needed one."

"And I can do more, a lot more, but it takes a lot of people helping down here. Hell, I have to pay teams to pull up Chambers' yard and street signs throughout the district every week. Other friends in and out of the Chamber of Commerce will have their hands out too, to lean on businesses owners who support Chambers. And you'd think the pride of being a published author would be its own reward. But, no, everyone who writes an op-ed for me or against Chambers wants their palm greased. No values anymore. What's this country coming to?

How many times do I have to listen to his damn campaign problems? "It's going to hell, Sonny, just going to hell. Nothing's sacred. People nowadays just don't take any personal satisfaction from a job well done. Absolutely no sense of public service, either."

"Jesus, they can't even cook up good stories – *I've* got to tell 'em how to make Chambers look like he's part of the swamp so shell organizations can print it on mailers. Then there'll be teams to canvass homes for the sick, lame, and lazy, and all those old folk's places - they expect to be paid to deliver, fill out, and collect residents' mail-in ballots too."

I've heard this speech so many times I could give it myself! "That's just another side of the same problem, Sonny. No one does their civic duty just because it's the right thing to do. No damn self-respect any more. No principles. Makes you just want to puke."

"And don't even get me started on the volunteer poll captains who I've helped forever. They won't jiggle a single machine or find a boxful of ballots without a handful of cash. Like you said, no one wants to do something just because it's the right thing to do."

"Do you think Putin has these same problems?" he asks sarcastically.

Sonny also has hecklers on the payroll to disrupt Mark Chambers' events. Sometimes his abettors turn off the electricity or activate fire sprinklers at a Chambers event, and they all have their dirty little hands out. A benefactor in a local fire department shut down an event that was just getting under way on the grounds that the facility wasn't up to code.

Sonny compensates many of his senior supporters with political favors like help with eminent domain decisions, below-market compensation for people's land for the road project, and inside information about federal contracts. He funnels cash to all the others.

The levers of power don't come cheaply, but players know the rewards of wielding federal authority are immensely lucrative.

Boggs understands completely, and has no reservations whatsoever about diverting union membership funds to secure a place at the table of power. He'll figure out some other day how to fund union members' health care, strike funds, and retirement, or simply pass those problems off to a successor.

"Boggs, the other matter we need to look at is this growing mess with the evidence for that federal lawsuit, the document. Why don't you get Luther in here to help us with that?"

Boggs steps out of the room to summon Luther and returns.

"You're right, Sonny. We've been making good progress with the contract talks, and should wrap it up in time for me to get re-elected. But that lawsuit's going to be a red herring they'll use to question the whole basis of the wage contracts. They'll make it very public, too, to get the news reports going their way, or at least confused enough to question us. Killing that goddamned document would leave 'em without any evidence - they'd *have* to drop the case."

"Luther's tried to get it the civilized way and the kids wouldn't play ball. Now it's time to knock some heads... or cave 'em in."

"You need to see me, Sir?" Luther asks when he walks into the parlor.

"Sure do, Luther. We're going to need some of your special tactical skills again. We've looked at this from a lot of different angles, but I think the best way is the most direct - just snatch the girl and use her as leverage to make her boyfriend give us the paper."

"Snatch the snatch... I like it, I like it a lot" Luther says, amused at his sophomoric play on words.

Boggs chimes in, "Why don't I get my union guy, Ivan, down here, too; he may be a little on the far side of his prime, but he's got the talent we need to get rid of the kids afterwards, and I mean without a trace. I think he's doing some work in North Carolina - practically next door."

"Good, do it, Boggs," Sonny replies. "This is our best option now - it's simple, quick, and guaranteed to get the results we need."

Boggs and Luther smile at another opportunity for licensed violence.

Chapter 40

Don't Be Stupid

E arly the next afternoon, Luther drives to Riggs' house, where Patina's about to kick off her cleated shoes after an intramural soccer match. It's a quiet neighborhood with a number of long-time residents, but few are out in the unseasonable heat and humidity.

Luther backs a nondescript van up the driveway and strides to the back of the house with a blanket under his arm. He knocks on the kitchen door, keeping the blanket low and out of sight.

Patina opens the door enough to ask, "Yes, may I help you?"

"You sure can, you little bitch..." he blurts out as he crashes through the door and smashes her against the refrigerator.

Patina reflexively kicks at his groin, narrowly missing his sensitive testicles. Almost simultaneously, she cups her hands and delivers a hard slap to his ears. Often, such a move can disorient and mentally stun an assailant long enough to escape, but Luther only shakes his head and continues holding on to her. She aims a thumb at his right eye, which Luther intercepts as he pulls her outstretched arm downward. Patina tries to bite him as he wraps her in a bear hug and covers her head with the blanket. Then, the suffocating blanket begins to exhaust her capacity to resist or escape.

She does manage to gouge the instep of her left shoe down Luther's shin. He swears and dips, but his jeans prevent the full effect. He slaps her covered face and secures her wrists and ankles with plastic ties. She can only manage a muffled outcry as he hoists her over his shoulder, carries her to the driveway, and vindictively heaves her through the back doors onto the van's bare metal floor.

Oh my God – what the hell's going on? Who is this demented freak, and what's this all about? Has he got the wrong person?

Driving out of the neighborhood, Luther takes a fiendish delight in abruptly accelerating, cornering, and stopping while he listens to Patina slam into the sides of the van, "Romeo shoulda taken the deal, but he didn't. Now *you're* the deal and you better hope to hell he takes this one."

Who is this cretin, and what's 'the deal'? Where are we going and what's he going to do with me... and Riggs? She shakes the blanket off her head.

Luther pulls out his cellphone and calls Riggs, "Hey Romeo, I got another deal for that old paper of yours, and this time you better listen up and take it."

Riggs is completely baffled by the call and the caller. *The voice is familiar.* "Who is this? What are you talking about, 'another deal'?"

Patina yells, "Riggs, help!"

Riggs instantly sits bolt upright in his office chair and immediately bristles with alarm and apprehension, "Patina!"

Luther continues, "I know it'll be hard for you, but try not being too stupid. Your little girlfriend's with me and if you don't want her wrestling alligators, listen up."

He's got Patina? What the hell is going on?

"Come by yourself with the document, you know the one I called you about before. And I mean *alone* to where I'm going to tell you. Now, numb nuts, can you do all that, or do I have to cut off one of those pert little nipples and send it to you? You've got 75 minutes, and don't even *think* about bringing the cops or she's automatic gator bait."

Riggs is stunned, even more so when he hears Patina cry out again in the background. "Listen, buddy, I'll do it, but don't hurt her. I don't have the paper here, it's in a safety deposit box in Charleston."

"Not my problem, buckwheat, 75 minutes and you'll need every one of them. Time's-a-wasting. Now listen up, because I'm not in the habit of repeating myself. Go west from the city on Savannah Highway to Toogoodoo Road. Drive 8-1/4 miles south on Toogoodoo to Parrishville Road and stay on that for a half-mile. You'll see Eddy Farm Road, we'll be at the end of it."

Riggs quickly plots the location west of downtown and sees that he hasn't got any time to lose.

Fifty-five minutes later, Luther arrives at the seldom-used dirt drive that leads to an open area by a tidal inlet. The small, isolated clearing is ringed with Spanish Oaks and cabbage palms on three sides, with a tidal inlet on the fourth. The trees provide a canopy over a dense, damp ground cover of palmettos and thorny wait-a-minute-vines. The area is alive with an ecosystem of trophy-sized cockroaches, spiders, rats, venomous snakes, and raccoons – each defending itself and preying on others.

Luther gets out of the van and sees Ivan ambling towards him with the chronic limp that Richard inflicted fifteen years ago.

"Hey big guy, you ready to go?"

"Yep, drove down this morning and got everything I'm gonna need: chickens, barrels, and clean-up supplies are all on the dock. Brought it here with Mr. Butler's boat, just like Mr. Colman said to."

"Great work, Ivan." Luther opens the back doors of the van and cuts the plastic tie that binds Patina's ankles together. He jerks her out of the van and she falls on the ground with a bone-jarring thud, "Get up, before I kick you up," he commands. She gets onto her knees, then stands.

Hmmm, even with a few bruises, she's still pretty damn fine. If Romeo doesn't show up on time, I just may have to tap this stuff.

"Whatcha got there?" Ivan asks.

"Romeo's girlfriend, the one who's going to make sure we get what we want."

"She's already *got* what I want," he says while making a gross show of rubbing his groin.

Luther laughs, "You're over the hill for this one, old man - she'd flat wear you out."

"Hah! I don't think so, but she looks a little skinny for me."

Luther pushes Patina towards the dock, "Walk, you little slut, and so help me I'll beat the living crap out of you if you try any bullshit."

Where am I? What's going on? What horribly crude, obscene people, she thinks nervously. *Who's that ogre on the dock? Chickens? What's he mean by 'cleaning supplies'? Are these the 'foreign interests' agent Haskell talked about?*

Ivan stares up and down at his newest victim, "Hell, girl, I may even hang you up on a hook like I did with some little price-gouging prick back in the day. The pussy didn't make it ten minutes before he cashed out. Think you'd last any longer?"

Even through her fear and pain, the comment instantly catches Patina's attention. *What'd he say? Hung someone on a hook? Good Lord, could it have been Richard? Is that even possible?*

Patina is frightened and nervous, but compelled to push her brutal captor for more information, "A hook, really? You've been watching too many horror movies - sounds like a bunch of BS to me."

Ivan stops, squints and moves his head forward, looking directly into Patina's face, "I'll show you some BS, you little tramp." He immediately slams the heel of his meaty hand across her face - a grating sound confirms the severe displacement of her upper and lower lateral cartilages: a broken nose. Patina recoils in intense pain and begins bleeding, but forces herself to stay on her feet.

Luther grins at her. "That face doesn't look quite so pretty now, does it cupcake? But I was really interested in other parts," he scoffs while crudely rubbing his hand between her legs.

Ivan holds both her shoulders and stares directly at her, "No, it happened alright, but nothing you'd know anything about. BC and I were in the trenches doing *real* work seven days a week while you were sucking frat boys all night at some fancy college."

Patina fights her pain and fears to keep a clear head and think, *God, my whole face hurts. Timing's about right, though - I <u>was</u> in college when Richard was murdered. Who's 'the boss? Who's this gorilla guy 'Ivan', and BC? What're they going to do to Riggs and me?*

Ivan forces Patina across the small, desolate clearing towards the small tidal inlet ahead.

He continues pushing her to the end of a 20' dock with a small shed at the end. Half way down the dock, *Sonny's Shangri-La* bass boat is moored with a sinister-looking, black 300hp outboard engine that can push it well over 50 mph in these calm waters.

Patina wonders, *'Sonny's Shangri-La'? Does Sonny Butler own that boat? Is <u>he</u> the boss, or the 'Boggs' guy? What are these animals up to? Damn, my face is killing me!*

Luther watches, then glances at his watch to see when Riggs is due. *Wonder if I've got time to bend her over a barrel for a couple of minutes? I bet that little wildcat could show me a trick or two.*

Ivan shoves her to the edge of the dock and slips a metal cargo hook under the industrial plastic tie that binds her wrists. The hook is attached to a braided steel wire that passes through a pulley on a davit to a hand-cranked winch. In the past, the apparatus was used to lower baitwells and such into boats and retrieve them. This is the first time it's going to handle human cargo.

Ivan cranks the winch to stretch Patina's arms over her head, then he faces a wide wooden railing. In a slow, almost ritualistic manner, he removes his watch and carefully arranges it on the railing, followed by his cell phone and sunglasses. Devoid of all mechanical devices that could fall into the salt water, he steps into *Sonny's Shangri-La* to retrieve a large croker sack of live, clucking chickens, then back onto the dock with the animated bag.

Patina's heart races as she tries to keep thinking straight. *What in the hell is going on?*

Ivan pulls the first fowl out by its neck, stares skyward, and closes his eyes. Looking like a 15th century Mayan nacom performing a sacrifice, he raises a worn machete, utters something unintelligible, and swings the blade down to decapitate the flailing hen. He begins chuckling while he hacks several more times and throws bloody, feathered pieces into the water beneath Patina's feet.

Patina is bewildered, puzzled, and verging on panic, but forces herself to look on, spellbound. *This guy is some kind of bizarre. Hell, this whole afternoon is bizarre and getting more so by the minute. What in God's name is going to happen to me? Is Riggs going to get here?*

Ivan pauses in his methodical slaughter of the birds and takes two steps towards Patina, "Little girl, you think the gators are getting hungry now? Oh yeah, you'll keep a gator full for two weeks!" he chortles sarcastically, looking like he's possessed by demons.

Oh my God, he intends to feed them a lot more than chickens... Riggs and me!

As Ivan ceremoniously butchers all the remaining birds, Patina watches the growing pool of blood spread around his feet. She can't help wondering if it's an omen of what's in store for Riggs and her - a dreadfully distressing omen.

She looks down at the water, distraught by how the next several minutes will play out, then continues scanning the area until her gaze stops on the shed. Beside it she sees a chainsaw, two rusty 55-gallon drums, about 20 one-pound containers of lye, and a hazardous fumes mask. *If he's part of a crew who killed Richard with a hook, what in God's name does he have in store for Riggs and me? Are we going to be Charleston's next cold cases?*

Ivan continues to fling the last handfuls of bloody chicken parts into the water and wipes his red-soaked hands on her shirt, pausing momentarily to fondle her breasts.

Within minutes, a nine-foot and an eleven-foot gator glide out of the mangroves towards the dock to investigate. Ivan steps right next to her and grins while pointing to the menacing reptiles, "If Romeo doesn't show up, you die, pretty girl. If Romeo *does* show up, then you *both* die," he mockingly jeers in her face.

Patina turns her head, closes her eyes, and struggles to keep her sanity.

Chapter 41

The Meeting

Agonizing over Patina's distressful plight and a deeply felt responsibility to defend the document, Riggs jams a 9mm Walther PPQ semiautomatic pistol inside his belt at the small of his back and an extra 15-round magazine of hollow point bullets in his pocket. *Should I bring him a fake package and keep the real one, to better support and defend the Constitution? Then I may be able to get Patina and the notes too. What would I use – what looks old? If I just had one of Patina's fakes... Would he check it? If he did, could he tell it was phony instead of the real thing? No, not enough time and too much risk to Patina.*

With remarkable sangfroid, he jumps into the company van and speeds to Patina's bank to retrieve the document. For once, there's no line to access safety deposit boxes and he's in and out in record time. He looks at his phone's GPS, *Already three minutes behind!*

Now, every red light and stop sign is an impediment, an obstacle standing between him and rescuing Patina. He's as alert for the police as he was for Taliban fighters in Afghanistan. *Focus, keep driving, keep your head on swivel... Pass this guy looking at his cell phone, get through the yellow traffic signal...*

Suddenly, flashing blue lights appear in his rear-view mirror.

Oh shit, a cop! This can't be happening, not now! Do I run? Try to lose him in traffic? Nope, not in this van, and can't outrun a radio.

Riggs slows to the speed limit and continues driving, but moves over to the right lane. The cruiser is only a half block behind him, catching up in the passing lane.

What do I tell him? That I'm on my way to rescue a kidnap victim and only have forty-five minutes left to do it? Hell, it'd take that long to explain everything to him... crap!

Riggs prepares to pull into a parking lot to avoid a useless, time-consuming chase when he sees the cruiser suddenly blast by him, intent on some other mission at some other place.

Thank you, God!

Riggs picks up speed and surveillance again, heading west out of metro Charleston on the Savannah Highway. He makes up a little time before turning onto Toogoodoo Road. With only twenty minutes left, an old pickup truck puffing blue smoke looms ahead on the twisting two-lane road. The grey-haired driver is sporting a well-worn baseball cap and crawling along at 30 mph with a death grip on the wheel. The posted limit is 45 mph and Riggs hasn't slowed below 60 even around the curves. *Not smart, but no other choice. Now, how do I get around this old fart?*

Riggs inhales, guns the engine and the van slowly accelerates. The van finally gains enough speed to chance a passing maneuver that Riggs carefully times for one of the few straightaways. *Patina would kill me if she saw me driving like this... right after she hugged me for saving her! Don't know what I'll do if anything happens to her, wouldn't ever get over it. Is that how she feels about her brother? What the hell am I going to see there? Is that guy alone, or does he have a crew with him? Gotta keep pushing...*

He feels like he's at the mercy of a large hourglass sand timer, whose grains are racing through the orifice instead of descending at a normal, measured rate. He checks his GPS Arrive Time – only eight minutes left.

Riggs turns onto Parrishville Road, then onto Eddy Farm Road, slowly driving ahead. His GPS shows a small clearing just ahead as his phone dies. *Damn it, battery's dead!*

Just before reaching the end of the dirt road, Riggs stops the van and silently gets out, sprints around to the back, and quietly opens the rear doors.

The sun's already about to dip below the tallest pines and Spanish oaks, signaling a transition to the desolate area's many nocturnal creatures. The warm, humid climate is perfect for dangerous Brown Recluse, Black Widow, and Hobo spiders. It also hosts, bellowing frogs, and a hundred other small critters, as well as the predators who feed on them: raccoons, snakes, opossums and an occasional fox. Riggs was familiar with all of them, but urban folks were rarely comfortable hereabouts.

He pulls an Inspire 2 drone out of its travel case, turns it and the controller with integrated mini iPad on, and launches the drone to recon the area. The Inspire captures stunning detail with its Zenmuse X7 camera and DL50 telephoto lens: the dock, a boat, two men, and a winch. It also reveals a bloodied Patina dangling over the water, *Oh my god! What the hell are they doing to her? One way or another, someone's going down today.* His senses are on high alert and he steels himself to enter the fray, take on the risks, and save Patina.

Riggs sets the drone on Active Track mode to autonomously follow Luther. Then he quickly logs into his YouTube channel with his mini iPad and allows it to access his account. Viola! He's now streaming live drone video to his YouTube channel. He glances at his watch - *Time's up!*

He puts the controller on the floor of the van and marches the final fifty feet of dirt road to the clearing, in plain view of Luther and Ivan.

Luther spots Riggs immediately, aims a large caliber handgun directly at him, and checks his watch. "Well, if it isn't Romeo, coming to save his little damsel in distress. And believe me, Romeo, she's in some *deep* shit. She'll be in even deeper if you get stupid or try being some kind of hero, right Ivan?"

Ivan waves, gives the winch handle a half turn, and laughs.

That voice – that's the guy who offered us a finder's fee for the document. I know government's full of bad actors, but this is a little much even for Washington.

"Riggs, they're going to kill us!" Patina manages to warn over the pain of her broken nose.

Luther looks over his shoulder, "Shut up, you mouthy little bitch." He continues, "I don't see the paper, tough guy, so I guess you don't want to see your girlfriend much longer. Alive, at least."

Ivan emphasizes Patina's peril by pointing at the two gators' gaping jaws, snapping at bloody chicken parts a yard below her feet.

"Kinda reminds you of Capt'n Hook and Tick Tock, doesn't it, Romeo? Now where is it, the paper?"

"Not on me, but close enough," Riggs manages to say as he tensely looks at Patina, Luther, and the pistol pointing at him.

"Didn't I tell you about being stupid? Apparently, you don't quite understand what's going on lover boy. I'm not here to play 20 questions. Give me the goddamn paper now or she's swimming with Tick Tock and his friends."

"Let her go, then you get it." His fists tense and vision sharpens.

Luther laughs, "Listen to the big war hero! Problem is, loser, you don't have any cards to play. And if I wasn't such a nice guy, I'd have done her already, dropped you like a 20-pound sack of shit, and then just got the paper myself. I know you didn't walk all the way from Charleston, so it's gotta be in your truck. What's it going to be?"

Every one of Riggs' senses is in overdrive. He's survived life-or-death ordeals before and fights to do so now by forcing himself to think clearly. It's no easy task, even with all his senses peaked.

"Yeah, it could be in the van, or I could've put it somewhere else, like in the palmettos for a little insurance. You think *you're* going to find it out here? It's already getting dark. You going to get the rattlesnakes and copperheads to help you search their nests? Good luck with that – and have you got any idea what a water moccasin bite does to you? Very painful and you'll lose the hand or arm, as a minimum. And what's your boss going to do when you botch the job and come back empty-handed?"

Riggs is sweating and nervous, but outwardly presents the same resolute demeanor he did to tribal councils in Afghanistan. He never knew for certain whether they were on his side, allied with the Taliban, or just in it for themselves. Either way, he knew the consequences for failure there could be the same as here – a fatal bullet.

Luther pauses to think about his options, not having considered this new twist. *Yeah, I know exactly what a water moccasin bite can do, but there's no way I'm finding out first hand.*

Riggs continues, "Like you said earlier, time's a wasting. I know the boss's ass is on the line, or he wouldn't make you stare at life in the pen for doing his dirty work. But, hey, what do I know... maybe you *want* to spend your next 30 years bending over for some big toothless bubbas."

Prison? Life? There's no way I'm gonna be some redneck's girlfriend. And Sonny and Boggs – he's right about their asses being in

---

188

the wind without this paper, and I'm not about to find out what they'll do if I come back empty handed.

"Look at it from where the boss sits, he gives you *the* big job and you blow it. You think he can afford to keep you around after that?"

Riggs' heart is racing, like it did during the tribal meetings, but he maintains his steadfast front.

Luther nervously puzzles over his dilemma, then says, "OK, you can have her, but I'm putting a .45 slug right in the middle of your boney chest if you don't get the paper. Then she gets one too." *Of course, by the time Ivan and I leave, they're both going to be gator bait or sludge in a barrel.*

Luther looks towards the dock, "Ivan, get her off the hook."

Ivan looks puzzled and hesitates, then grabs the davit with its human cargo dangling over the water and swings it to the dock.

Patina agonizes, *They're never going to let us go – the gators, the saw, lye, guns; there's <u>got</u> to be something I can do.*

Patina reaches for the hook with her bound hands, quickly lifts her knees to her chest, and explosively launches her cleated shoes squarely into Ivan's vulnerable right knee. The intensely-painful blow shocks his entire leg. He screams, curses, and falls sideways - slamming his head into the rusty metal davit.

Luther looks on from the clearing while still having to keep his pistol trained on Riggs, *What the hell?*

Dazed, Ivan shakes his ringing head and struggles to regain his faltering balance when his feet slip on the pooled chicken blood. Patina kicks him repeatedly. He tries to plant his hands on the dock and push himself up, but they too slide in the red ooze. Disoriented now, Ivan loses his balance. His throbbing knee hits the edge of the dock and he slips off amidst another flurry of curses. Ivan stretches his arms, struggling with slippery hands to hold onto the base of the davit and avoid the gators he just lured to the water below him.

"Help! Luther! Can't hold on, I'm going down. Quick - get over here, help me get back up!"

"OK, hold on Big Guy!" Luther anxiously glances back and forth between Ivan and Riggs, momentarily shaken, confused as to what he should do next. *Got to get the damn paper!*

Ivan glares up at Patina with the most threatening look she's ever seen, "You goddamn bitch, you goddamn little whore. That other guy, the one I hooked, he was the lucky one next to what you're in for. I'm gonna filet every inch of your skinny carcass and feed it to the gators piece by piece."

Patina kicks his still-ringing head and stomps her cleats into his meaty hands to complete his full descent into the water.

"Luther, kill 'em both, help me. Gators! Luther..."

The larger of the two ravenous reptiles closes in on the panicked, thrashing quarry before him, assessing which flailing appendage to attack first. The big bull gator spots Ivan's right arm and closes its powerful tooth-studded jaws on the appendage with a force of over 2,500 pounds per square inch. The pressure instantly crushes his humerus as the gator goes into a death roll – a spinning and convulsing move to tear the arm from its body.

As soon as the gator wrenches the arm free at the shoulder, Ivan's deep brachial artery spurts blood into the water – further stimulating the carnivorous reptiles into a feeding frenzy.

Ivan manages one last gasp, "Kill her, kill 'em both..." as he and the gators become an indistinguishable swirl of torso, extremities, jaws, and thrashing tails, where a pink foam marks the epicenter of the struggle.

James Blaisdell, AKA Ivan, will commit no more sins.

Luther watches in stunned disbelief, wondering again whether he should go to the dock and shoot Patina, keep a bead on Riggs, or shoot them both and take his chances with finding the paper. Infuriated, he says, "Damn that little slut, I knew I should've wasted her as soon as we got here."

Riggs quickly speaks up to re-focus Luther's attention away from Patina and back on the document, "He's gone, Luther, but the paper isn't, you still need the paper, right? Or your boss does, and he's counting on you to deliver it. Today, now! Right?"

Luther hesitates for another moment to quickly reassess his options. He turns his eyes and pistol directly back on Riggs, "Yeah, yeah, you're goddamn right, I *am* getting it." *Then I'm going to double-tap both of you.*

Patina extends her feet to the dock, stands on her tip toes, and lifts her hands free of the hook. She briefly catches her breath and runs past Luther to Riggs. She's terrified, shaking, and queasy. She throws her bound hands over his head and hugs him so hard he can barely breathe. He gently wipes blood from her face, being particularly careful to avoid her radically mis-aligned nose.

He quickly kisses her forehead and whispers, "Patina, go up the road beyond the van and stay low to the ground." *She'll be safe, I've saved her.*

She looks into his eyes with a quizzical stare, "Riggs... be careful, he's crazy, like bat-shit crazy."

Riggs winks an assurance that he's got a plan.

Founders' Intent

—

Chapter 42

The Trade

As Patina hurries towards the van, Luther turns his menacing pistol on Riggs from a scant eight feet away. "Well doesn't that just warm the cockles of your heart - Romeo to the rescue… *now cut the shit!*"

Riggs looks very uneasily at Luther and the .45 caliber muzzle pointed directly at his face. Harrowing memories return of heavily-armed tribal guards leading him into and out of meetings. *Focus on the mission; support and defend the Constitution against all enemies, foreign and domestic, the team.*

"Play time's over, hero, now it's back to business - the paper. And don't think I won't hesitate to put a couple of slugs right between your eyeballs."

"You were right all along, Luther, it's in the van, on the floor next to the driver's seat. I'll get it." Riggs starts to turn back towards the dirt road.

Luther quickly steps forward as if he's going to intercept Riggs, "No, I don't think so, funny guy – you trying to run game on me? You're staying right here in the open, just where you are so I can keep a bead on your ass. *I'll get it.*"

Luther thinks, *Good, now I can waste him; but wait, what if he's jerking my chain and it's not really there? I'll shoot him as soon as I've got the paper.*

Keeping his eyes and aim squarely on Riggs, Luther walks to the van, opens the driver's door and leans in. During the moment Luther's gaze dips below the dashboard, Riggs pulls out his pistol, bolts towards the tree line, and dives headlong into a dense clump of palmettos.

The Walther PPQ, or Police Pistol Quick is named for its extremely short $1/10^{th}$ inch trigger re-set distance that allows the user to fire successive shots very rapidly. Riggs does exactly that, with a speedy four-shot fusillade towards his foe.

Completely astonished, a bewildered Luther immediately stands up, turns, and instinctively returns fire. Several shots tear through the palmettos and one rips at Riggs' rectus femoris – his right thigh muscle. Still firing, Luther rushes towards the dock with the paper. *I can't believe Romeo pulled a piece on me... that little son of a bitch pulled a piece on ME.*

With adrenalin pumping, Luther fires several final suppressive shots behind him while running to the dock. All accomplish their goal of keeping Riggs' head down. He races down the dock, unties the single mooring line, jumps into the boat, and speeds towards the channel. The wake washes ashore a lone shoe with a foot inside as feasting gators continue dismembering the rest of Ivan, ingesting whole chunks of fresh flesh and bone that'll satiate them for weeks.

Patina stands up and runs towards Riggs, "Riggs, are you alright? You're bleeding, he hit you!"

"Patina, what did he do to *you*? I didn't know *what* to think when I heard you in the van – I just ran on instinct. Your face is bleeding and… your nose. We need to get you to a doctor." Riggs holds her and lightly kisses her forehead.

"You're bleeding yourself, Rambo – my god, he shot you."

"Yeah, in my leg, but no bones or major vessels, more like he grazed me. He wasn't even aiming, just firing – spray and pray and got lucky. I'll take my belt off so you can use it to hold a compress against the wound to stop the blood flow."

"A compress?"

"Use my shirt." He takes it off and hands it to her, "Just fold it over a couple of times." The zip-tie on her hands makes it more difficult.

"We *both* need to get to a doctor. I think I'll be OK, but right now my face hurts like hell. Do you think we're safe?"

"For the moment, yes. He took off in the boat and has the document, though. There's no way he's going to just let us walk out of here after what he's already done and his buddy dying. We can't call - my cell phone's dead. Help me to the van." Riggs is unaware of, and Patina doesn't think to try, Ivan's phone.

In the van, Riggs uses a pair of diagonal pliers to cut the zip-tie binding Patina's wrists, just as the drone controller begins chirping a low battery signal. Riggs uses the controller to retrieve the drone, quickly inserts two fresh batteries, and re-launches it towards the direction of Luther's escape.

Looking at the controller screen, Riggs quickly finds the wake of *Sonny's Shangri-La* in the otherwise placid waters. The Inspire 2 tracks the boat from a distance... with the HD video recording everything it sees and streaming the signal to Riggs' YouTube channel.

"Let's track him for a minute while I catch my breath. I really want to find out who that guy's working for."

"Riggs, don't be ridiculous - you've been shot, for God's sake. We need to get you to a hospital right now and hand this whole thing over to the sheriff."

"I know, I know, we will. But if we leave right now, we'll lose the video signal and may not have anything *for* the sheriff."

"I never knew you could be so hard-headed."

Founders' Intent

Chapter 43

Rearview Mirror

L uther calms down a bit, then suddenly wonders, *Jesus Christ, what if the package is empty, and those two shit-birds pulled a fast one on me?* His pulse quickens as he imagines how Sonny and Boggs would react to failure – especially after his blundered effort with Senator Chambers.

He eases back on the throttle, pulls the page out of the envelope, and momentarily panics when a slight gust pulls it out of his hand and swirls it above his head. He immediately idles the big outboard engine and looks up at the paper. Luther breathes a grateful sigh of relief as it wafts low enough for him to grab from the stern of the boat. He looks at what truly seems like an actual old document.

Luther cringes when he recalls Ivan's last words from his deadly watery vortex, but smiles at the prospect of killing Riggs and Patina. *Maybe just shoot 'em both, put them into the plastic drums and let the lye turn 'em into goo. I still may nail her, though – just for all the trouble she's caused – and make Romeo watch before I plug 'em both.*

For the next six minutes, Luther scans the water ahead and warily steers the boat around sand bars, shallows, and partially-submerged logs. There's noticeably more debris in the water following the thunderstorms that blew through three days ago and left branches all over Sonny's golf course. He cruises past two small peninsulas to Sonny's waterfront house.

Luther guides the boat up to the dock, where Sonny, in a silk evening jacket, and Boggs walk down to meet him, "Did you get it? Any trouble? Do we need to do any more clean-up? Is Ivan bringing the van back?"

"Yes sir, I got it right here," he says while thrusting the envelope towards Sonny in an effort to deflect attention from his multiple failures. "But some really bad news for Ivan, boss. He slipped off the dock into some gators and I couldn't get him out in time. Tried to help, to pull him out, but he was just too far away; I almost fell in myself. I saved the paper, though, right here – just like you both needed."

A stupefied and disbelieving Boggs immediately steps forward, glares into Luther's eyes, and interrogates him, "Wait a minute, Ivan's *dead*? Alligators *ate* him? Did I hear that right, Luther - is *that* what you're telling me?"

"Yes sir, Mr. Colman, I'm really sorry, but that's exactly what happened. I tried everything, just couldn't get to him. Shot at the gators to kill 'em or run 'em off, but they just went under water. I'm really sorry, never seen anything like it - I know he was a really great guy."

Boggs' hatred of Riggs and Patina intensifies ten-fold. "What about the kids, did they go in with the gators too?"

"It turned really crazy, really fast. That damn punk Romeo came at us with a pistol and started firing at Ivan and me. The paper was the most critical thing, so I had to go for that. I know I hit him, just don't know if he's already dead or just dying. I'll go right back and make sure they're both finished, then clean up the place all neat and tidy like."

Sonny reaches for the envelope. *Ivan just fell into the water? Finish the kids off - you didn't already do that when you got the envelope from 'em? This sounds like a bigger mess than the Chambers debacle. Exactly what the hell happened there?*

"Let me see this damn thing," Sonny orders. "Can't believe this 230-year old paper's caused us so much trouble,"

He opens the envelope, examines the page, and struggles trying to read the cursive text. The paper feels substantial and it certainly looks old to his novice eye. Boggs, still visibly shaken and dejected, steps next to Sonny and rubs a page corner between his thumb and fingers.

Riggs and Patina, sit in the van and stare into the drone controller screen, *Who are these two guys? One of them looks like Congressman Butler. Is one of them 'the boss'?*

"OK, Luther, go back and finish the job and make sure it's clean when you leave. As for the paper, burn it, but not anywhere around here. I don't even want an ash on this property for some FBI tech geek to find. Take that damned thing out to one of the islands and burn it, then stomp the ashes and scatter them in the water."

Boggs begins to return to the house when a visceral urge for lethal revenge overcomes him. The imminent life-or-death struggle with the troublesome Riggs and Patina also unleashes his primal lust to dominate others, especially through brutal, uncompromising force.

"Luther, hold on, I'm coming with you. After what happened to Ivan and the trouble those little shits caused us, I'm going to help you with the solution, then I'll drive the van back." Boggs cautiously steps onto the boat, sits in the elevated rear fishing seat, and fastens a seat belt Sonny installed for his niece.

"Sure, Mr. Colman," Luther grins, "hop in - no reason for me to have all the fun, none at all."

Boggs manages a thin smile too. *Goddamn shame about Ivan, but the week hasn't been a complete loss – played a round of cooterball with Starburst, slept in late, drinks, seafood, and now I can waste those little pricks who've been such a damned pain in my ass. I do another term as union president to shift more bucks into my retirement and... God, how I love America.*

Sonny returns to the house for a celebratory drink and continued antics with Caprice and another caddy girl who're staying over at *Waterside*.

Luther backs the boat into the channel and steers it towards deeper water. Once underway at 45 knots, he scans ahead for other traffic... nothing. He glances down at a rearview mirror to see if anyone's behind him.

Nothing on the water, but wait - there's something foreign in the mirror, something that shouldn't be there... two small colored lights about 100' behind and above him. *What the hell...?* He steers a bit to port, then starboard. The lights on the drone precisely track both turns. *What is it? Where'd it come from? How long's it been there? What's it doing? Who's controlling it?* Too many unknowns.

His neck hairs stand up and his heart races. For the first time, Luther realizes *he's* now the prey. This time *he's* being stalked – *he's* in the crosshairs. It's an alarming, totally foreign sensation and extremely troubling. The fact he's at a complete loss on how to deal with the unrelenting electro-mechanical predator intensifies his growing anxiety.

Panicked by the sight of the drone, Luther doesn't see the semi-submerged cypress trunk that the outboard engine strikes so violently that it practically rips off the boat's jack plate and transom. The engine instantly kicks out of the water and partially breaks the lower drive unit from the rest of the engine.

Simultaneously, Boggs' upper body heaves forward and down, held at the waist by the straining seat belt. Momentum flips the heavily damaged lower drive into the stern of the boat. The Yamaha Turbo 1 propeller, still rotating at more than 4,000 revolutions per minute, bores into Boggs' back like a meat slicer into sausage. The three curved stainless-steel blades instantly drill a 13 ¼" diameter cavity through his spine, ribs, and lungs before the lower drive snaps back into the water. After slinging small hunks of flesh and bone off its bloody blades, the engine dies, along with Boggs Colman.

The extreme impact has a different, but equally devastating, effect on Luther - an incomprehensible experience that plays out in milliseconds. Every sensation is too foreign and sudden for him to process - an overwhelming and simultaneous bombardment of intense sounds, blurred objects, and powerful forces wrenching a vulnerable body he can't possibly control. All coupled with excruciating pain.

Luther Phillips' momentum hurls him completely through the windshield, across the seat in front of it, and into the water. He suffers multiple deep facial lacerations, a broken left shoulder and ankle, and comes to rest in a semi-conscious state. As his feet brush the sandy bottom, he feebly strains to hold his head out of the water. He fights to comprehend what just happened and where he is, then senses progressively-intense pain throughout his body.

Sonny's Shangri-La wallows to a complete stop, like a stumbling, mortally-wounded big game animal. As Luther slowly turns towards the remnants of the boat, he's barely aware of motion on the water just in front of his face. *What the...? Too small to be a gator, what's out here? Crabs? I can't see it..."*

A brief moment of partial clarity returns to his bruised and disoriented brain and he's aware of something that is vaguely familiar. *Aaaah! Holy shit! No, no, no! Not happening, just can't – water moccasins!*

Terrified of the serpents and having very recent personal knowledge of their debilitating potential, Luther strains to move but his traumatized limbs and body simply will not, cannot, respond. Though normally solitary creatures, two of the deadly pit vipers open their jaws to bare their cotton-white mouths and needle-sharp fangs. Each snake injects Luther's face and neck with 3 milliliters of powerful cytotoxic venom. Feeling threatened, three more snakes attack him over several minutes, sinking their twin fangs into his barely flailing hands and arms.

Recovering from her own moccasin attack, Sheila Chambers is completely unaware of the poetic justice of the agonizing bites into her unknown assassin.

Two maimed corpses, one floating and the other collapsed in a bleeding heap, draw an inevitable cloud of ravenous flies. Crabs begin to sidle towards the inanimate flesh, joined by two small gators.

Nature has dealt with Boggs Colman and Luther Phillips as other adversaries couldn't. They will commit no more sins.

Chapter 44

Crash Landing

R iggs reclines in the passenger seat of the van, elevates his wounded leg, and tries to settle down while Patina monitors the controller screen.

"Oh my god! Riggs, I don't believe it - you've got to see this," Patina gasps as she leans over with the controller. She's breathlessly followed the entire grisly spectacle in real time and can hardly believe the traumatic ending.

Riggs immediately sits upright, "What's going on? Is he coming back already? Bringing anyone else with him?"

"Not anymore; he just met two guys on a dock, showed them the document, then got back into the boat with one of them and sped away. A minute or so later, the boat hit something and killed both of them. It was utterly horrible."

"One of the guys could've been Sonny Butler, since the boat was *Sonny's Shangri-La*, I wonder who the other one was," Riggs says.

Throughout the drone's flight, the light off-shore breeze carried the rotors' buzz away from its three subjects, but it also forced the drone to work a little harder when hovering. That, and the high-speed pursuit after Luther have all but depleted its two on-board batteries.

The controller begins its annoying Low Battery signal again and displays a visual warning on the controller screen. Patina doesn't have a clue how to avoid a crash and preserve the vital video evidence on the drone's microSD card. She thrusts the beeping controller towards Riggs, who monitors how far away the drone is and its remaining battery charge.

When the battery charge reaches a critically low level, the drone begins a self-landing procedure. Riggs sees that it's over water and he quickly changes its heading to route it over land. Within seconds, the high branches of a Spanish Oak tree snare the descending craft. The drone's speeding rotors momentarily thrash to escape, lash at a number of twigs, and the Inspire 2 falls through the canopy.

As soon as he sees that the drone is in distress, Riggs turns the motors off, and the Inspire hits the ground.

"Have we lost it?"

"It's getting too dark to start looking for it now, but we can search for our flying witness in the morning. Tonight we can still see the video that's been streaming to my YouTube channel."

"No way mister, you're still oozing blood. The sheriff can hunt for the drone; I'm taking you straight to the hospital."

Chapter 45

Joining Forces

After hearing Riggs' and Patina's story later that night and watching the YouTube video, Charleston County Sheriff Barry Cobb and two detectives ride to the wreckage of *Sonny's Shangri-La* to secure and investigate the scene. They're able to precisely locate on a map where the accident occurred, but know that tidal currents will have moved the boat up to several hundred yards away. They spot it with their lights and slowly cruise towards it, careful not to contaminate the scene or disturb any evidence that may have been thrown from the boat.

Accompanying the lawmen, the Charleston County coroner has been calculating the amount of flesh that teeming crabs will have eaten, and he confirms his estimate as he pulls on his waders before stepping into the shallows. The water comes alive with scurrying crustaceans and the air is thick with flies. He expects to see maggots burrowing through the dead flesh in as few as six more hours unless he can secure the bodies in the morgue's refrigerated storage lockers.

Riggs' detailed YouTube footage significantly helps the coroner with identification and cause of death, "Yep, same clothes as in the video – it's them. Let me get a few pictures for the record, though. If you'll lift the guy in the rear fishing seat, I'll get his face. There's not much face left on the one that went through the windshield. Then let's get them into remains pouches and back to the morgue. I'll fingerprint them there and check the floater for powder residue, if the crabs have left enough of his right hand and forearm."

It's a grisly business, but absolutely necessary to document what happened, especially if foul play was involved and it ends up in court.

Sheriff Cobb reminds the crew, "These two are high profile – especially the guy in the water, he's Congressman Butler's Chief of Staff. This is going to be all over the news tomorrow, so let's do it all by the book." *Better wake up Dorothy to put a press release together,* he reminds himself.

"Hey, sir, here's the envelope we saw in the video. Looks like it's still in one piece," a deputy inside the boat reports to Cobb.

"If that's what got them mixed up in all this, there's got to be something to it. Bag it, tag it, and personally make sure it gets properly logged into evidence with SGT Winters before you clock out."

Another team heads to the clearing and dock. They're also aided by Riggs' YouTube video and set up lights to confirm where the perpetrators and victims stood, moved, and what they did. Luther's van was still there, of course, which they check for fingerprints. They find the cut plastic tie that Luther used to bind Patina's ankles, the blanket he covered her with, casings from Luther's pistol and the three items Ivan left on the railing at the end of the dock.

Before securing the crime scene for the night, one of their flash-lights illuminates the shoreline where the last remnant of James Blaisdell, AKA Ivan, lies: a large shoe with the stump of a foot inside. They'll test the DNA for a positive identification.

Just before midnight, Sheriff Cobb informs Congressman Butler that two male bodies were found earlier in the evening just minutes from Waterside aboard a boat registered to the congressman. Then he calls his counterpart in Silver Spring, MD to effect notification of Boggs' next of kin. At 0730 the following morning, Cobb releases a statement,

> *"At 1937 hours last night, the Charleston County Sheriff's office was notified of a boating incident that oc-curred earlier in western Charleston County. At the scene, detectives found a badly damaged boat with two deceased middle-aged males, and the partial remains of a third male nearby. Names are being withheld pending notification of next of kin. Further details will be released as they become available."*

By 0630, an investigative team was already headed to the coor-dinates that Riggs supplied for the downed drone. The team finds the slightly-damaged craft 15 minutes later and returns it to the Sheriff's

Department. Riggs, in a wheel chair with his wound dressed, is there to explain how to recover the video footage. Using that as evidence instead of the YouTube will preclude any accusations that Riggs may have tampered with the video file.

"The video is recorded on a microSD card in this slot," he points out to the tech. He's careful not to touch the drone and create another possible allegation of evidence tampering.

The detective removes the card, places it in a reader, and displays the entire episode on a large monitor - from the time Riggs walked into the clearing to Ivan lowering Patina with the winch, the shooting, the escape, the meeting with Sonny and Boggs, and collision with the submerged cypress log. It all plays out in living color and HD detail. The detective, a native Charlestonian, murmurs, "Luther Phillips and Butler's old pal Boggs Colman - two perps in a pod. South Carolina's a better place this morning. Now we'll just have to pull enough evidence for the sheriff to nab Sonny Butler, too."

So that's who they all are, Riggs concludes.

When the video's loaded on the lab's computer, the technician notifies Sheriff Cobb.

"You got it, huh? Everything look like what I saw on YouTube last night?" Cobb asks.

"Yes sir, take a look." The video starts re-playing on the 27" high resolution monitor as Cobb intensely views the detailed action.

"This is all at or around Sonny Butler's place. That's awfully good video footage. I'm not used to seeing quality like this in crime scene movies - usually grainy or shaky stuff from a cell phone or cheap security camera."

As the action continues, Sheriff Cobb can't believe he's got such compelling evidence on the three felons.

"Sheriff, here's the part showing Sonny Butler," the technician says. And indeed it does: Luther driving the boat straight to Sonny's dock, handing him the paper, conferring with Sonny, and Sonny examining the paper before motioning for Luther to leave with it in the boat.

"It certainly looks like a gang of conspirators to me," Cobb announces. "Since a federal employee's involved, I'm calling Will

207

Haskell, he needs to see this. Make a certified copy of the video for them, will you?"

"Yes sir, too easy," the technician replies.

FBI Agent Will Haskell from the FBI Regional Office on Belle Isle Avenue in Mt. Pleasant takes the call from Sheriff Cobb, "Hey Barry, what've you got going on so early today?"

"Good morning, Will. Haven't put every piece of the puzzle together yet, but U.S. Representative Sonny Butler's chief of staff and one of Sonny's long-time cronies died in the congressman's boat last night. Looks like the deceased had kidnapped a young lady and were planning to murder her and her boyfriend to get a document. Shortly afterwards, the kidnapper drove the boat to Butler's place and met Sonny and the friend of his, Boggs Colman. Boggs and the kidnapper died a few minutes later when they took off in the boat and hit a log."

"All three dead, huh? Sounds like that'll save a lot of man hours and taxpayer dollars – great!"

"I have preliminary statements from the victims and they're both very credible – he's a former Army officer and she's a smart cookie. On top of it all, one of them managed to record the whole thing with a drone."

"You've got drone footage? That's super, sounds open and shut."

"It never is, but this may come pretty close. They also had an old paper that all the perps were very interested in. Looks like they were all neck-deep in something and Butler's a co-conspirator."

"How do you want to play it, Barry?"

"If you're amenable, let's run it together. I've got plenty of boots on the ground and you've got access to unique federal resources to find out why the paper was so important to them. I can bring one of your agents up to speed and we could present the evidence to the U.S. Attorney."

"Always like working with you, Barry. I'll send an agent over to review the accident report, the victims' statements, video, and the mystery document."

"Frankly, Sonny's a real slippery fish. If he's the kingpin behind this, South Carolina needs him off the streets. Have your agent ask for me personally and I'll update him on what we've found. Thanks, Will."

Early that afternoon, Agent Haskell reviews the evidence and meets Sheriff Cobb at the offices of Shyrel Hayden, U.S. Attorney for the South Carolina District.

It's rare for both senior lawmen ask to call on her, so she greets them personally, "Hello Will, Sheriff Cobb, you said you had a high-profile matter involving a congressman and his federally-employed Chief of Staff?"

"Yes, we certainly do, Shyrel." Haskell and Cobb begin showing her the video and a photo of the document.

"One of the intended victims captured this video with a drone. In fact, that operator is an FAA-certified drone pilot. He pointed out that he was flying in class G airspace and observing all relevant FAA flight rules."

"Class G airspace? What's that and why does it matter?"

"I had the same question. It means he was authorized to fly there, so his lawyer won't be able to get it tossed for flying illegally."

Hayden sits through the video, "That's quite a lot of activity, even for someone with Sonny's reputation. What's the federal tie-in?"

"We believe two of the deceased perps facilitated criminal activity by communicating across state lines with cell phones. One was Boggs Colman, who placed the call from Sonny's house to a James Blaisdell in North Carolina. Blaisdell's the guy you saw in the video who put his watch, glasses, and phone on the shelf before he fell into the water."

"That doesn't prove Sonny was in on the call, though."

"True, but when you combine those circumstances with his activity on the video, it's very reasonable to conclude that he was part of the whole thing from the beginning."

"I agree. I'll get an AUSA[4], to prepare the complaint and affidavit for the magistrate judge. I'm confident he'll issue a warrant, then

---

[4] Assistant U.S. Attorney

your agents can make the arrest. Barry, I imagine you'll work with Solicitor Williams to pursue state-level charges?"

"Yes, Ma'am, though I think she'll probably see how the federal case goes before asking for a warrant."

Congressman Sonny Butler is completely unaware of what's about to come down on him. He is, however, *very* aware that Luther didn't destroy the document and he needs someone to do that to sustain the flow of union contributions.

In desperation, Sonny calls Jim Sparks.

Chapter 46

We Have Questions

B y the next morning, the breaking story reverberates throughout local, state, and national news networks.

"Charleston, SC: Last evening, South Carolina Congressman Sonny Butler's Chief of Staff, Luther Phillips, and President Boggs Colman of the Food Services Union of America were found dead about a half mile from Butler's waterfront home. Both men died in a boat owned by the Congressman and authorities recovered a third body nearby."

Of course, the stories were the absolute talk of the political crowd... and certain very invested individuals.

Wealthy and influential developer Everett Pelletier is aghast at the news coming across the TV in his spacious, luxury Charleston office. Pelletier has a much more direct concern than most viewers, and calls his brother and partner, "Davey, get in here, quick. Have you seen this news about Sonny's Chief of Staff and his old pal Boggs Colman?"

"Hah! What'd they get caught doing this time?"

"I don't know what the hell the back story is, but Colman and Luther died last night... in Sonny's boat."

"What? No way! Probably drunk and hit something – like an island."

"Maybe, but they're also talking about some paper they had with 'em." Everett's brother Davey immediately gets more serious.

"Knowing Butler and Colman, it was probably a crooked union contract. So long as the paper doesn't have *our* names on it..."

"That's exactly my point: whatever it is, and whatever they were up to, you can bet they'll put Sonny through the ringer before it's all over."

"Yep, but he's pretty slippery – no one's ever been able to get any *real* goods on him. He's been in some pretty tight spots when he worked on city council for us, and remember the shopping mall deal that started going south when he was a senator?"

"Jesus, I thought we were all cooked on that one, but he wriggled his way free from that one too."

"That's all true, bro, but there's no way we can afford to have our names come up during the investigations. He's pulling some real shit for us with the Charleston Air Force contract and I hope to hell he's covered his tracks."

"You got that right. And the $200,000 we funneled to him – are we covered? It's a clean transaction – no tell-tales hanging out?"

"I *think* we're good there, but there's nothing like three deaths to bring every snooping cop and auditor out of the woodwork. I'm just not sure everything's buried deep enough for *that* kind of scrutiny."

"Better set up a chat with him, we've got way too much to lose if the state or the feds unravel everything. But be careful how you contact him – I bet the dicks'll start checking every phone call, email, and text from here on out and back at least a year."

"Roger that, I'll run over to the Charleston Club, and maybe out to his house to see him in person."

"No! Not the house, that place will be swarming with cops and reporters already."

Similar scenarios play out a dozen more times in a dozen more offices before it's even noon.

6th District Field Representative Ripp Jennings is on the phone non-stop to reassure donors and supporters, "John, at this point we just don't have any more information on the tragedy than you've seen on the news, but I can assure you the congressman is as surprised and saddened as you are, and just as anxious to learn the facts. We're staying in close touch with the investigators and we'll let you know something the moment we do."

"Yes, Walter, I'm looking at the news again, too. I know they said something about Sonny's boat, but we just don't have the facts yet. At this point we believe it was simply a very unfortunate accident. I'm sure we'll know more soon. Yes, the fund raiser's still on."

Sonny's supporters wonder, *Were Luther and Boggs doing something illegal? If so, was Sonny involved? What paper did they have with them? What'll this do to his narrow campaign margin - can he win another term? If he doesn't, what'll it cost me to get Mark Chambers to steer tax money into my project?*

Sheila Chambers, still recovering from her snake bites, also wonders, *Is that lowlife finally going to get his due? Will the public finally recognize what a sleaze he is? Will it wipe out his incumbency advantage? Will his fat cat donors pull back?*

Stories and every shred of breaking news about Sonny's demolished boat, the human remains, the document, and local theories continue to run on local TV, blogs, radio and newspapers.

As Patina and Riggs watch the same news, Patina runs an idea by Riggs.

Founders' Intent

Chapter 47

All About Me

P rofessor Dale Hartman is one of the many Charlestonians glued to news that mentions the document found at the accident scene. To him, though, the document isn't an ancillary detail of the story, it *is* the story.

Damn it, the cops have it! he fumes. *What's my play now, how do I get in front of this?*

Hartman thinks for a while, then picks up the phone.

"Hello, WCHS television? This is Professor Dale Hartman at Charleston State University. I have some vitally important information regarding the accident story you've been reporting all morning. I need to speak with your news director immediately; put him on the phone, please."

"Who is this?" station assistant Jimmy Cooley asks.

"Like I just told you, I am Doctor Dale Hartman, from the Charleston State University history department. It's urgent that I speak with the news director about the Luther Phillips boat accident story. I have key information about it that he's going to want to hear."

"That'd be Betsy Harker. She's awfully busy with that one today, but let me see if I can track her down. What'd you say your name was?"

"Hartman, Doctor Dale Hartman." *God, I detest having to deal with such mentally-deficient cretins.* "I'm a professor at Charleston State University. This is vitally important, you need to hurry."

Several very long minutes ensue.

"Hello, Professor Hartman is it? This is WCHS news director Betsy Harker. Jimmy said you had some important information about last evening's accident?"

"Yes, thank you, Ms. Harker. You briefly mentioned a document during your coverage. I'm quite familiar with that newly-surfaced paper because I'm the first person to have read and studied it. My conclusion is that it's from the Constitutional Convention of 1787, was written by five Founding Fathers, including South Carolina's own John Rutledge, and will have a direct impact on a number of pivotal U.S. Supreme Court decisions." *That ought to get her attention.*

"That's very interesting, may I ask how you know all this?"

"Very recently, I photographed and transcribed the document as part of my research for an upcoming treatise about its impact on the nation. I wrote my PhD thesis at Stanford on the Convention and I'm the foremost authority on that gathering to draft the U.S. Constitution. I'm unquestionably the best positioned authority to examine the paper and determine its significance. While the loss of two lives is certainly regrettable, the real, far-reaching story is the document they had."

"I see. Do you know how they came to be in possession of it after you photographed it? I'm just asking because an attorney for some association in Washington asked about it in regard to a federal lawsuit."

"No, I don't have any idea, but I'm sure the detectives will discover all those answers during their investigation. That's not really the issue here, though."

"Would you be available to come by the studio for a live interview today?"

"Yes, certainly. To serve your viewers, I'll do it. What time should I come? Hartman is almost salivating. *This is it, I'm on my way! My big break. But wait a minute Dale, remain calm, thoughtful, and very professorial. By tonight, all those sneering pretenders will see YOU on national TV, breaking the biggest constitutional story in decades! Or should I be calling myself Chairman Hartman?*

Walking into the WCHS building, Hartman is absolutely giddy and rehearses lines to maximize his role and reputation. He hasn't felt this way since he first examined the document in his office. *Tonight, I'm actually going to ask Dr. Cochran out to dinner! Hell, everyone likes being with high achievers, and that'll describe me to a T.*

Jimmy meets Dr. Hartman in the lobby of the television station and escorts him to a lounge. Several minutes later, a young lady appears.

"Hi, Mr. Harmon, I'm Jen Rose, newsroom assistant. I'll take you back to the news studio now."

"It's Hart-man, young lady, and my title is Professor or Doctor," he interrupts. *Doesn't anyone here listen? No, Dale, remember to be patient with those of limited mental capacity.*

"So sorry, Dr. Hartman." *Great, here's another pompous buffoon I've got to deal with.* She attaches a lapel mic to his jacket and reviews a few on-air basics prior to introducing him to the nightly news anchor.

"Betsy said you have new information about something found at last night's accident site?" Jen asks.

"Not just something. It's a vital U.S. historical document that I discovered and examined in some detail."

Jen leads Hartman to the studio news desk, where a technician sound-checks his mic before she introduces him to news anchor Jovita Schorre as a commercial break is about to end.

Jovita welcomes him and resumes her broadcast, "Welcome back to the WCHS news hour and a story we've been breaking live throughout the day. This afternoon we have Dr. Dale Hartman from Charleston State University and an authority on the U.S. Constitution. Dr. Hartman, you have information about the document that investigators recovered from last night's tragic boating accident and that is apparently evidence in a federal lawsuit, correct?"

"Yes, I do, Jovita. I'm very familiar with the document and I was the very first, and the only expert authority, to initiate a scholarly examination of it. My research, based on my PhD work at Stanford University and decades of constitutional study, concludes that it's genuine and a vital factor in reconsidering the Supreme Court's decisions on the federal minimum wage."

"That's very interesting, Professor, what sort of document is it?"

"I've taken a very detailed photo of the page," he says into the camera as he holds up Patina's picture. "The Founding Fathers wrote these notes while drafting our U.S. Constitution. They're so significant because they provide added detail about the federal government's authority, or more precisely, lack of authority, to regulate certain aspects of interstate commerce. Most significantly, they plainly preclude the federal government from setting a minimum wage."

"Well that certainly *is* controversial, and I'm sure it'll open much more than the proverbial can of worms."

"Yes, Jovita, and I'm meticulously researching those and other aspects of the document, which will all be included in my in-depth treatise on the matter. It should serve as the definitive piece on the subject and will no doubt be used by the Supreme Court when they're called on to reconsider prior seriously-flawed decisions on a federal minimum wage."

"Thank you again Dr. Dale Hartman of Charleston State University, we look forward to reading your analysis as soon as it's published. And now, a word from one of our sponsors."

Jovita stands up and shakes Hartman's hand, "Well done, Professor Hartman. Would you mind if we kept your photo to use on the late-night news?"

"I've only got the original, Jovita..."

"Can't you just print another one from your camera?"

Hartman sputters, "I've always kept the first print for archival purposes, it's an old researcher's superstition. Why don't you just make a copy here at the studio?"

"I guess we could do that, sure. Jen, would you please make a couple of copies of this photograph?"

"Certainly Ms. Schorre, be back in a minute."

"Now, Jovita, one more detail. For maintaining factual accuracy, may I ask that you credit the pictures to me?"

"I suppose we can do that, sure Dr. Hartman."

Congressman Sonny Butler will face much more intense media attention.

Chapter 48

Spotlight

W ith news of Luther's and Boggs' deaths running all day, a veritable army of reporters incessantly hounds Ripp Jennings for a press conference with Congressman Sonny Butler.

"Sir, they're ringing the phones off the hooks. I've stalled them until I could find out how you want to handle it."

Without even pausing, Sonny shoots back, "Schedule it, Ripp. Let's get the damn thing done and over with – just like ripping off a band aid." *The quicker we get it done, the less evidence and time the investigators will have, and some reporters won't even get the word in time to attend. Let me practice my bereavement face. If this performance lives up to my others, I may be able to get enough sympathetic votes to knock Chambers off his pedestal and save money on those damn TV ads in the process.* "The sooner the better; hell, let's do it this afternoon, before tonight's fund raiser."

"Oh, and Ripp, get me out of here and back to Washington as soon as the fund raiser's over – even if it means going by limo. If anyone asks, tell 'em I was called back to D.C. 'on urgent House business', of course." He manages a brief, unexpected smile.

Two hours later, Ripp welcomes broadcast, internet, and print media reporters to the hastily called news conference. *They look like a school of starving piranhas – just can't wait to devour Sonny for a lousy byline and moment of fame.*

"Ladies and gentlemen of the press, while Congressman Butler is still mourning the loss of both his Chief of Staff Luther Phillips and dear friend Boggs Colman, he has graciously agreed to make brief remarks and take a few of your questions." Ripp steps aside – Sonny's cue to come to the podium.

Sonny steps forward in authoritative, measured steps with a look of sorrow and heartbreak, but also standing erect and meeting the stare of every reporter in the room. He maintains a command presence, as if he's completely in control of the calamitous situation that was thrust upon him. He does it all with a dash of sincerity for two trusted people who'd done his bidding, but it's mostly fabricated to garner compassion, donations, and November votes.

Sonny speaks in a slow cadence as he carefully assesses the reporters' expressions, "I open my meeting with you this afternoon under particularly solemn and painful circumstances. I do so with a special and very heart-felt message to all the loving family, friends, and colleagues of Boggs Colman and Luther Phillips." *There, that's the reaction I'm looking for – quiet, melancholy, looking up to me as the authority for answers, rationale, and to calm their undefined fears. Everyone's afraid of the monster under the bed, and looks to a leader to calmly assure them it's not there tonight, that they're safe as long as I'm in charge.*

Sonny gauges the reporters, knowing he's really playing to their much larger audience of readers, viewers, listeners, and bloggers. "Those friends and family have suffered an unspeakable loss in a tragic accident yesterday, two loved ones who sacrificed so much for America through their decades of selfless public service to us and all other Americans. *They really don't want the truth - that there are extremely evil people in the world who do very wicked things. They all want to hear a fairy tale with a happy-ending - a bedtime story to allay their fears of random violence and death. Subconsciously, they want me to tell 'em that story so they can avoid uncomfortable controversies, conflicts, and tough realities, so they can focus on what they can control in their mundane little lives. I'm here to do exactly that!*

"We will remember and honor Boggs and Luther with our prayers, thoughts, condolences, and unwavering support for their families. I thank you for being here to seek and report what we know, and I shall provide a brief statement before taking a few questions."

Sonny scans the pool of reporters, from front to rear and side to side. *They seem to be buying it; so far, so good.*

"All day yesterday and this morning I was making final preparations for tonight's event with a group of civic-minded South Carolinians who I've been scheduled to meet with for some time. My Chief of Staff, Mr. Luther Phillips, has been under an extreme amount of pressure orchestrating those efforts here in the district and simultaneously overseeing a number of vital matters in Washington."

A few reporters who are on a tight deadline begin to fidget, waiting for some substance and to ask questions.

"Luther Phillips was the kind of dedicated public servant who'd never give less than his best or ask for a break when there was work to be done. Knowing that, I insisted early yesterday morning that he relax for a bit and let other staff members shoulder the load for the rest of the day. Perhaps he sought to relieve some stress by getting away for a few hours of quiet boating in our district's soothing waterways, away from phones and television."

The reporters listen, still waiting to hear something meaningful.

Sonny filibusters on, "I can only assume that my long-time friend Boggs Colman, a supporter, and champion of tens of thousands of working men and women, apparently joined him in the boat. His loss will be especially hard hitting to all those hard-working Americans whose lives and interests were so dear to him." He conveniently omits everything about Ivan and the felonious crimes at the clearing and dock.

With his deadline looming ever closer and tiring of Sonny's platitudes, a reporter stands up and blares out, "Congressman, the last time you saw them was yesterday morning?"

Sonny shoots an icy glare at the reporter, then answers, "Yes, that's right." *That little turd - what I'd really like to tell him is to sit down, shut the fuck up, and show a little respect for a U.S. congressman!*

The floodgates have opened, other reporters immediately follow up.

"Was it unusual for them to take out your boat? Did they know how to operate it, and what the hazards were?"

"Representative Butler, did you know he was using your boat?"

"Was he familiar with the local waters?"

"WCHS television just broke a story about a historical document they had with them. How did they come into possession of it? Were you aware of the document? Did you know it was evidence in a federal lawsuit? Were they tampering with evidence? Isn't that highly illegal?"

Crap! This is headed off in the wrong direction! Butler tries to cut off the barrage, "I haven't seen anything the sheriff's office recovered, so I really can't say any more about what they may have found. I've pledged to support the investigation in any way I can, of course."

The reporters are unrelenting, "Couldn't the document impact the on-going contract Mr. Colman's union is negotiating?" Is it possible there's some foul play afoot?"

Sonny jumps right back in, "The union's counsel would have to address your legal questions, but I have absolutely no knowledge whatsoever of Boggs Colman knowing anything about a document you're alluding to."

Butler continues with his drivel, trying to stay ahead of the questions, "I only learned about the tragic incident through a notification by the sheriff and I'm looking for answers too. I have no earthly idea how it could possibly have come about. Their tireless efforts on behalf of working men and women across the country will be sorely missed. I was happy to let Mr. Phillips and Colman use my personal boat for the day, and didn't see them after we had breakfast together. I can't imagine either one of them being involved in any illegal activity, and will of course cooperate in every way I can to resolve this terribly regrettable matter. To that end, I'm confident that our law enforcement professionals will conduct a thorough investigation of the entire matter."

The room quiets for just a moment.

"Frankly, I have just as many unanswered questions about all this as you do," Sonny adds.

"Representative Butler, Mr. Colman's come under scrutiny a number of times as union president and you've had a close relationship with him over the years, haven't you?"

"Of course I have. As a member of the Education and the Workforce Committee that represents all labor, and Mr. Colman's direct and indirect representation of millions of American workers, you should be concerned if we *weren't* close."

Sonny's feigned surprise and contrived sympathy roll off his tongue with innate ease and practiced refinement. To most, it seems genuine. Those who really know him, of course, recognized long ago that he's simply perfected his deceitful, double-dealing, self-serving opportunism to an art form.

Ripp Jennings knowingly smiles in the background at another virtuoso performance – a rehearsal for Sonny's final role when the curtain rises at tonight's fund-raiser.

Founders' Intent

Chapter 49

Grand Event

An hour after the press conference, the fund-raiser starts promptly at 6:30 p.m. It's a luxurious affair for Sonny's most generous supporters. Each $10,000-a-seat guest will dine in the Charleston Club's elegantly decorated main hall, tastefully adorned with spectacular ice carvings and exquisite arrangements of freshly-cut local and imported floral arrangements.

Checkbooks should loosen up even more after enjoying exotic hors d'oeuvres selected especially for the occasion - including light grey caviar from the Beluga sturgeon, Basque white almond gazpacho, foie gras patè, verrines filled with sweet and savory delights, and fine cheeses.

Sonny's well-heeled contributors will dine on Versace Butterfly Garden china with hand-polished silver utensils, all meticulously arranged on fine Irish linen tablecloths. Their contribution will provide them the freshest salads, soups, direct-from-the-Atlantic seafood (or aged Kobe filet mignon for those who prefer it), and a baked Alaska or Bananas Foster dessert. The open bar's top-shelf spirits and wines and a live five-piece combo should provide further stimulus for last-minute payments to Sonny's campaign, charitable fund, and supporting PACs. Ahh, the perks of office.

Sonny puts on his best smile to work the arriving donors. "Jack, and Marsha - you look just as lovely as always, thank you so much for coming tonight. I was thrilled when I saw your names on the guest list; both of you have always been such faithful friends and supporters."

"Wouldn't miss it, Sonny," Jack says while leaning in closer to Sonny, "and I have to thank you for putting your thumb on the scales for the eminent domain project."

"Don't thank me at all, Jack - just doing my duty as your representative in Washington and happy I could be of help. Always feel free to contact me directly." *And keep those checks coming…*

Sonny greets another guest and his wife, "Prescott, Julie, what a pleasure to see both of you, it's been way too long."

"Couldn't agree more, Sonny. You and Dana need to join Julie and me on the boat again." *Please, please don't take me up on the invitation, you degenerate.*

"Unfortunately, Dana had to stay in Washington for some volunteer charity work she just couldn't delay or delegate, but I'm sure she'd absolutely love to." *Christ, that's the last thing we want to do – bob up and down on your damn boat listening to Julie's incessant blather. She's got a smokin' hot body, but I can't figure out when that woman has a chance to inhale.*

"Listen, Sonny, I'd like to talk to you for a minute sometime real soon about a federal project that needs some funding so they can hire my outfit to do the work. It'd be a multi-year deal; could we get together to talk about an earmark in an appropriations bill?"

"Say no more, Prescott, that's why I serve. Why don't you call me at the D.C. office next week?" *Reminder to self: have staff confirm the amounts of his latest contributions.*

After receiving another thirty minutes of additional thanks for past meddling and requests for future favors, Sonny excuses himself from another wealthy couple to move to the front of the ballroom. Ripp Jennings takes the stage to welcome the donors, express his sympathy for the family and friends of Luther Phillips and Boggs Colman, and to deliver a few introductory remarks.

Sonny foregoes the usual forced energetic ascent he uses to appear younger, more virile, and physically fit. Tonight's audience demands a different act, so he deliberately times his pace up the steps with a cadenced, dignified pace.

After hearing Sonny's remarks at the press conference, the donors are even feeling a bit compassionate for the man who all but extorts them in exchange for federal favors. *What else will he say? What else <u>can</u> he say? Seeing your friends for the last time yesterday morning... what a tragedy.*

On stage, Sonny contrives a modest, warm-looking smile to the audience and begins with no small amount of feigned sadness, "My dear friends, my fellow Carolinians, I most humbly thank each of you again for your generous support of me over the years so I can continue serving you and our great state. May we now take a minute, though, to pause in silent prayer for our two lost friends and patriots, Boggs Colman and Luther Phillips."

The room goes quiet until Sonny resumes, "As soon as I learned of yesterday's tragic incident, my immediate thought was to notify each of you that I was cancelling our time together to give us all more time for prayers and mourning."

The audience remains absolutely quiet.

"As I reached for the phone, I reflected on the service, character, and motivation of Boggs Colman and Luther Phillips, their tireless efforts to serve all of you here and so many other Americans who are beyond these walls. I had to ask, 'Would Boggs and Luther want us to stop moving forward on their account?' Or would they want, no, demand, that the work go on in spite of their fateful departure? If you knew them, if you knew their hearts, as I'm confident so many of you do, the answer was clear - they would absolutely insist that we continue." There's not a word about Ivan and activities at the clearing.

Looks like they're buying it; God knows I didn't want to pay the outrageous cancellation fees to the Charleston Club, the caterers, and the band. And some of them, the short-sighted, self-centered ones, would have demanded I refund their $10,000. All about themselves - no loyalty.

The donors politely applause, look approvingly at their dinner partners, and nod in mutual agreement.

Ripp takes a step forward and speaks, "We all know the grief that's in your heart now, Congressman Butler, and recognize your courage to persevere in the face of such hardship."

Sonny turns his head towards Ripp in thankful acknowledgement, then looks down in an attempt to appear humble and returns to the head table. It plays out just as they'd rehearsed it before the doors opened.

Ripp looks at the donors, "I know all of you here, so I also know your appreciation for what Congressman Butler's done for you, your families, your neighbors, and your businesses. But you may not know what he's done for others. To highlight this past year's work for South Carolina and the country, I'm going to ask our technician to start a very brief presentation. Ma'am, if you'll lower the house lights, let's begin."

Lights dim and stirring music begins as all eyes turn to the big screen at the front of the room. The substitute audio-visual technician with a bandaged nose confidently and methodically flips the switches and pushes buttons on the Club's array of computers and panels. She obviously paid attention to the regular tech's demonstrations six weeks ago, and starts the very laudatory video highlighting Sonny's work - absent his many illegal and unethical behind-closed-doors activities. There wasn't a hint, of course, of Sonny's lewd golf tournament.

The presentation opens with a montage of lower and middle-class workers contrasted with horseback riders on Seabrook Island's beaches, golf courses, and yachts. Questions fade onto the screen, "Is this fair? Is this right? Is this the America we want for our children?" Audience members, many of whom own similar or larger yachts and thoroughbred stables, collectively murmur, "No". What they mean, of course, is that it isn't fair for *others* to enjoy a lifestyle that's so much more lavish than that of the wage-earners in the video.

Representative Butler, obviously not in his silk robe for the video, but clad in jeans and a work shirt, is shown joining a group of manual workers, clerks, and fast food employees, appearing to intently listen to their concerns and nodding sympathetically.

Ripp Jennings smirks at the unwitting audience that's listening to every line of the contrived propaganda. *As long as they're on the receiving end of legislative favors, they'll keep lapping up this hype – they want to believe it, or just don't want to consider the consequences of it being lies. Funny, because there're some smart guys and gals here. The competitive side of human nature, it never ceases to amaze me - the instinct to make sure I get more than my share even if I have to turn a blind eye to its source.*

While pictures of legitimate campaign expenses cascade into view, the on-screen narrator chimes in, "We need Sonny Butler fighting for us in Washington, and that takes everyone's help."

In addition to their per-seat donation, some faithful beneficiaries and those needing an immediate favor have tucked away signed checks for tonight's event. They know the lofty cost of favors and favored causes, and are more than willing to deal with the familiar Sonny over his unknown conservative challenger.

Sonny looks from side to side to read the faces in the crowd and see how many are reaching for donations from their coat pockets or evening bags.

Suddenly, shockingly, the dignified and thoroughly orchestrated world in the Charleston Club's main ball room is irrevocably shattered.

Founders' Intent

Chapter 50

We Interrupt This Presentation

Right before the audience's riveted eyes, the video presentation unexpectedly morphs from Sonny's aggrandizing promo to an aerial view of a small clearing in the woods, a dock, and three figures. In the booth at the rear of the ballroom, substitute technician Patina Gregors has seamlessly transitioned from Sonny's presentation to Riggs' drone video - clearly showing Ivan brutally breaking her nose and lowering her towards two alligators.

The audience is completely baffled, of course, but remains spellbound - glued to the screen and more attentive than ever. *What am I looking at? Isn't that Luther Phillips from the newscasts? Did that other guy just smash his hand into some woman's face while she's got her hands tied? What's this got to do with Sonny's work in Washington? I'm not following any of this...*

Sonny sees an abrupt, confused change on the face of a nearby donor, and all the other guests at that table. He quickly scans other tables and sees the same bewildered expression on everyone's face. *What the hell?*

He looks back at the screen and instantly recognizes Luther. He sees, but cannot comprehend, how Luther's deeds are playing out before everyone, and in such detail. Sonny instantly assesses the severity of the threat to his campaign, his office, his wealth, lifestyle, and his very freedom. Every survival instinct kicks in. Adrenalin pumps, heart pounds, sweating, narrowed focus.

Key snippets of the drone video churn on, showing Riggs' arrival, Patina kicking Ivan into the water, the shoot-out, and Luther jumping into *Sonny's Shangri-La* with the document. Everything.

The audience is confused, of course - nothing's making any sense to anyone. *Why is Luther shooting at someone? Is that the document the professor told us about on WCHS's afternoon news?* The guests now begin to understand that this has nothing to do with

Sonny's work in Washington and begin to feel like Dorothy Gale –
spinning wildly in a tornado from Kansas to Oz.

Sonny shoots a baffled, menacing look at Ripp, who returns an
equally-bewildered expression. Without waiting to see any more of
the completely unexpected footage, Sonny leaps up from the head
table and begins running towards the audio-visual booth. *Goddamn
it! What the hell's going on? Is this really happening? How? Who?*
Lots of questions, no answers.

His face reddens further as he crashes between tables of confused supporters, *Gotta stop this, got to! They've already seen too
much! Am I finished? Can I salvage it?*

The screen fills with more high definition video of Luther talking
to silk-jacketed Sonny while he and Boggs examine the document.
Nude caddy girls linger on the porch. The fading light of day confirms
they're all together in the late afternoon, much later than Sonny told
the world just hours ago at the press conference. Then they see Sonny
examine the document and deliberately motion for Luther to take it
away in the boat. Sonny returns to the adoring company of the two
nude caddy girls.

This is a political death sentence! Sonny continues his rampag-
ing charge past tables full of astonished guests, *Gotta stop that
goddamned thing! Gotta kill it! I'll come up with excuses later, just
gotta stop it now!*

Sonny reaches the audio/visual control booth and nearly rips the
door off its hinges. Veins on his neck bulge even thicker and sweat
pours from his brow. He looks directly at Patina and tries to decide
whether to choke her on the spot or destroy the presentation. *Gotta
stop the goddamn show – can't have it running another second.*

Patina vaults out of the front of the booth as Sonny lunges for
the first computer he sees and violently rips out every cable he can
put his frantic hands on. Like a demented psychopath, he vainly
pounds on switches to end the damning show and screams at Patina,
"YOU GODDAM LITTLE BITCH, *YOU* DID ALL THIS! YOU
AND YOUR PUNK-ASS, LOW-LIFE BOYFRIEND."

The video continues from Patina's laptop, out of sight on a shelf
under the Club's sparking, smoking equipment, exposing Sonny,
Boggs, Luther, and Ivan. It glaringly presents his interview as blatant

lies: seeing Luther late in the day, examining the document, and sending Luther and Boggs away with it. The audience has now witnessed everything.

Even the oldest, most loyal and fervid supporters stare in utter disbelief.

Agape at the detailed spectacle of contradictions, they push back from their tables in stunned, embarrassed silence. A common thought pervades the audience, *The stories, the rumors, the innuendos are all true – South Carolina's U.S. Representative Sonny Butler really is the stereotypical garbage politician people whisper about.*

I 've got to put as much distance between him and me as I can. Is it too late to cancel my last donation? Is he going to be arrested? Will Sonny try to save his own skin by spilling his guts about our pay-for-play deals? Is my name going to be on tomorrow's news?

Donors and their spouses get up, nearly in unison, to leave in abject disgust. *Oh my God, he's finished, he's cooked, and so is his ability to pull strings for me. I wonder how much Mark Chambers is going to expect for his support? Can he do anything to salvage the deals I've got going with Sonny?*

Founders' Intent

Chapter 51

End of the Line

Within mere minutes, only a handful of people remain in the ballroom with the shell-shocked Sonny. A half dozen of them are Charleston County Sheriff's deputies and two FBI agents are in jackets. Sonny reflexively takes a step away from the deputies towards a side door, only to find that escape blocked too. He's cornered like the despicable sewer rat he is.

Senior FBI Agent Will Haskell nods for his partner to restrain Sonny. As the cuffs are tightened, Haskell steps in front of Sonny and looks him squarely in the eyes, "Sonny Butler, I have a warrant for your arrest for conspiracy to kidnap and to murder Patina Gregors and Riggs Blanding."

The FBI? Holy shit, where'd they come from? How'd they even know to be here? And I thought all these sheriff's deputies were here for security – the SOBs are here to run me in!

Suddenly, like the transforming Dr. Jekyll to Mr. Hyde, Sonny's demeanor instantly transforms from cowed suspect to his pompous high-handed self. He begins shouting at the agents, "You're cuffing me up? Which one of you wanna-be Dirty Harrys is the ringmaster of this outrageous sideshow? You have *no* idea what you're getting into, this is absolutely the most outrageous thing I've ever seen! No, it goes *beyond* outrageous! I'll have every one of your tin badges by morning!"

Haskell continues telling Sonny his rights.

Sonny is red-faced, absolutely livid. Standing fully erect with a self-righteous air of superiority, he shakes off the agent's grip, "Get your goddamn hands off of me you lousy, two-bit flatfoot; I'm a United States Congressman. I'm protected from arrest under the U.S. Constitution, it says so right in the first part."

Agent Haskell glares into Sonny's eyes and with immense satisfaction informs Sonny of the reality, "Privilege from arrest only applies when the House is in session or you're on your way to, or returning from, a session. The Constitution also clearly states that privilege from arrest does not apply to felonies."

Sheriff Cobb looks on approvingly.

The agents direct Sonny through several photographers and reporters to an awaiting black SUV; the press will document a second big story in as many days.

The agents drive Sonny to the Sheriff Al Cannon Detention Center on Leeds Avenue in North Charleston for in-processing and weekend detention. There, Sonny is visibly shaken as the staff collects his valuables and other personal items, and completes accession forms. Then he finds himself in front of a camera for a mug shot and providing a DNA sample for the FBI's Combined DNA Index System (CODIS). Fingerprinting and a physical exam round out the process. Only then does the staff allow him to call an attorney and Sonny cannot dial the numbers fast enough.

"Gordon, I might have really stepped in it this time. I need you - I need you bad and I need you *now*."

Gordon Asner has represented defendants of dubious character in a number of high-profile circumstances throughout the southeast, and has occasionally represented Sonny over the past two decades. This is the first time he'll have to argue for Sonny's release on bail, though.

"Who is this... Sonny? Is this you, Sonny? It's one o'clock in the morning."

"Yeah, Gordon, it's me and I need you to wake up and listen. I need your help. The feds just arrested me and I'm in their miserable damn jail in North Charleston. I won't tell them anything, but I need you to get me out of here - on my own recognizance or at least on bail. You also need to call Ripp Jennings and help him with some damage control. Blood-sucking reporters were covering the arrest like stink on shit, and I know they're drooling to run the story all over the papers, TV, and internet first thing in the morning. Ripp's got to get ahead of it."

"Jesus, Sonny, what's it all about, sounds serious."

"It *is* serious, and the election that I still intend to win is just around the corner. Oh, and Gordon, call Dana in the morning. I'm not

sure I'll be able to talk to her before the news runs with this – the
D.C. press will probably be knocking on her door as soon as the sun
comes up."

"Sure, Sonny, but this may be tough going…"

"Of course it will, that's why I pay you so much; just get down
here so we can put our heads together."

"I'll see you in 45 minutes, Sonny."

Monday morning, a pair of U.S. Marshalls escort Sonny from
the detention center to the J. Waties Waring Judicial Center at 83
Meeting Street for his initial court appearance.

When Sonny's case comes up, an AUSA urges the judge to deny
bail on the grounds that Sonny has the means and incentive to pose a
flight risk from the very serious charges against him. The judge listens intently.

Attorney Gordon Asner addresses the judge next, "Your honor,
I respectfully request that my client be released on his own recognizance as a long-standing leader in the City of Charleston, throughout
Charleston County, across the great state of South Carolina, and as a
United States Congressman representing 668,000 fellow citizens. He
has always faced his responsibilities in a forthright, honest manner
and has no prior convictions or history of violence. He will pledge to
this court, as he did when he assumed office in Washington, to obey
the law."

Again, the judge listens carefully.

"I would be negligent, your honor, if I didn't also remind the
court that Congressman Butler remains responsible to his many constituents, a responsibility that he takes extremely seriously. It's a
responsibility he cannot possibly fulfill from the confines of a jail cell
to the extent that nearly three quarters of a million American citizens
rely on him to do. Again, then, we ask the court to give the people's
representative his ability to carry out his trusted duties by releasing
him on his own recognizance."

The judge reviews several pages submitted by the AUSA and Gordon Asner prior to the bail hearing and weighs both arguments before announcing his decision.

"Mr. Asner, your client is released on $200,000 bail under the following conditions: he will obey all state and federal laws. He shall relinquish his passport. He may travel to, work at, and return from his official work places in Washington, D.C. to attend called sessions, to his current residence there, and to his place of worship. He may travel throughout the 6th U.S. District in the state of South Carolina. He is to get the court's permission beforehand if his official U.S. Representative duties require him to travel beyond these limits. Does your client understand and agree to the conditions of his bail?"

"Yes, your honor, he does. Thank you."

After arranging bail, Sonny is exuberant, "Hot damn, Gordon, I knew you'd pull a rabbit out of the hat – you always do. Now, when can you get the charges dropped?"

Gordon turns to Sonny in shocked disbelief, staring at him for a full 10 seconds before saying a word. *He has no idea what he's facing – thinks it's another political game, like steering a contract one way or another.*

Gordon steps closer to Sonny and stares into his eyes, "Sonny, like the AUSA told the judge, those serious felony charges alone are enough to make you a flight risk - you're *very* lucky the judge didn't bang down his gavel and deny bail altogether."

Sonny looks surprised and puzzled. He's always been able to grant or withdraw some kind of favor to get whatever he's wanted. Sonny's expression and manner become more serious.

"There's *no way* the U.S. Attorney's going to just drop the charges. The best we can do is negotiate a favorable deal that avoids hard time. The most likely outcome is time at a medium or minimum-security federal facility."

"Facility? *A facility?* You mean prison, right, Gordon?"

"Yes, Sonny, prison, federal prison - that's *exactly* what I mean. The video's going to be awfully persuasive and you've got a reputation for doing lots of off-book deals for friends and supporters. A couple of neighborhood groups in Mount Pleasant are still keeping your name in the news about the highway project. And there're some rumors about an air base construction contract."

Sonny becomes increasingly sullener as Gordon continues.

"Rightly or wrongly, jury members might consider all that when they deliberate. If they come out with a guilty verdict, I'll certainly push for probation within your district and D.C. The Federal Bureau of Prisons will decide *which* facility you spend time in, but regardless of where it is, you're going to be spending time in *one* of them, even if it's at a country club jail."

A much more sobered and dejected Sonny Butler returns to *Waterside*. Given the clarity and completeness of the video and his many past deeds, Sonny Butler is on the verge of trading his life of power and prestige for years in a federal cell.

There will be no more perks, peddling political favors, silk jackets, or cooter-ball tournaments... or *will* there?

Chapter 52

Your Vote Counts

W ith her snakebite wounds healing, Sheila Chambers is released from Tidewater Memorial Hospital and her candidate husband Mark reviews their options. "Sheila, what do *you* think? This journey involves you just as much as it does me and the rest of the team."

"I'm with you either way, honey, but would you even have to *do* any more campaigning - can Sonny even run for office as a criminal? I know he hasn't gone to court yet, but you couldn't ask for any better evidence than that video tape at the Charleston Club – it's more reliable than eye-witness testimony. I mean, he's formally accused of multiple felonies by federal authorities and the state's still looking at its options."

"Sheila, do you remember the 1994 mayoral election in Washington, D.C.? The FBI had a video of the guy smoking crack cocaine and he served six months in federal prison. After all that, citizens *still* re-elected him to the D.C. Council and then for another term as mayor."

"What? So Sonny could still be our congressman even if he's convicted of multiple felonies and serving time in a federal prison?"

"There're only three eligibility criteria and he meets every one: be at least 25 years old, have been a U.S. citizen for seven years, and be an inhabitant of the state. If he gets a majority of the votes, he's in. Elections in a constitutional republic have always been a participatory venture. So what do you say, have you had enough, or are you ready for more?"

"Mark, you... no, *both* of us... have put in far too much to drop out now. There's just too much at stake. You were unopposed in the primary, so if you drop out now, Sonny Butler would be the only candidate on the ballot. All it'd take is one vote, his own, to get him re-elected for another two years. I don't think the 6th District and South Carolina can stand any more Sonny Butler."

"I'm with you, hon. Let's do a joint announcement and push hard for the last week."

Out on bail, Sonny Butler hungers to rise like a Phoenix from the ashes, and stumps before crowds who are now more curious than supportive. *Got to get all of this behind me and get back to 'life before the video'.*

He tells a modest crowd, "Innocent until proven guilty, that's how we do it here in America!"

Sonny expounds on his innocence every chance he gets, and Ripp schedules plenty of chances throughout the 6th District. The press, of course, is elated to get more sound bites and headlines and ask more questions, "Congressman, the video tape looks awfully incriminating and calls your credibility into question, doesn't it"

"No, not at all, and thanks for that question. I've seen the tape, of course, and it doesn't prove a thing. Absolutely nothing. Look at it yourself, closely and objectively. It shows nothing more than me at my house talking to a couple of colleagues, that's it. I may have been off a little on the time of day when I spoke at the news conference, but as you recall, it was an especially busy day, as they all are when working for the good people of the 6th District."

"Representative Butler, it also showed two nude ladies on your porch..."

"Yes, I saw that on the tape too - absolutely appalling! I have no idea who those utterly indecent women were, and, as you and I clearly saw in the video, I went directly to the porch and confronted them. If the video had sound, you'd have heard me sternly demand they put their clothes on and immediately leave the premises."

"Why would they be nude on your porch in the first place?"

"I wouldn't put it past some unscrupulous, overly-ambitious people who considered me an enemy to send those two disreputable ladies to my house to create scandalous stories. It's downright pathetic what some people will do – lie, cheat, and disparage someone's good name. At any rate, I prepared for my fund-raiser and relied on my staff to promptly escort the two of them completely off the premises."

"What about the document, the one that's evidence in a federal suit? The video shows you looking directly at it."

"The video shows what actually happened – that I looked at a piece of paper. I had no idea what Luther showed me on the dock. It had nothing to do with me personally or my work as your representative. I told him he should return it to whoever its rightful owner was. End of story. Or, more correctly, there is no story."

"What about the brutal events at the dock, before they showed you the paper?"

"That's a complete mystery to me too, because as all of you saw, I wasn't there. I have every confidence the sheriff will get to the bottom of it."

"If the video is irrelevant, how do you explain your violent actions to stop it at the fund-raiser?"

"Violent? No, not at all - let's not overstate or embellish the facts, my friends. Was I driven and passionate? Yes. Highly motivated? Of course. I was extremely involved with the hard-working folks who made the promotional video, and was appalled that some substitute technician with opposing political views would sabotage the entire evening with some of her boyfriend's spy pictures. How would you behave if those millennial peeping Toms used drones to spy on *you* and *your* family, and then hijacked your evening with friends to push it in everyone's face? I know it may have *sounded* like I overreacted, but I was unapologetically incensed at their brazen arrogance, especially the night after a terrible tragedy took two of our own."

The room grows quiet and he surveys the reporters, *Sonny, old boy, you've still got it!*

"Everyone in that room was a dear friend who I've known for years, and they'd made substantial contributions of their valuable time and resources to advance the agenda we've worked so hard for. I was momentarily overcome, and acted uncharacteristically when I saw the kid in the projection booth attack them and their dreams with that spy video the way she did. I admit I'm human, I'm imperfect, like you, but I'll do everything in my power to support my constituents."

He made it sound so believable, as he always did.

"Thank you so much, and remember to take a friend with you to vote Sonny Butler – I'd be honored to continue serving you."

Ripp steps in, "Thank you again, members of the media. As you can imagine, Representative Butler has a very demanding schedule these last few days before the election and is already late for his next appointment. Thank you again, everyone."

"How do you think it went, Ripp?"

"Right on target, Sir, and a nice job pointing the finger at the kids and shifting the focus to everyone's fear of drones."

I kind of liked that myself. Everyone's afraid of what they don't understand, I'm just smart enough to take advantage of it!

Chapter 53

Next Moves

"Gordon? Sonny here. Listen, I need to see you again right after lunch. Can you come out to *Waterside* about one o'clock?"

"Certainly, Congressman. Anything in particular I should be prepared to discuss?"

"Just these ridiculous charges and some thoughts on what I should be doing before the election."

Gordon inwardly groans at the prospect of putting himself on the line for Sonny Butler under these daunting circumstances.

"Welcome to Waterside, Mistuh Asner; Mr. Butler's inside waiting fo you."

"Thanks, Jasper, I know the way. How's the family?"

"All doing right well, Suh."

Gordon strides past Jasper and turns left into the living room.

"Well hey there Gordon, sorry to call you on such short notice, but I'm really down to the wire on this election."

"So you're definitely going ahead with it, despite the federal charges and all the evidence? You know that video's going to be very convincing to a jury, right?"

"That's why I have the best criminal attorney in the southeast, Gordon. I'm counting on you to pull another rabbit out of the hat, maybe make it inadmissible."

"Let's stay realistic, Sonny." Gordon grumbles.

"Gordo, I've spoken at a couple of modest campaign events to test the waters, and it's going much better than even I expected." Sonny goes on to relate his newly concocted version of events, as told to the crowd earlier in the day.

"What do you think, Gordon?"

"Well Sonny, that's a start. The felonies on the dock are certainly a problem. Just say you had absolutely no idea anything like that was going on; say any more and someone's going to find a discrepancy and pound you with it."

"You mean pound *us*."

"Your next step is to see an anger management counselor, or at least get an appointment with one for PR purposes. That's something that always pulls at a few heartstrings – it'll show people you recognize you reacted strongly and want to make sure you can continue dealing with pressure in productive, non-violent ways. I've got a couple of names I'll give you."

"Yeah, sure, I'll do it – just let me know who to call."

"Get your wife to come down and stand with you at the big news conferences and rallies. She doesn't have to say a thing, just stand beside you and confidently look up at you."

"Already done, Dana flew down the day after the arrest."

"We also need to go after the girl and her boyfriend. I ran her name and found out she had a brother who was murdered about 15 years ago. They found his gun at the scene, so we'll make it sound like he was part of a criminal shoot-out. That'll start to smear her."

"I didn't know that - great work, Gordon."

"And her boyfriend was a major who got out of the Army after about 13 years on active duty; we'll paint him as a quitter who took the easy way out and left his men back in a combat zone."

"Nice – I like that! Americans can't stand a quitter, especially an officer who runs out on his troops."

"Then we'll say both the kids are irresponsible, having found a historical federal document related to our most cherished Constitution without immediately turning it over to a proper official at The Library of Congress, the Archives, or the like."

"Hell, *I'm* their federal representative, they should've presented it to *me*!"

"Yeah, exactly, great point; saying that'd be a nice touch. Instead of accusing you of improprieties with the damn thing, we flip it so they're trying to cover *their* asses and trying to smear *you*. Hint that they were trying to make some quick bucks by selling America's history to the highest bidder."

"And his father's been whining for years about an eminent domain case, the one through Park West," Sonny adds.

246

"We'll say he's fighting progress that would unquestionably improve the quality of life for people in the 6th District. Your support of the project gave him all the motive he needed to go after you and he got his disgraced drone-snooping son to help him."

"Great stuff, Gordon. How about Chambers? Anything we can do there?"

"People still see him as lily-white, and then there's that whole snakebite thing with his wife - so don't go straight for the jugular. Sound sympathetic to 'the dreadful accident she had'. Having served in D.C., tell people that every candidate needs to be at the top of their game to face the heavy 7-day-a-week demands of the job. It's in the best interests of candidates, their families, and the good people of the 6th District for him to be completely focused before taking on all that pressure. Tell the audience you relish a tough campaign – to openly debate the issues - but only in a fair contest, that's the only way you do it. Tell people that Chambers needs to put his family first, and that you look forward to a hard run in 2022."

"Yeah, good angle. I'll ask folks, 'How can you expect someone to take care of you in Washington if they don't care for their own family in the 6th District?' Now, Gordon, two questions: can you pull this all together in the short time that's left, and will people go for it?"

"I'll need to call in some favors and put extra people on it. Good people, mind you, and they don't come cheap – especially on such short notice.

"I'll find the money, just don't let it get *too* far out of hand. Now, will people go for it?"

"Let me answer this way. A wife comes home to find her long-time husband in bed with a gorgeous 25-year old. The wife stops dead in her tracks, completely shocked. The girl casually gets out of bed, dresses, strolls right past the stunned wife and out the front door. The husband calmly sits on the side of the bed, lights a cigar, looks straight at her, and says, 'Dear, are you going to believe your lying eyes, or what I'm about to tell you?' Make the story believable and tell it with conviction… works every time."

"Yeah, you're right, Any successful politician can do that in their sleep." Sonny shakes his head up and down and smiles, much more confident than he was 30 minutes ago.

"Sonny, you may have to call in a big favor, or promise one, because it'd be a big help if you could get a couple of high-profile party loyalists to publicly support you. Let a crowd see 'em doing that, and the herd instinct will take over from there. Hell, most people don't even bother voting. And most of the ones that do vote run straight down the ticket."

"I think I can arrange that."

"Finally, and this is absolutely *crucial*, Sonny, is there *anyone* who could say something we're not already aware of - anyone at all? Is there any new twist that we don't know about? If so, it could be absolutely fatal."

Chapter 54

Quiet Time

S onny takes to heart Gordon's stern warning about potential talkers and thinks about where his story could spring a leak. *Jasper? Naw, he's seen a lot over the past 25 years and never said a peep. Other house staff? They aren't close enough to see anything worth talking about. Ripp? No, he's been a willing accomplice on a few actions that could get him jail time, too... unless he did a plea bargain; I'll need to remind him of just how that'd turn out for his young ass.*

Satisfied that he's covered his bases in Charleston, he feels even more confident while driving from *Waterside* to his next speaking engagement. A self-satisfying grin illuminates his face as he passes the private golf course where he played just a week ago, *Now that was a great day, and Boggs, old friend, we had a super last round there with Starburst and Caprice!*

Suddenly, out of the blue, it dawns on him, "Holy crap!" He slams on the brakes and skids to a stop in the stark realization that there's one key person who knows much more than he'd like her to – Caprice! *Jesus, just how much does she know - what's she overheard in the golf cart and around the house? What do I really know about her? She's been good so far, but the chance to sell out a congressman may prove just a little too tempting. Holy shit!*

Sonny grabs his cell phone and dials City Concrete, the cover name he gave her in case Dana ever scans his contacts list.

Caprice picks up on the second ring, "Hello, Big Guy, tell me what I can do to make you feel better," she answers playfully.

"Listen Darlin', there's something I need to talk over with you, in person and soon – like this afternoon."

"Today? It's my day to get groceries, laundry, and do my hair. Can we do it tomorrow morning?"

"I'm sorry, sweetie, it's gotta be today; I'll make it up to you."

That sounds promising, he's a great sugar daddy when it comes to gifts and cash.

"OK, if it's got to be today. Do you want me to come over to the house?"

"No, no, not at the house. Plug this into your GPS: Ernest F. Hollings ACE Basin, it's on Willtown Road out beyond my place. Be there at 3:00 p.m.. Can I count on you?"

"I've never let you or *it* down, have I?"

Sonny acknowledges her attempted humor with a twisted smile, "You're a doll Caprice, see you at 3:00."

Sonny finds the Hollings Refuge ideal for his most off-book meetings because it's away from the city and doesn't have any security cameras or weekday crowds.

Caprice was curious why he'd want to meet her at a wildlife preserve on Jehossee Island – it didn't have a golf course and sounded a little too public a place to pleasure him. But Sonny was a powerful man and the location was wherever he said it was.

At the Basin, Sonny backs his car into a corner of the small sandy parking lot to hide his congressional license. He looks around and doesn't see anyone, so gets out and walks towards the Alexander Pond Trail, out of anyone's direct line of sight.

At 3:05 PM, Caprice pulls in, parks, and gets out. She looks from left to right and can't see Sonny. But Sonny sees her, and walks over to greet her.

"Caprice, darlin', thanks for driving over here on such short notice, we need to talk."

'Need to talk?' What is this - is he dumping me?

"Sugar', as you know, a lot of bad people are saying a lot of terrible things about me, and they'd like nothing more than to add fuel to the fire. We've enjoyed each other and had our fun, and you've done the right thing by keeping it strictly between us."

Then Sonny's demeanor changes abruptly; he becomes cold and much more intent. He turns and peers deeply into her eyes with a threatening look and holds her arms in an unusually firm grip.

Caprice's idle curiosity evaporates and she begins to worry. *This isn't like Sonny at all, what's going on? What's this all about? Of course I've never told people about what we do together. And that goes triple for his wife. Is she what this is really all about?*

Sonny looks to his left and sees three naturalists ambling in his direction. *Crap...*

He turns back to Caprice and walks her off the path. "Unfortunately, we can't see each other or even be seen *around* each other, darlin' - at least 'till this whole mess blows over. Do you understand, I mean *really* understand? No one can hear a thing about us," he coldly glares into her eyes with a threatening intensity she's never seen before.

Caprice's neck hairs stand straight on end and she feels her pulse race. There's an immediate adrenalin rush – a fight or flight sensation. *This isn't like him at all, not even the time his wife paid a surprise visit the weekend we were at Waterside. Something's definitely different! Is he scared of me, of what I know about him? I wonder if he was scared of the guys who died, and had something to do with them? Was it really an accident? Am I going to have an accident?*

"When it's OK, I'll call you. Until then, we don't know each other, right?"

"Sure Sonny, I understand. You know I don't talk about anything."

"And this meeting didn't happen, either," he tells her while peeling five $100 bills from his wallet and tucking them into her hand.

Sonny walks back to his car and drives to his campaign meeting. Caprice stands alone, confused, shaken, and terribly frightened. *Holy crap! A girl tries to have a little fun and pick up a few bucks; all of a sudden, she's a liability - a serious liability. What can I do? He's a U.S. congressman, for god's sake.*

Caprice becomes increasingly more anxious and fearful as she thinks about Sonny's chilling tone, the intimidating conversation, and the three deaths that are constantly on the news.

Maybe I'm lucky that he or someone else didn't do something terrible to me right here and now... 'local woman found strangled on Jehossee Island'...

As she plays out various scenarios, she's on the verge of panic by the time she returns to Charleston. *Is it safe to even go into my apartment? What about Starburst, has he talked to her this way too?*

Chapter 55

Unexpected Gift

A fter a very tense hour of driving and reliving her meeting with Sonny, Caprice passes the road to her Charleston apartment and arrives at a parking lot at 3691 Leeds Avenue North. She nervously enters the lobby and meekly approaches the receptionist of the Charleston County Sheriff's Office.

"May I help you Ma'am?"

"I think so. I, I, I need to see the sheriff about something very important."

"He's busy right now, Ma'am, let me get a deputy for you."

"No, it's got to be the sheriff, the sheriff himself, only the sheriff. I, I won't see anyone else."

"OK, Ma'am, suit yourself. It may be awhile, but you're welcome to sit over there in the lobby."

After 25 minutes of fidgeting and almost walking out twice, a door opens and Sheriff Cobb appears.

"Hi, I'm Sheriff Barry Cobb, and I understand you need to see me, not anyone else, only *me*?"

"Yes, thank you, Sir. It's about the two men who died on Mr. Butler's boat. Can we talk somewhere else?" Caprice nervously looks around the lobby and at the door,

"Congressman Butler's boat, that case?"

"Yes sir, that one."

"Follow me, then. *Is this a nut job, some conspiracy theorist, or a political operative?*

On his way to the office, he leans over a cubicle, "Jeanette, would you come with us for a couple of minutes?"

"Certainly, Sir," she says as she stands up and follows Cobb and Caprice. Cobb leads them to his office and closes the door.

"Ma'am, this is Jeanette, one of my most trusted and capable detectives. Anything you want to tell me, you can say in front of her. Now, tell me who you are and what I can do for you."

"I'm Caprice Flowers and I live here in Charleston. I've heard all the news about Sonny Butler's friends dying on his boat, and everything they say he's done. I know that it's all true and I can prove it, but I'm scared that something like that might happen to me. He told me to meet him today, and he told me not to say anything to anyone. I wasn't going to, but he changed and I'm really scared." Caprice nervously squirms and looks down, then at Jeanette and Sheriff Cobb.

Cobb is skeptical, but feels a professional obligation to follow up.

"You know *what's* all true? And how can you prove it?" We can protect you, but I need to know just what I'm protecting you from."

"I've been seeing Sonny Butler for a while, especially when he comes down from Washington without his wife," she says, continuing to fidget.

"Go on," Cobb says.

"The night Sonny came home from playing golf, before the big weekend fund-raiser, I was at his house - in the parlor when he was on the phone with his wife. I had my phone with me, and when I set it on a table in the room I clicked an app so I could record us while, well, you know, while I made him feel good when he was talking to her. I thought it'd be good to have in case I got caught somehow and he denied everything."

"OK."

"You must think I'm just terrible, but I did like him and he said he really liked me."

"No one's judging you, Ms. Flowers, go on."

"When he hung up, he sent me out the other door, to the foyer, and told me to come back in thirty minutes to finish. I couldn't get to my phone from the other side of the room, so it just kept recording. The two guys who died in the boat came into the room and started talking with Sonny. Afterwards, I went back in to spend some more time with him and when he left, I got the phone. Everything they said is on my phone."

"You've got their conversation recorded on your cell phone?" Cobb asks, astonished at the evidence that may have just fallen into his lap.

"Yes, Sonny and the other two men were planning to kidnap the girl and kill her and her boyfriend, I have it recorded on my phone."

"You have a recording of the three of them talking about how they were going to kill the girl and the guy?"

"Yes, that's what I'm telling you. One of them also called someone in North Carolina to come help them. I kinda got it by accident, and they had no idea I did. But I have it, and if Sonny can do that to other people, I'm scared what he might do to me."

"OK, OK. Do you have the phone with you?"

"Yes Sir, in my purse…. here it is."

"You'll have to unlock it and show me how to play it – you've probably got a ton of apps on it."

"Yeah, I guess I do. Here, let me put it on speaker," she says as the recording starts.

"Boggs, the other matter we need to look at is this growing mess with that federal lawsuit evidence – the document. Why don't you get Luther in here to help us with that?"…

… Why don't I get Ivan down here, too; he may be a little on the far side of his prime, but he's got the talent we need to get rid of both the kids afterwards, and I mean without a trace."

Cobb is absolutely stunned – an admissible recording of perpetrators planning their felonies in crystal clear language. He thinks about the crimes, the evidence his detectives collected at the boat, Riggs' video, and this recording. These were very serious crimes, planned by three dead conspirators and one live U.S. congressman.

While Jeanette sees to Caprice's safety, Cobb tells FBI agent Haskell about the recording and they agree to meet U.S. Attorney Shyrel Hayden at her office.

At the Liberty Center Building in Charleston, an assistant meets the two lawmen in the lobby, "Good evening, Agent Haskell? Sheriff Cobb?

"Yes, that's us, in the flesh, thank you."

"Please follow me, the U.S. Attorney's expecting you."

The three of them take an elevator to the 2nd floor. When the elevator doors open, they pass through a secured door and checkpoint to the U.S. Attorney's suite of offices.

"Ma'am, Agent Haskell and Sheriff Cobb are here," the assistant announces to the U.S. Attorney.

"Good evening, always a pleasure to work with both of you. I understand you have new evidence in the Sonny Butler case. He's out on bail, isn't he?"

Sheriff Cobb responds, "Yes, he is, and trying to steer the story away from himself and towards the victims. But late this afternoon I received a voice recording of him conspiring to kidnap the young woman and murder her and her boyfriend. Looks like our 6th District congressman got a little careless."

"That sounds almost too good to be true. Do you mind if I bring one of my AUSAs in?"

"Not at all."

"And the recording is admissible? You had a warrant for it?"

"Don't think there's an issue with a warrant, a 'lady friend' of Sonny's made the recording and brought it in voluntarily."

"Sounds like you've covered the bases. Let's hear it."

After listening to the recording, Hayden is as pleasantly surprised as Cobb was, *Rarely do you ever see such clear, compelling evidence against a high-level perp,* she thinks. "The chain of custody's solid on these, and there won't be any sustainable challenges?"

"It's tight. The video literally fell out of the sky and the recording walked through the doors."

"Sheriff, I think we have an extremely tight case that may not even go to trial, thanks to you two. Now I'm concerned about the young lady who recorded and provided the audio. Butler will be facing life in prison, which is certainly more than enough incentive to harm her while he's out on bail."

Chapter 56

Checkmate

As soon as the U.S. Attorney's office advises Gordon Asner of the newly-discovered evidence and tells him he can come by to pick up a copy, Gordon immediately calls his dumbfounded client.

"Sonny? Gordon here. There's something going on I don't know about. The U.S. Attorney's office just called me with new evidence – another recording. I'm going over right now to pick up a copy."

Within a half hour, Gordon's at the U.S. Attorney's office, "Ms. Hayden, I'm Gordon Asner, counsel for Congressman Butler."

"Yes, I know who you are, you're here to pick up a copy of the recording?"

"Exactly. Is it another video those eavesdropping kids made to frame my client?"

"Mr. Asner, I've already heard the congressman's fabrications about being attacked by his victims. What I hadn't heard was Sonny himself giving directions to kidnap the young lady and kill her and her friend."

"What the hell are you talking about, Hayden?"

"New evidence has come to our attention – an audio recording of your client conspiring to the crimes he's charged with."

An AUSA hands a copy to Asner.

Gordon is completely dumbstruck. He doesn't say another word, turns pale, and picks up the copied audio CD. On the way back to his office, he calls Sonny and insists he join him there.

Sonny angrily bursts into Asner's office just as an assistant walks in with the CD player, inserts the disc, and leaves. "What the hell's so damn important that I had to cancel an appearance with voters?"

Without saying a word, Asner presses the Play button on the device. Asner is astonished. Sonny is completely dumbfounded and visibly shaken, *What the hell? How? Where'd it come from? How'd the feds get it? Can Gordon get it thrown out? He's GOT to get it tossed.*

"Damnit, Sonny, I thought we had an understanding – you were going to tell if there was anything else hanging in the wind. You didn't say a thing about a recording of you actually planning to murder two people and get rid of them... permanently. Who made it and how the hell did the feds get it? You were going to lay everything on the table so I could fight this battle without one hand tied behind my back. With the video and this I've got *both* hands tied behind my back, I'm blindfolded, and have a gag in my mouth, too!"

Sonny paces and blankly stares down at the floor. *Who was around the room when we were saying all that? Caprice! It had to be her, that little whore. Just when you think you can trust somebody, they screw you. No morals. No values. No sense of loyalty.* He wipes his forehead and visions arise of a jury triumphantly announcing his guilty verdict.

"I really wish I'd known about this from the beginning, Sonny."

Sonny turns towards Asner and erupts, "JESUS CHRIST, GORDON! Don't you think I'd have said something if I knew about it? Believe me, I'm more shocked than you are because I'm the one dancing on the end of a rope here. Can you get it tossed? You've *got* to get that goddamned thing thrown out."

"They have to tell me how they got it, and I'll go through the chain of custody with a fine-toothed comb. There *may* be some problem with all that, but realistically, you've got to start looking at the other side of this... if it *is* admissible. It's ten times worse than the video, and *that* was pretty damn bad."

Sonny frantically stares back at Gordon and grouses, "Just who's side are you on?"

"Sonny, you want me to level with you, and that's what I'm doing. That tape is *your* own voice laying out *your* own plan, and the person who made it is *your* girl. Hayden will crucify you in court. You need to face reality."

"Reality? If you can't get the recording tossed, at least get me a couple of years on parole."

"Sonny, if the recording's admitted, there's way too much for a jury to ignore. The judge could easily hand down a life sentence in a federal lock-up. This is serious stuff."

"Can you convince him to confine me to the 6th District and Washington?"

Gordon glares directly into Sonny's face, "Damn it, Sonny, *listen to me!* You're *going* to federal prison. We need to look at a deal with the feds that at least gets you into a low-security facility for as few years as possible. Are you listening? Do you understand what I'm saying?"

"But won't they cut me some slack as a congressman?"

"They're probably going to come down harder on you because you *are* a congressman – you know, all that crap about holding public leaders to a higher standard. Hell, Judge Wooten sent the Lexington County Sheriff in a federal prison just for helping illegal immigrants avoid detection while they were in jail. And he'd been the sheriff for 42 years. What do you think a judge will do to you for conspiring to kidnap and murder two people?"

Sonny sits down and sinks back in a chair, visibly drained. He can see the dominoes starting to fall and his bravado quickly evaporates. He thinks about Dana, the parties, the favors, and taking down enemies. Cooter-ball and junkets. Silk pajamas and jackets, *Sonny's Shangri-La.* Everyone kowtowing. And then… a cinder block prison cell with uniformed strongmen directing his every move all day long, every day.

"Can you feel the feds out, see what they'll offer?"

"Let's talk to her."

The U.S. Attorney agrees to meet Asner and Sonny the following morning. "Shyrel, we may be able to resolve this whole matter right here, right now without going through an expensive, laborious trial and appeals. My client's never been convicted and has earned the citizens' trust through elections at the county, state, and 6th District level. That's all got to count for something…"

"Let me stop you right there. I've heard the sales pitch before, so I'm going to save us both some time and cut to the chase."

Hayden stares directly at Sonny, "A few people elected you just to gain favors, but most voted for you because they thought you'd do what's right by the office. You blatantly abused their trust, conspired to commit multiple felonies, and you're going to face the consequences."

Then she pivots to Asner, "Here's what I'm offering: your client pleads guilty to all charges. Under the federal sentencing guidelines, kidnapping and murder are level-32 and 33 offenses. That's *before* we consider aggravating characteristics that'll raise the offense by two levels for the broken nose, two for using a dangerous weapon, and two more for wounding the kid with it.

Sonny wonders, *What the hell does a 'level-32' offense mean?*

Shyrel calmly informs Gordon that his client's looking at a life sentence.

Sonny's jaw drops, *Life? In a federal prison? Is she kidding? Is this some good-cop, bad-cop play?*

"I'll recommend the judge sentence your client to 420 months in a federal facility here in the state. If he keeps his nose clean, he may get that reduced by up to 15%. That's a great offer, if the judge accepts it, and it's the only one you're going to get. I've got to get back to work now, so talk it over with your client and I recommend you don't sugar-coat it." Shyrel and the AUSA leave the room.

After one last half-hearted plea for Gordon to 'do something', Sonny inescapably realizes he's his own worst enemy - he's literally convicted himself. He closes his eyes and sees a jury box stuffed with political enemies who're salivating at the prospect of taking down the invulnerable Sonny Butler and licking their chops in anticipation of reading the guilty verdict and imposing the stiffest possible sentence. It finally sinks in - he's finished.

In a stupor, Sonny stares out the window for a full minute. Then, in an uncharacteristically muted voice, he slowly and reluctantly says "I'll take the deal."

Gordon breathes a sigh of relief.

Despite all of Sonny's foul deeds, Asner still feels a measure of compassion for his deceitful client and lays a consoling hand on his sunken shoulder. Sonny slumps in the chair and tries to fathom his shattered world; a tear rolls down each cheek. He slowly stares up at Gordon with a bewildered, hollow gaze and searches for an answer to his only remaining question, "Who's going to take care of everybody in the 6th District?"

As soon as the judge reviews the case and approves the plea bargain, South Carolina hears the complete story.

Mark Chambers edges Sonny in the election, prepares for his first term in Congress, and graciously accepts The Tidewater Preservation Corps' invitation to speak at their January event.

Everett and Davey Pelletier waste no time seeking an audience with the new Representative-elect.

Sonny Butler begins the next thirty-five years of his life at the Federal Correction Facility in Estill, SC, hoping to earn as many of the 63 months reduction for good behavior as he can. Soon after he's processed-in, a burly guard escorts him to his cell.

"Inmate 27316-193, this is your cell and cellmate - Buster Givens. He's in for molestation, rape, and assault in two states; he despises politicians."

Sonny reactively takes a step backwards and sheepishly looks up at the muscled Givens.

The guard turns to Givens, "Buster, meet Sonny Butler, a U.S. Congressman until the end of the year."

The heavily-tattooed Givens looks down at Sonny and smiles ear to ear. Sonny's eyes bulge open and his anal sphincters involuntarily constrict especially tightly.

WCHS television runs a brief story of the evidence, Sonny's sentencing and subsequent incarceration; stock prison footage appears beside Sonny's mugshot. The case is closed; Sonny Butler will commit no more sins.

Dana files for divorce when she learns about Sonny's golf tournaments and amorous adventures with Caprice. As part of the eventual settlement, she's awarded title to *Waterside*. Dana never cared for the area's heat, humidity, critters, and solitude, so she took a tax break by donating the property to the Tidewater Preservation Corps for their use as a retreat and education center. She couldn't resist sending Sonny an invitation to the dedication ceremony, where Congressman Chambers would conspicuously serve as the honored guest.

Chapter 57

We Need It

Within another week, the stories about the three deaths and Sonny's arrest are replaced with new and different events that command the headlines and television news. Patina returns to her academic studies, work at the Historical Society, and begins packing some things to move to Riggs' house.

Professor Dale Hartman takes immediate notice of the closed case, and hopes for an opportunity to once again obtain the original document, write his new treatise, and ascend to the level of academic prominence he's convinced he deserves. He wastes no time calling the Charleston Historical Society.

"Good afternoon, will you put me through to David Arkin?"

The receptionist responds, "Yes Sir, may I ask who's calling?"

"Don't you know who I am by now? It's me, Doctor Dale Hartman at Charleston State University," he states indignantly. *As often as I call there, you'd think that pedestrian little flunkey would finally recognize me.*

Melba puts him through, *I love jerking that fool's chain!*

"Good morning, Dale, David here, how can I be of service?"

"I see the Sonny Butler case is closed, which means the document isn't needed as evidence any longer; can you text me your intern's phone number so I can proceed? I'll have some time next term to get started and I'd really like to thoroughly research the whole matter… to advance the cause of Constitutional research, of course."

"I'll ask her to send it to you."

George Wickley, Chief Counsel for the National Association of Restauranteurs, is also intent on obtaining the document for the Association's complaint in federal court. He knows that he can't compel a disinterested party to provide it unless they're a party to the lawsuit.

"How do we get around that?" Neal Tanner asks him.

"We convince them to join us as plaintiffs in the civil suit."

"What if they don't want the hassle, or just choose not to?"

"I'll make them a very lucrative offer, and all they have to do is sell us the paper or sign on with us – they don't really have to actually *do* anything. If you concur, I'll go as high as $50,000. Seems like a lot, and will be to them, but it's a pittance compared to what we gain."

"OK, George, go ahead."

Eight other large owner/manager associations have pledged their full support to overturn the SCOTUS rulings. News stories of the boat accident and Sonny's incarceration, along with a quick internet search, provides him with Riggs Blanding's drone business phone number.

Patina arrives at Riggs' house 20 minutes after he does, and they're both ready to relax before starting dinner.

"Riggs, guess who's asking for my phone number?"

"Professor Hartman – still looking for the document, I bet."

"Do you think I should give it to him, meet him, or just ignore the guy?"

"What a coincidence! I had a call at the business today from some attorney – his association offered us $50,000 to sign on with them as plaintiffs in their lawsuit."

"Really? That's a lot on money, why on earth would they do that?"

"So they can use our document to challenge Supreme Court decisions. Without us giving it to them or becoming a party to their lawsuit, they can't get the document as the evidence they need."

Patina digests that fact.

"I also had another call from the lawyer we talked to last month – Rudy Hayes. He wants to represent us against any ownership challenges."

"Well, aren't we the popular ones today! We still don't know if anyone will challenge us for it.

Chapter 58

Dominoes

A fter taking Sonny's phone call the day after the boating accident, Jim Sparks began developing his own plan to recover the document. With the case now closed, he's also well aware that any related evidence can be returned to its owner. He contacts an associate to forge an official-looking authorization letter and takes it to Charleston to complete his mission for David Wang and the Chinese government. *Just have to beat the kids to the paper...*

Within minutes of arriving at the Charleston International Airport, Jim drives a rental car directly to 3691 Leeds Avenue in North Charleston. He gets out of the car and begins walking to the headquarters building of the Charleston County Sheriff's Office. Jim's always wary around law enforcement activities, and this one's especially imposing - where a large, fenced detention complex dominates the campus. While walking to the headquarters, he barely notices a young woman with a baseball cap and sunglasses walking towards him. She's completely absorbed in her cell phone and runs into Jim, dropping a large, clear bag.

Surprised, Jim graciously blurts out, "Oh, excuse me, Miss, I'm so sorry - I guess I wasn't paying attention. Here, let me get that for you." Jim stoops down to sneak a look at her toned, tanned legs and retrieves her bag.

"Oh, thank you, Sir, that's very kind of you. But, it's entirely my fault. I was paying way too much attention to my phone instead of looking where I was going. No harm done, thank you again." She takes the bag and continues across the parking lot.

Inside her SUV, Patina opens the evidence bag and reads the sheriff's accompanying paperwork. Nothing unusual there. Then she pulls out the old waxy envelope and examines the historical page inside. After looking at it thoroughly, Patina is satisfied it hasn't suffered from Luther's handling, the boat accident, or its overnight exposure on the tidal flat. *That's a minor miracle!*

Jim enters the building and follows the receptionist's directions to the evidence room.

"Sergeant, I'm here to pick up a personal paper that's been released as evidence in a closed case. It's under the name Patina Gregors and I'm her agent." Jim produces his official-looking authorization letter with Patina's forged signature and bogus notary stamp on it.

"Well that's a real coincidence," SGT Winters says.

"What do you mean, what kind of coincidence?"

"It usually takes weeks to get rid of stuff like that, but she just now signed for it - I'm surprised you didn't run into her on the way down here."

Damn it! That's who I bumped into outside - the great legs! Hell, I just had it in my hands and gave the damn thing away!

Jim executes an abrupt about-face and sprints down the hall. He bursts out the front doors and scans the parking lot for Patina or a vehicle she might be driving away in. She and the document are nowhere in sight.

Confused by the visitor, Sgt. Winters calls Patina and tells her about the mysterious stranger and his unusual inquiry.

Patina immediately goes on guard. *That's strange - very odd. Who was he and what did he want the document for? I wonder if he was the foreign interest the FBI agent told us about? I need to take some precautions.*

Sparks plots his next move. *Where would she go – to her apartment? The Society? School? No matter what, I bet she ends up at her boyfriend's house.*

He drives to Riggs' house and waits almost two hours before seeing Patina pull into the driveway and get out of her SUV with the all-important evidence bag in hand.

Just as she turns to walk towards the front door, Riggs pulls into the driveway and parks behind her, "Hey, Patina, I picked up some things for dinner, give me a hand, will you?"

"Sure, anything for a Riggs' special home-cooked dinner."

She tosses the evidence bag onto the front seat of her Honda and walks over to hug Riggs, give him a kiss, and pick up two arms full of groceries, "I got the document and stopped by the Society for a while. Afterwards, it was too late to put it in the safety deposit box, but we can toss it in your safe tonight; I'll run it over there in the morning."

"Sounds like a plan; let's get these things in, I'm really hungry tonight."

From two houses away, Jim watches her movements in detail and realizes that a rare opportunity may have just fallen into his lap. *Every now and then, a minute's worth of luck beats a week's worth of planning!* He drives his car just beyond Riggs' house, then anxiously waits for them to go inside. When they do, he quickly gets out of his car and briskly starts walking towards Patina's Honda when three kids bear down on him on hoverboards.

"I'm sorry, sir; Evie, Bobby, Jax - be careful! If you don't watch where you're going, the boards go back in the house," their mother tells them. *Crap!* Jim mutters." *Where the hell did they come from?*

When mom and the kids pass, Jim again steps towards the driveway and is just about to walk up it when Riggs comes out the front door. *Jesus Christ! Can't that guy just stay inside and put his damn groceries away?*

Riggs walks past Patina's SUV to his Camry and retrieves two bottles of wine and the last bag of groceries. Seeing someone by the base of his driveway, he politely manages a perfunctory wave in the stranger's direction and returns to the house. *New neighbor? Someone's house guest?*

As soon as Riggs goes inside, Jim rapidly takes the few remaining steps to Patina's SUV and spots the evidence bag. Forty minutes later, he's at the airport to board a return flight to Ronald Reagan Washington National Airport.

That evening, Jim Sparks calls David Wang's executive assistant to coordinate a drop-off and payment. David's EA, anxious to complete this vital task for his boss, meets Jim the following morning at the nearly deserted National Mall. Without saying a word to one another, the EA leaves a payment envelope on a bench as Jim leaves a wrapped page on an adjacent bench. Both retrieve their respective packages and leave.

The EA returns to Sunrise Mechanical and proudly presents the package to David Wang. David opens it, peers inside, and looks at the paper. *Who'd ever think this could cause the Middle Kingdom such problems... problems that are now completely avoided.* He smiles with satisfaction for promptly fulfilling such a crucial mission and tells his EA to schedule an appointment with Juinjun at the Chinese embassy.

The next day, David brings the page to Juinjun, who beams with the thought of a job well done and the accompanying recognition it'll shower upon him. *Finally, there's some positive news on an otherwise cloudy economic battlefield. This will assuredly earn the ambassador and me high praise from the Central Committee.*

Within 24 hours, an embassy courier puts the wrapped page and other sensitive documents into a diplomatic pouch for his regular flight to Beijing.

On Tuesday of the following week, an influential member of the Communist Party of China's Central Committee makes an exceptionally irate call to the ambassador. Without any customary courtesies or small talk, he gets right to the point, "Your subordinate Zhu Jianjun is either unacceptably negligent in his duties to the Middle Kingdom or a disloyal imposter who is deliberately trying to play us for complete fools! And you are *personally culpable* for allowing such ineptitude within the embassy!"

The ambassador is completely shocked and utterly confused, "This lowly official is most sorry for any possible misunderstanding. Comrade, what can he possibly have done? He's always been one of the most trusted and effective members of my staff. Do you suspect he has embarrassed us by a scandal with an American?"

"The document he sent us - the one the American businesses are going to use to reverse higher federal wages – *it is not real*, a complete fabrication. All of you should have checked it."

Juinjun, of course, was predisposed to regard it as genuine and simply passed it along after his cursory examination. Forensic examiners in Beijing, however, correctly concluded it was counterfeit.

The Central Committee Party member continues to berate the ambassador, "Does Juinjun take us for absolute fools? Did he think we wouldn't examine it? Or perhaps you and your staff have been living as decadent Americans and fail to see the serious economic consequences we face here? You don't appreciate how a fall in American wages would bring us even greater problems?"

The ambassador remains completely dumbstruck, particularly after Juinjun's earlier assurances that the matter was completely resolved in their favor.

The Party official goes on, "When Juinjun called Beijing of his success, I informed other members of the Central Committee that we cleverly interceded in the American trade association's petition to the federal court. Now they all know I was duped and am not worthy! For that, the Party will reassign me to the Xizang Autonomous Region of Tibet – the middle of nowhere! But I will not be alone. Since you have demonstrated that your leadership does not conform to the high standards of duty and detail that the Party expects and demands, I have named you as the third assistant to my household there."

The Central Committeeman hangs up in disgust.

The ambassador cannot contain his shock and anger; he is absolutely livid and angrily directs his aide to summon Juinjun to his office at once.

Juinjun leaves two guests in his office and bounds down the hall to the ambassador's office, glowing in anticipation of the very favorable news he knows he's about to hear. *Perhaps even a new posting?*

His reception is anything but warm. "Zheng, enter and close the door."

The ambassador paces behind his desk before turning to Juinjun with a frigid stare and throbbing neck veins. "You were to send a most important document to the Party that should have eliminated any future U.S. court challenge to America's high wages?"

Juinjun is caught completely off guard and searches for clues why the ambassador addressed him much more formally than usual, and in a tone he reserves for only the most serious matters.

"Yes, yes, this lesser official did."

The ambassador slowly sits down, barely containing his anger.

Juinjun asks, "Didn't Beijing get the document and realize how we have averted a major economic issue in the future? They must be most pleased – maybe offer you a position within the Central Committee?" Juinjun smiles broadly, anticipating what success will mean for him too.

"Did you not examine the document? You dunce! It is a complete fake, a forgery. You have been tricked! You should have noticed the hoax immediately and taken stern measures with those who brought this deception to you – they have seriously insulted you, me, the Middle Kingdom, and the Party!"

Back in his own office, a thoroughly dejected Juinjun immediately phones David Wang, who calls his EA on the carpet. After a very stern, one-sided conversation, the EA contacts Sparks to berate him and demand a full refund.

Sparks is utterly embarrassed and fuming that he's been duped, by an amateur, no less. He's always much more critical of his performance than any client could be – he lives for and takes pride in being a consummate professional, it's how he fulfills himself. Jim Sparks cannot abide failure, especially as glaring as this with such a high-profile client.

Sparks responds, "I looked at the paper myself. I'm no professional examiner, but I've seen a lot of forgeries and it looked awfully damned good. Listen, I'm more surprised than you are; I'll fly back down tomorrow morning to find out what the hell's going on. If I don't come back with the real paper, you'll get every nickel back. Give me two days." Now Jim Sparks isn't concerned about doing an elegant job; rage and self-criticism displace his normal meticulous planning and rage drives him to just act.

Sparks had no way of knowing that SGT Winters alerted Patina about the stranger trying to obtain the evidence she'd just picked up.

Sparks was also completely unaware that she stopped at the Society to create the fake and switched it with the authentic notes in the evidence bag before arriving at Riggs' house. The authentic document was locked in the trunk, to be returned to the safety deposit box the following morning

Sparks won't have the time or disposition to conduct his normal detailed planning, but as he told Boggs Colman, he knows how to play hard ball too.

Founders' Intent

Chapter 59

Final Trip

As soon as a still seething Jim Sparks lands in Charleston, he drives to an outdoor sports store and expertly peruses an array of automatic knives – those with blades that spring from and retract back into the handle with the push of a button. He selects a Microtech Combat Troodon with a dagger-shaped blade just under four inches long.

Thusly armed, he cruises by Patina's apartment, but doesn't see her SUV, the one he took the forged document out of ten days ago. *Let's try the boyfriend's place again.*

Riding by the house, he sees Riggs carrying a clear plexiglass cover from his garage to Patina's SUV. Of even greater interest, however, is Patina following him with a large envelope.

What's he doing? And more importantly, what's she got and where are they going?

Sparks follows them for twenty-five minutes as they drive into Charleston. Riggs and Patina arrive at the Historical Society parking lot, grab the plexiglass display cover, and walk inside. Sparks drives past the Society to park on a side street a block away.

"Dr. Arkin, here's the finishing touch to the display – the cover Riggs made for the document."

"Hello, Patina, and thank you again Mr. Blanding, you've been all too kind to us."

"Happy to help out, Professor. Patina brought the document too, so we can see how everything looks together."

"Splendid, I've prepared the arrangement in the Rutledge Room, please follow me."

Named after Charleston's favorite son, the Rutledge Room was chosen for its north-facing window to preclude direct sunlight from falling on the document. A completed fully uniformed mannequin of Colonel Henry Rutledge stands guard at the double-wide entry off the main hall. Shelves along the walls hold a number of irreplaceable personal and professional relics, maps, and references.

Dr. Arkin leads Riggs and Patina to the double doorway and gestures to the display stand, centered on and facing away from the window. On the sides of the document space are a brief biography of John Rutledge and an explanation of his notes and their significance to the Constitution. Arkin has arranged three flags behind the display: an American flag stands to the display's right and a South Carolina state flag is on the opposite side. Between them is the South Carolina Revolutionary War flag.

Dr. Arkin basks in satisfaction – deservedly quite proud of everyone's efforts and he can't wait for the donors and public to share that pride.

Patina steps inside the room and approvingly takes it all in, "This looks wonderful Dr. Arkin, and Riggs' project is perfect for it!"

Riggs is also quite satisfied with his new piece, especially seeing it with the several flags that remind him of so many military ceremonies. The hallowed memory of his machine gunner's memorial service in Afghanistan flashes before him.

Patina unwraps the document and carefully places it in the center space of the display. Riggs fits the plexiglass cover over the notes and screws it in place. Patina, Riggs, and Arkin step back and admire the completed exhibit centerpiece. "You've both done a tremendous service for the Society, South Carolina, and, if I may say so, to the U.S. Constitution," Arkin adds.

Down the hall, Sparks walks through the front door of the Society and directly over to the receptionist, "Hey there, I'm looking for a Founding Fathers' document that one of your staff just brought by; do you know where it is?" He grips the new knife in his pocket.

Her curiosity piqued, Melba replies, "Why yes, Sir, just down the hall to your right – in the Rutledge Room. There's a mannequin of the colonel there, you won't miss it." *He doesn't look like the professorial type or the history buffs who come in, and I haven't seen him with Dr. Arkin. How'd this guy even know we <u>had</u> a new document?* Her eyes follow him down the hall as she strains to hear why the stranger is asking about the document.

Patina acknowledges Dr. Arkin's compliment and suddenly spots a vaguely familiar face at the room's entrance - the very man she bumped into outside the sheriff's campus ten days ago. *Is this the guy SGT Winters called me about – the one with a phony authorization and my forged signature? What's he doing here? Is he the 'foreign interest' the FBI warned us about? This can't be good...*

Sparks surveys the room and its three occupants, instantly targeting that Riggs as his primary adversary.

Seeing Patina's surprise and having no idea who the man is or why he's there, Dr. Arkin asks, "May I help you?"

Sparks takes a step forward, "You sure can, old timer, I just need a piece of paper and I think I see it right there." Pointing to the display, he gruffly orders, "Get it out."

Confused, Arkin asks, "And who are you?"

Sparks glances at him and forcefully shoves him aside while continuing to scrutinize Riggs.

Patina takes a step, "You're the guy from the sheriff's office, the one who forged my name, aren't you?"

"Yep, sweetie, in the flesh. And you're the klutz with the extra fine legs. Should've just grabbed the damn paper then so I didn't have to make a second trip."

As Riggs moves to intervene, Sparks bounds beyond the confused Arkin and grabs Patina. He pulls one of her arms behind her in a painful hold.

"Let the lady go!" Riggs commands loudly as he steps towards the two of them.

Sparks glares, "Not so fast soldier boy. You just get the damned paper." He pulls the knife from his pocket and presses the slide switch to project the gleaming blade.

Riggs takes instant notice and hesitates a few seconds to quickly assess his options. He sees the intensely determined look of a cold-blooded sort who's familiar, even comfortable, with violence, *Like the Afghani tribal warriors again, who had no hesitation to kill everyone who's any sort of obstacle... or a loose end.*

"Yeah, sure, whatever you need." Riggs steps over to the display, "But let her go - you can have the paper and get out of here without things getting sticky."

"Don't kid yourself, pal, I'm the guy who *makes* things sticky."

"Don't get all crazy, we can all come out of this with what we want." Riggs methodically unscrews and removes the cover - stalling to find some sort of equalizer to combat Sparks' gleaming dagger.

As Sparks reaches for the document, he cuts one of Patina's arms and pushes her to the floor. Riggs drops the historic paper and begins to rush towards her when Sparks blocks his path, threatens him with the blooded knife, and stares at him. "You on a suicide mission, soldier boy?" he taunts in a steely, menacing tone.

Riggs has another flashback of Afghanistan, Memories return and heighten his senses, his eat-or-be-eaten instincts and imperative to survive, to defend his team, and accomplish his duty. He grabs the first object at hand - an old tome off a bookshelf - and hurls it at Sparks, with a follow-up salvo of colonial tableware.

Dr. Arkin winces as the priceless relics sail across the room, miss their target, and crash into pieces against the nearby wall.

Sparks grins and his eyes go cold, "You better bring a whole lot more than that to the fight, champ."

As Sparks circles and measures his adversary, Riggs eyes the Revolutionary War flag and staff with its spear tip. He yanks it from its base and aims it at his modern-day enemy, just as a bearer would've done two centuries ago. Sparks lunges with his knife and Riggs parries with the staff, pulls it back, then quickly attempts to harpoon Sparks.

Jim reacts instantly to barely deflect the thrust – suffering only a torn shirt and a superficial laceration. Riggs' powerful effort, however, solidly embeds the expedient weapon into the prized uniformed figure of the state's most famous colonel, and he can't pull it back out.

Arkin gasps in disbelief at the staff running completely through his elegant restoration - piercing the colonel's original Civil War tunic.

Sparks and Riggs stare at each other from opposite ends of the pole, both panting with heightened pulses and beads of sweat running down their faces. Sparks lunges forward again with his knife and slashes across Riggs' arms, forcing him to let go of the flagstaff. Now he's completely unarmed against his vicious assailant.

Riggs' vision narrows on Sparks' red knife blade and he backs up against a bookshelf.

Patina braces herself on the floor with her bleeding arm, desperately searching for some way to help. *What can I do... there's got to be something!* She looks at the only object she can propel at Sparks – the wooden document display between her and her target. She draws her knees up to her chest and kicks it with every effort she can muster. It crashes against Sparks' thigh, but only delays his attack on Riggs for a moment. Sparks curses her and quickly returns his attention back to Riggs.

Patina trembles at what's sure to be Sparks' final, lethal assault.

Riggs grabs a silver tray from the shelf and holds it up as a last-ditch shield against the inevitable attack. *Is this it? I survive two combat tours in Afghanistan... and die here – back home in some exhibit room?*

Sparks flashes a perverse grin at his cornered foe and savors the moment before the coup de grace.

Riggs desperately grips the tray and focuses on Sparks' movements to defend himself against the imminent strike.

Sparks slowly and methodically waves the knife from side to side to confuse and intimidate his victim. He glares into Riggs' eyes, looks for any slight loss of focus, and tenses himself for the fatal lunge.

With blood running down both arms, Riggs continues to measure his attacker, *How's he going to come at me? What's my best move?*

The moment Sparks senses Riggs' deliberation and uncertainty, he springs forward.

Riggs focuses on the lethal blade, but blood loss slows his reflexes - he can't move the tray into position fast enough. *Will the first strike be the last, or will it take more than one?*

Then, abruptly and inexplicably, Sparks stops in mid-thrust and his mouth gapes open without uttering a single syllable. He simply gasps, quivers, and awkwardly stumbles ahead for two final, faltering steps. Trembling, he slowly looks down at five inches of Colonel Rutledge's sword protruding from his profusely-bleeding abdomen.

Sparks and Riggs exchange confused, blank, incomprehensible stares. Not emitting another sound, Sparks drops his knife and collapses with a completely perplexed look on his tortured face.

Patina sighs in relief.

Mild, soft-spoken Professor David Arkin is aghast. He's shaking and shocked at the effect of his deadly thrust with Colonel Rutledge's historic weapon. He half-steps backwards, trembling, and sits on the floor among the shards of broken colonial artifacts.

Riggs manages a thankful nod and staggers towards Patina. She almost passes out with relief and covers his wounds with her hands as he strains to pick up and secure John Rutledge's secret notes.

Within another minute, the Charleston Police respond to Melba's call when she first heard the commotion. They pour into the building, secure the room, and immediately usher in the EMTs.

Sparks is the first casualty they encounter, and the lead medic checks him for a pulse, "All this one needs is the coroner."

Leaving the corpse, the EMT rapidly dresses Patina's wound. The second EMT assesses Riggs, "This one's lost a lot of blood - he'll survive, but he's got to go to Tidewater Memorial *right now.*"

Both medics load the fading Riggs onto a gurney and wheel it to the ambulance. Patina continues to hold his hand and assure him she'll keep the document safe. As he loses consciousness, his thoughts are of his dearest Patina, protecting her and Arkin, and of his duty... *to support and defend the Constitution against all enemies, foreign and domestic.*

Chapter 60

End of the Dream

As Riggs and Patina battle Jim Sparks in the Rutledge Room, Professor Dale Hartman eagerly pulls his newly-arrived copy of Stanford Magazine from the rest of his daily mail. He quickly scans the table of contents to find a story about the remarkable discovery.

He's stunned, absolutely stunned, "What ... what the hell?" He reads aloud in disbelief, then curses at the article. "Stanford's giving *David Arkin* credit for his paltry role in shedding new light on the Constitutional Convention? They tag *him* for his historical opinion of John Rutledge's document and its relationship to SCOTUS interpretations of the Constitution?"

"Dammit!" he shouts, and hurls the magazine to the floor. Hartman paces his drab little office, looks at all his walls full of diplomas, certificates, and plaques, then picks the magazine back up. He pores over the text for his name, line by line, only to find it in a brief footnote,

> "In a strange and unexplained twist of events, Stanford alumni Dr. Dale Hartman publicly claimed to have discovered and immediately photographed the document. Inspection of sensor smudges on the photo, however, conclusively proved that the image was taken with a camera owned by one of Dr. Arkin's interns."

Hartman storms out of his office to his final lecture of the day, angrily snapping at anyone who so much as glances at him. He's in absolutely no mood for small talk or pleasantries... until he looks down the hall at Dr. Robin Cochran. She's her usual vision of beauty and charm, leaning against a classroom doorway as she playfully talks to someone just inside.

Hartman's instantly-transformed mood ascends to a dizzying peak when he sees her smile broadly, throw her head back, and laugh out loud. Suddenly, he's walking a foot off the ground and the magazine article is completely irrelevant. He walks up to her and boldly asks, "Robin, what a genuine treat to run into you, let's get that lunch, about 11:30?"

"Oh what a lovely offer, it really is, but I've got a transfer student I've been tutoring who's just invited me for soup and a sandwich - we're reviewing his extra credit work so he can graduate next spring. Billy Jackson, may I introduce Dr. Hardmen?"

Hartman's shocked – his jaw drops and his mood instantly reverts to a fuming passion to wring Billy's neck. *That impudent little prick! Quitting my class AND moving in on Cochran!*

He barely has the presence to correct Robin, before striding off, "It's *Hart*-man, not Hardmen," he mutters over his shoulder. Returning to his office, Hartman finds a memo on his desk.

Professor Dale Hartman,

The Faculty Review Board has completed its consideration of your unauthorized disclosure of another student's personal information, your highly irregular action with a student, and your false claims of academic discovery. I have studied all their findings and approved their recommendations:
- You are immediately relieved of all your responsibilities as a doctoral advisor.
- Beginning with the upcoming term in January, you are relieved of all duties and responsibilities as a graduate-level lecturer, and are offered a teaching position as a primary instructor of U.S. History 101 if you choose to continue your employment with this institution.
- Your application for tenure is returned without action.
- You are herewith placed on conduct probation for one year.

Dennis Belton
Dennis Belton
Chairman, History Department
Charleston State University

Soon afterwards, Dale Hartman finds an expensive-looking envelope atop a pile of papers, addressed to him in hand-drawn calligraphy. *What could this possibly be? It looks awfully interesting, and I'm certainly due for some good news.*

He carefully opens the envelope with curious anticipation and pulls out an invitation,

Mr. & Mrs. Gerald C. Cochran
Cordially Invite You To
The Wedding of their Daughter

Miss Robin Cochran, PhD
To
Mr. William Edward Jackson IV

June 26th at 3:00 PM
At the Charleston Club
40 Prioleau Street, Charleston, SC

Reception to Follow

Founders' Intent

Epilogue

A week after her near-death battle with Jim Sparks, two additional events change Patina's life.

That Friday, she receives a small box delivered to her apartment, *What in the world is this, did Riggs send this to me? What's that guy up to? Wait a sec, it's from the Charleston County Sheriff's office.*

She tears off the shipping paper and sees a beautifully wrapped gift box that she opens immediately.

"An alligator purse? What the… ?" she says aloud. More puzzled than ever, she looks inside the purse and finds a note,

Dear Ms. Gregors,

    This is my very personal 'thank you' for your courageous role in closing a long-standing felony case in Charleston County.

    The DNA of the man who tried to murder you on the dock matched that from a 15-year old cold case. The earlier sample was from skin tissue found under the fingernails of Mr. Richard Gregors, who I believe was your brother. Both samples belonged to James Blaisdell, AKA Ivan, of Tacoma, WA.

    While no measure of justice can return your brother, I hope this information brings you some degree of closure and that you're not offended by the poetic justice of how I packaged this expression of my sincere gratitude.

Yours in Service,

Barry Cobb
Barry Cobb
Charleston County Sheriff

Patina goes inside to sit down, takes several very deep breaths, and contemplates the magnitude of what she's just learned. Richard's cold case is finally solved – his murderer has been identified and paid for his crime. She buries her face in her hands and tears run down her cheeks. *I'm relieved, I'm sad, I'm not really sure how I feel right now or what to say or do. It's over, finally over - Richard can rest in peace.* She wipes away tears and calls her mother in St. Thomas.

She stops short of calling Riggs with the news - she needs some time to think about and digest it, then talk with him in person.

Suddenly she realizes that she, Richard's younger sister Patina Gregors, was the Marshal Raylan Givens who finally brought justice to her brother's killer. By her own hand, when he was intent on killing her too, she prevailed and conquered the monster.

She appreciates the closure, of course, but it cannot compensate for the tragic loss she and her mother have endured for well over a decade.

Patina walks outside to the parking lot to her SUV and heads downtown for work at the Historical Society. On the way there, she hears her "Music of the Night" ringtone; it's Riggs, and he sounds irrepressibly excited.

"Patina, can you meet me for lunch at Ahab's, even if I don't crash into you?"

Three hours later, they sit across from one another at the restaurant. Riggs can tell something's on Patina's mind and it's something serious.

"What's up Babe, you look lost in thought? Is it anything at the Society, or school?"

"No, nothing like that, something so much different. Kind of good and bad at the same time."

"OK, I'm listening, tell me what it is and how I can help."

She holds up the alligator purse, "I received this in the mail today from the county sheriff."

"The sheriff? Well, that *is* strange. Do you know why?"

"Yes, he had a note inside, it's still there – go ahead, you can read it."

Riggs reads the note, then looks at Patina. He stands up and steps around to her side of the table to warmly hug her.

"I don't know what to say, Patina. Of course it's got to be some kind of relief to know the guy's finally been identified and he won't ever hurt anyone ever again. But it's also got to bring back some awfully upsetting memories."

"Right on both counts," she says while hugging him back.

He looks at her, squeezes her again, then kisses her on the forehead before returning to his chair. He reaches across the table and holds her hands. They quietly look at each other, down at the table, and out at the river.

"May I take your order, or do you need another minute?" the waitress asks.

"Patina?" Riggs defers.

"Something light, a half seafood salad today and I'm going to splurge with a piña colada, please."

"The same." Riggs adds.

Patina enjoys Riggs' company, support, and genuine affection. She's already feeling somewhat better, but realizes she's still got a lot of emotions to sort out. She knows that will not, cannot, happen in a day.

"I'll be fine, with time. All the events over the past couple of weeks have just been so unimaginable – both when we were going through them and thinking about them afterwards. I'm so grateful you were with me all the way."

"Patina, I was scared to death - at a complete loss when I heard your voice in the van, and terrified at what could've happened at the dock. We're through all that now, though - thank God. We're both healing and I have so much to look forward to with you."

She manages a smile and blows him a kiss.

"Riggs, do you think we did right by the document – giving it to the Library of Congress, along with the FDE's report?"

"Yes, absolutely, I sure do. We weren't in it for money or headlines – it just fell into our laps. Marjorie Tanner said there's a very good chance the Library of Congress will reimburse the FDE fees since they'd have to pay them anyway. I'm no expert on constitutional documents, but it certainly seems like it's going to be a significant addition to a more thorough understanding of the intent and limits of that commerce clause."

"That's true, and I'd much rather spend time together doing what we both want instead of slogging through years of lawsuits and ownership claims that may pop up."

"Yep, I hear you. Looks like all the interested parties are involved: federal government, business owners, labor, and academia. Let's have another piña colada while they follow all their processes and agendas. I'm glad the media ran stories about the donation, now maybe everyone will finally stop chasing us."

Patina leans back, finishes her first drink, clears her head, and looks squarely across the table.

"Now, Mr. Riggs Blanding, tell me why this lunch date was so important today – you sounded on top of the world when you called."

"Maybe this isn't the right time, Patina…"

"This is the *perfect* time for me to get some good news, especially from my special guy."

"Well, thank you," he says while blushing.

"OK, Patina, here's the deal. It's an off-shore job for both of us."

"A job? You know I'm still in class until the term ends, right?"

"Sure do, that's what makes it so perfect. I'll be healed and you'll be done with classes before it starts. You, Miss Patina Gregors, now have an all-expenses paid offer plus a generous technical fee for two weeks in the sun."

"Riggs Blanding, what on earth are you talking about?"

"I just booked a drone assignment to survey, photograph, and take videos of high-end beachfront properties in Eleuthera. It'll be easy enough to fly the missions, but I need a tech-savvy partner to transfer and edit all the image and video files."

"Eleuthera? I've never heard of it. Is it a city or a country? Where is it?"

"It's an island in the Bahamas, about an hour's plane ride from Fort Lauderdale."

"Would I be going with you just to edit drone files?" she asks with an alluring little smile.

"Oh, there'd be plenty of time for beach walks, swimming, maybe even renting a sailboat."

"And afterwards, at night?"

"Night life in Governor's Harbor is pretty tame and shuts down early, but I think we could figure out something to do at our place."

They both grin in the shared expectation of time together on the tropical island.

"What do you think - pack your bikini and sun screen?"

"Absolutely, I'm in. But let's get a place where I won't need the bikini - just extra sunscreen and you to rub it on."

Within a day of arriving in Eleuthera, Patina updates the face-book cover photo of her and Richard on the beach in St. Thomas. In its place is one of her on a beach hugging the other guy she loves – Riggs Blanding.

Founders' Intent

End Notes

To satisfy readers' curiosity about which elements of the story are real and which are fictional, I've included these several notes.

The U.S. Constitution

Chapter 14 accurately discusses the Articles of Confederation, which was the agreement the original thirteen colonies created to provide a modicum of centralized political organization in their revolution for independence. As Dr. Hartman correctly explains, a few delegates attending the 1787 Constitutional Convention in Philadelphia, PA intended to replace that document and create a new type of government.

While we take key provisions of the Constitution for granted, they were quite novel at the time. Jefferson, for one, studied Greek, Latin, and French to learn the strengths and shortfalls of their governments.

The 55 delegates' understanding of human nature, such as Madison's observation that "Men are not angels", lead to the idea of separating the powers of legislators who write the laws, the executive who carries them out, and the judiciary that rules on conformity with the Constitution.

A unique aspect of the Founders' view of federalism is the federal government's limited authority - having only those powers enumerated in the Constitution. A frustrated Sonny Butler is correct in Chapter 32 when he muses on federal limitations.

Professor Hartman accurately explains the use of committees during the convention, and the convention delegates did appoint South Carolina delegate John Rutledge to chair, along with the four other named delegates, to the Committee of Detail and charged them with drafting the U.S. Constitution.

Rutledge composed a draft upstairs in his house on 116 Broad Street in Charleston. He built the house as a wedding present to his bride, and the structure operates today as a bed & breakfast.

Convention and committee business was conducted in secrecy, so no actual notes are known to exist. Although it is entirely plausible for the committee chair to have made notes, those in the story are my own creation.

The Rutledges of South Carolina

'Rutledge' is a storied family name in South Carolina history, and for good reasons.

John Rutledge, 1739 – 1800, was a prominent lawyer and President of the colony of South Carolina before he was elected Governor when it became a state. He served in the various high-level state and federal offices stated in the story.

One of John's ten children was Frederick Wilkes Rutledge, who married Harriott Pinckney Horry; she inherited Hampton Plantation, bringing it into the Rutledge family. A 1786 inventory of the plantation lists a mahogany desk on one of its many pages of property.

Frederick and Harriott had eight children of their own, and one of their grandchildren was Henry Middleton Rutledge II (1839 – 1921). At the age 22, the men of his regiment chose Henry as their colonel, and the unit went on to fight on the side of the Confederacy during the Civil War. Henry's military service gave rise to my idea of a mannequin made in his likeness.

Colonel Rutledge and second wife Margaret Hamilton Seabrook had five children, one of whom was Archibald Hamilton Rutledge Sr. Archibald was born in McClellanville, SC, attended Porter Military Academy in Charleston and Union College in NY.

After teaching at Mercersburg Academy in PA, Archibald, returned to Hampton Plantation in 1937 with an eye to restoring the property. He lived there for 34 years and did indeed auction off many of the furnishings to buy Little Hampton, his birth home in nearby McClellanville.

As told in the Prologue, SC named Archibald as the state's first Poet Laureate and he was the last occupant of Hampton Plantation. The Plantation house and grounds, near the Santee River, are open for tours.

In 1973, Archibald Rutledge died at Little Hampton, the same house where he was born. I had the privilege of discussing Rutledge family history with Archibald's grandson, Henry Middleton Rutledge on the back porch over a Dr. Pepper. We also talked about drones and he proved to be an adept student pilot – flying one I had with me.

The Charleston Area
With the exception of Ahab's Restaurant, the Charleston State University, and the Charleston Historical Society, and Waterside, the named locations are real: Ernest Hollings ACE Basin, New Britton Island, the rivers leading past the island to the Atlantic Ocean, the FBI, Sheriff's Office, U.S. Attorney's Office, and the J. Waties Waring Judicial Center.

At the time of this writing, there's an on-going debate over a major road project in Charleston County that is affected by heirs' land, as described in Chapter 2.

Characters
Riggs Blanding is a purely fictional character, as is his father, Galen Blanding. I took their last name from Camp Blanding, Florida, where I trained as an ROTC cadet.

Galen's military unit is real: the 4-64 Armor Battalion/1st Brigade was a unit in the 24th Mechanized Division, which conducted the 'Hail Mary' encirclement of Saddam Hussein's Republican Guards during Operation DESERT STORM.

The manner of Richard's brutal murder developed from an account of Zulu warriors' decisive victory over British forces at the 1879 Battle of Isandlwana, South Africa.

"One sight, a most gruesome one, I shall never forget. Two lads, presumably two little drummer boys of the 26th Regiment, had been hung up by butcher hooks which had been jabbed under their chins, then they were disemboweled: all the circumstances pointed to the fact they had been subjected to that inhuman treatment while still alive."

Samuel Jones, 45th Regiment.

Patina Gregors is also a purely fictional character. Her last name is that of a Danish businessman I knew years ago in St. Thomas, USVI. Patina's athletic heroine, Mia Hamm, played forward for the United States' women's national soccer team and was a two-time gold medalist.

Ivan. The owners of the B&I Department Store in Tacoma, WA acquired an infant gorilla in 1964 as a pet., Their simian, Ivan, had grown too big for their home by age five and they moved him to an enclosure in their department store. My family saw Ivan in 1981 when we went to the B&I's pet store and bought an American Eskimo pup. In the early 1990s, the ape's plight attracted international sympathy, and his 1994 transfer to the Atlanta Zoo brought even more notoriety.

Crowds-on-demand services (Ch 11) are real and easily found with an internet search. The CEO of one such company stated he's worked with a number of political candidates. My fictional character Hondo is operating an ethically-challenged such service.

Marion Barry (Ch 47) served as Washington D.C.'s Mayor from 1979 – 1991. The year before his term ended, he was convicted in federal court for possession and usage of crack cocaine. After release from federal prison in 1992, Barry ran for D.C. Council and won with the slogan "He May Not Be Perfect, But He's Perfect for D.C."

In 1994 he successfully ran for mayor again, serving from 1995 – 1999. After leaving the mayor's office, Barry ran for his old Ward 8 city council seat and held it from 2005 – 2014.

Federal Minimum Wage
The origin of the federal minimum wage is accurately cited in the story, as are the SCOTUS cases that confirmed it and extended the fed's reach into the world of commerce. The federal minimum wage is currently $7.25 an hour for covered personnel, and $3.25 for workers who receive tips (their employers are required to make up the difference if they take in less than a total of $7.25 an hour).

The account of President Roosevelt's effort to install up to six more Supreme Court justices is true.

China
Some Chinese protocols differ from those most Americans are familiar with, and one difference is in introductions. In Chapter 17, Dr. Hartman would have made a much better impression had he graciously accepted Professor Zheng's business card and attentively read it, instead of simply cramming it into his trousers pocket. His failure to reciprocate with a card of his own and backslapping Zheng would also have held him higher regard with Zheng.

China is facing the serious concerns mentioned in 19: disputed territorial claims in the South China Sea, the possibility of an exodus from North Korea, civil unrest in Hong Kong, and the magnitude of its aging population.

Miscellaneous:

Sonny Butler had good reason to tread carefully in Chapter 3 when planning to meddle with awarding a federal contract, citing Korean construction giant SK Engineering and Construction. Key personnel in that company and the federal government were indicted in 2017 in regard to bribery and other crimes related to one of the largest construction projects in the Army's history.

Yes, water moccasins can tolerate chlorine.

The National Security Agency, or NSA, operates signals collection and processing sites on the Hawaiian Island of Oahu. Contract employee Edward Snowden walked out of the facility in 2013 with classified government information that he revealed to journalists and, as of 2017, he is residing in Moscow.

The Inspire 2 drone is manufactured by DJI and has all the capabilities described in the story: flight time, speed, and Active Track flight mode (the ability to autonomously follow a subject designated by the pilot). It can also live-stream video to a YouTube channel.

Boggs Colman's death. Fortunately many modern bass fishing boats are equipped with outboard engines designed to prevent them from rotating into the rear deck area if they strike a submerged log. Too bad for Boggs Coleman that *Sonny's Shangri-La* wasn't one of them!

Shyrel Hayden, the U.S. Attorney for South Carolina, is a fictional character. Interestingly, as of this writing, that office is held by Sherri A. Lydon. Prior to her appointment under President Trump, Lydon was in private practice and one of her last clients was James R. Metts - the Lexington County Sheriff for 42 years. In 2015, Metts was convicted of conspiring to harbor illegal aliens and Chief U.S. District Judge Terry Wooten sentenced him to a year and a day in federal prison.

Founders' Intent